THE BILLIONAIRE PACT

AFRO LUV BITE 3 IN 1 COLLECTION

UNOMA NWANKWOR

KEVSTEL PUBLICATION

Kevstel Publications

info@kevstel.com

Thankful to God from Whom the gift comes.

To Kevin, Fumnanya & Ugo

And finally, my readers. I love & appreciate you.

NOTE TO READER

This is different from my other works. It's a fun, flirty, sweet romance under my Afro Luv Bites Collection.

This collection contains the three books in the Billionaire Pact Series

Vegas Nights: Book 1

Second Shot: Book 2

Pretend Bae Book 3

Enjoy!

VEGAS NIGHTS

Billionaire Pact Book 1

ONE

"I'm about two seconds from strangling you!"

Safiya Nadar narrowed her eyes at Layla Assan, her best friend. She intended the look to be intimidating, but it didn't work. It only made Lay, as she called her, cackle. Rolling her eyes, she returned her focus to the treadmill to get her mileage in.

"You should know by now that I'm not scared of you," her friend replied.

Safiya shook her head and stopped the machine she'd been on for the last several minutes. She turned to her side and looked at Layla. They had been best friends since elementary school. Layla and her mother migrated to Atlanta from Ethiopia when she was nine. Safiya met Layla when she stuck up for her while she was being teased about being the newest kid in school. An experience she knew all too well since she, her grandmother and her dad had migrated from Tanzania two years prior. The little girls hit it off immediately and had been inseparable ever since. They had experienced almost everything together – lots of laughter, tears, arguments, heartbreaks and death. Their friendship stood the test of time. They were both the only children of their parents, opposites in behavior, but blood couldn't have made them any closer.

"Lay, I can't just go running off to Vegas."

"Who said anything about running off? We're strolling through the airport and getting on a plane." Layla gave her an incredulous look.

"You know what I mean—"

"Actually, I don't." Layla cut off her machine and turned. Her chest rose and fell, trying to fill itself with oxygen. She stepped down and wiped her face with a towel.

Safiya smiled. She always admired how well put together her friend was. Her long, honey-dyed hair was in a bun on the top of her head. Loose springy tresses fell all over her face. Her mocha skin shone and had a glow that was enhanced by the perspiration from her workout. Compared to Safiya's slender, five-foot, six-inch frame, Layla was a curvaceous five feet four, but her personality and confidence made one think she was well over six feet tall.

"Remember my dad? Who will take care of him while I hop off to Las Vegas with you?"

"I've told you we're not running or hopping anywhere—"

"Be serious, Lay."

"I am being serious. You know your dad loves when you take time for yourself. Unc is always complaining how you're so bogged down taking care of him, even though the nurses do their jobs well. He's not an invalid. Stop making him feel like one." She rummaged through her backpack and retrieved her wireless ear pods case.

"It's just for the weekend."

Safiya massaged her forehead.

"Or, I'll tell my mother to check up on him. You know he'll hate that, but I'll do it."

Safiya widened her eyes and shook her head. She remembered the last time she had Layla's mom check in on her dad. He didn't let her hear the end of it. He said she nagged him more than her late mother.

Layla laughed. "Okay then, stop making excuses. It's been a year since your divorce. And might I remind you, Justin is in Boston enjoying his newfound freedom and you're here wallowing as if the world has come to a halt."

Safiya creased her eyebrows. The excitement she used to feel in her heart at the mention of that name had been replaced by a hollow of regret. She and Justin had been college sweethearts. Layla had never liked him, but tolerated him because of her. She thought Justin was trying to create a wedge between them. And although that was true, it wasn't something Safiya shared with her best friend. She wanted her man and her girl to get along. Like most love stories, theirs was a match made in heaven, until it wasn't. They had gotten married barely six months after meeting, against her father's wishes. A month later, her dad became sick and she was all he had. Justin knew that, but her having to sacrifice time to take care of her dad angered him. Let him tell it, he was being neglected.

Justin was a budding musician and he was used to Safiya being able to bar hop with him and go on impromptu trips to pursue opportunities he felt would lead to something more. With a dad recovering from a stroke, she just couldn't do that anymore. As time went by, Justin sought the comfort and support he claimed she wasn't providing from another woman. It wasn't until two years into that relationship that Safiya found out.

"Look, you need to live. Life is short and things don't always go as planned, as you know. All you've done since the divorce is go to work, take care or rather smother your dad and repeat."

"That's not true," Safiya said.

"Name one thing you do that I don't have to force you to do. I'll wait." Layla put one hand on her hip and shifted her weight to one leg.

Safiya knew her friend was right, but she didn't want to admit it. The failure of a divorce weighed so heavily on her that she shielded herself from the public. Even though the circumstances of the demise of her home wasn't her fault, she couldn't help but wonder if she should've done things differently to save her marriage.

A beat passed between them. "I thought as much," Layla said. "Look, I have to write this article about the grand reopening of the *Walden Luxury Hotel and Casino*. Come with me. I'm scheduled to talk to the owner on Friday afternoon, then we'll have the whole weekend to ourselves. Sunday, we'll be back."

"I have to work Friday," Safiya countered.

"Call in sick. You hate that job. The only reason you're still there is we haven't hit the lottery." Layla laughed.

Safiya rolled her eyes. "Let's go, cause you're seriously wrecking my nerves."

The two friends walked toward the exit of the gym they visited twice a week.

"You know I'm telling the truth." Layla stopped walking and placed her hands on her hips. She cocked her head to the side and creased her brows. "And how many times will I tell you I'm not scared of you."

As they stepped out into the cool March evening, Layla's phone rang, interrupting their conversation. With the smile on her face, Safiya knew immediately it was Todd, her fiancé.

She walked ahead to give her friend some privacy and let her mind wander to the comment about the lottery.

"When will that be?" she muttered to herself.

Hitting the lottery was a standing joke they had about being free to buy a building so they could open their own businesses. Layla, who was a journalist for *Lifestyles of the Wealthy*, had a dream of starting her own media house. A place where she could write articles about things that mattered and not the frivolous lifestyle of the rich and simple, as she called them. Safiya, on the other hand, worked for *Fragrance & Things* as a mixer and tester of fragrances for candles. She had the dream of opening her own candle making business where she could make products with ingredients that were healthy and smelled good. Opening her own business would not only give her something she was happy with creating, but it would allow her to properly care for her aging dad, make a real difference in her community and have the flexibility to spend more time doing things she once loved.

"I see you smiling. Todd must have been his nasty self on the phone," Safiya said as Layla approached.

"And you know this." Layla raised her hand for a high five, which Safiya gave.

"I love the two of you together. You took your time and got to know him. He treats you like a queen and I'm so happy for you."

"I know you are, and I love you for it. However, I'm tired of not telling you about the freaky stuff, so we need to find you a man and quick."

"Nope, we are not looking for a man. There's so much I have to focus on right now and a man isn't one of them. I'm happy living vicariously through you." Safiya walked over to her grey Altima and pressed the key fob to unlock the car. She opened the back door and threw her gym bag in.

"Whatever. So, Friday are we on?"

"Only if you promise it's just a girl's trip and you won't try to set me up with anybody."

Layla sighed and shrugged. "Okay, whatever...your loss. Ms. Kitty will soon close up with the way you're going."

"Oh my gosh. On that note, I'm going home." Safiya opened the car door. Layla naming her body parts shouldn't be new to her, but it still shocked her every time.

"Hmm, yeah, bye. Talk to you later. Kiss my Uncle poo for me. I'll come get you from work early on Thursday. We need to go shopping."

Safiya looked down at the old tee and black leggings she was wearing. She bugged her eyes, looking back up at her friend.

"Yeah, don't look at me like that. You're not going to Sin City like...ugh. I don't even know what to say. But yes, we're giving you a makeover *rafiki*."

"You do know I don't own my job, right? I can't just leave whenever."

"And you do know I don't care. Figure something out. Before Justin, you were daring and resourceful. I don't know how he sucked out your soul, but we're getting it back. Love you, *dada yangu*." Layla strode off to her Jeep Cherokee, not waiting for her response.

Safiya sighed and got in her car. *Vegas, here I come.*

She started her car and pulled out of the parking lot headed to her dad's house. She had been pulling double shifts a lot lately, so she looked forward to spending the day with her favorite person.

TWO

"You're a freaking genius!"

Darius Gray raised his champagne flute in salute to his best friend and investment advisor, Hakeem Richardson.

"Cut it out, man. I only brought you the deal. It was your signature ruthless business strategy that made it all come together."

The friends clicked glasses and took a sip. Standing at the huge window of his penthouse suite, Darius took in the view of the city he had spent a lot of time in over the last year.

"So, you ready for tomorrow?" Hakeem asked, taking a seat on the couch.

"As ready as I'll ever be. It's going to be lit."

"It wouldn't be you if it wasn't." Hakeem chuckled.

"You're as bad as I am, so don't throw stones."

"I never said we were bad," Hakeem grinned.

Both men shared a laugh. Darius met Hakeem and his brother Brice in an orphanage during their preteen years. The three of them grew up together and formed a strong bond in the process. Darius and Hakeem, who were closer in age, naturally gravitated towards each other and became best friends. The three of them went through so much together. Right before an angel took Darius in, they agreed to stay in touch. And they did, resulting in a brotherhood spanning more than a decade.

Darius pulled out his phone. He needed to call his assistant to make sure everything was in place. Julia was always on top of everything, but the perfectionist in him always had to be sure. He looked at the reminder notification he'd just received.

"Oh, shoot."

"What is it?"

"I forgot I have this interview with some reporter from that lifestyle magazine."

"When?"

"Tomorrow at noon."

"So, what's the problem? Still gives you plenty of time for the opening in the evening. Is Vanessa going to be back by then?"

Darius ran his hand over his head he kept clean shaven. In the early days, he loved the press and interviews, but now he shied away from them. One wrong quote and his stock would plummet. He learned that the hard way a couple of years ago.

"You know I don't like this press thing. I don't know why I agreed to this one."

"Because it's the magazine you vowed to get on the cover of," Hakeem replied. "Speaking of, how does it feel?"

"What?"

"Hitting the billion-dollar mark before thirty-five. That was your goal and you did it. All by yourself." Hakeem paused. "I'm proud of you, man."

Darius who was now the Owner and CEO of *Gray Holdings* remembered the day he told Hakeem he would be a self-made multi-millionaire by thirty and would hit the billion mark by thirty-five. In fact, all of them had made that pact. They each landed in the orphanage due to their parents not making the best decisions. The desire to leave a legacy and be there for their own kids, when they had them, propelled the friends. It was a mission they had all accomplished.

For Darius, after being rejected for adoption so many times, he became a runaway and lived on the streets. He knew what it was like to go hungry for days. He also knew the torture of sleeping on hard surfaces with little or nothing to shield him from the cold. He remembered days when he saw a rat and wished it was a juicy steak. He'd experienced hunger pangs so painful, it felt as though his intestines were feeding on themselves because there was no food for them to feast on. He survived by pick-pocketing to buy what he could, or shop lifting food and others essentials. It was during one of his thefts that he met the angel who would make a lasting impression on him. Although she was with him for a brief time, she gave him what he'd always longed for – a home.

"None of this would have been possible if you didn't invest in my first venture," Darius said.

The friends, though poor, were smart. They ended up getting scholarships and attending college together. Hakeem, who dabbled in trading stocks, made a huge profit right after college and agreed to invest in Darius's first flip job.

"You were good with your hands. So, when you talked about flipping houses and I could help, why wouldn't I?" Hakeem finished off his drink. Then stood and walked to the bar to refill his flute. "Now look at you, acquiring and flipping real estate all over the world."

"You didn't have to invest in me...so thank you."

Several moments of comfortable silence passed between

the pair. Darius was lost in his thoughts of what the weekend held. He would finally be done with Las Vegas for a while and could head back to his home base in Georgia. His schedule rarely kept him in his ten-bedroom mansion located in the city of Johns Creek, but that was also where his center and real heart was and he was looking forward to spending some time with her.

"You've avoided two of my questions now."

Hakeem's voice brought him back to the present. "What questions are those?"

"Vanessa and how does it feel." Hakeem counted off his thumb and index finger.

"I feel accomplished. And Vanessa man...I don't know. I think she's beginning to want what I can't give and that's my cue to let her go."

"You're telling me as beautiful as she is and all the years you guys have been doing this off and on thing, the fear of loving someone trumps trying to make it work?"

Love? That was a taboo word for him. Love made a person weak and vulnerable. It made one relax and not take precautions, thinking the one you love will have your back. His angel had loved and look where it left her. Six feet under. So, yes, he'd pass on the weak emotion.

Darius took a deep breath. "That's exactly what I'm saying."

"One day, the money won't be enough. You'll want more."

"And until then, I'll keep acquiring the money. With a clear head." Darius studied his friend. "What's with all the love talk? Are you ready to settle down?"

"I don't know. Some days I am. Bed hopping every night is getting old." Hakeem rubbed his arm absently.

Darius watched as his friend's eyes sunk with regret, as they always did with this topic. That could only mean one thing – Mariama Niang. Over the years, Darius had become convinced she was Hakeem's true love. Darius swallowed a lump in his throat. If he could wish for anything, it would be to go back to that night and make it right for his friend. But even he couldn't. He'd advised Hakeem to move on, but he didn't seem to be able to do it.

"Who knows? You might meet her tonight at the after-party." Darius winked.

Hakeem groaned and Darius laughed. In his opinion, they were still young, but if his friend wanted love, who was he to tell him different? As long as cupid knew to stay miles away from him.

***

"I SAID no cheese and no onions!"

Darius heard the raspy voice as he walked into the hotel's restaurant the next morning. His newest luxury hotel had a soft opening two weeks ago, and guests have been arriving by the thousands since then. Later in the evening was the grand open-ing, so now was not the right time to have dissatisfied customers.

"We're so sorry about that—"

"That's what you said the first time you brought me the omelet with cheese. You went back to fix that and now you're bringing me the omelet with onions. I told you the first time I didn't want either in my omelet."

Darius stood against the table in the back as he noticed the two women. He was walking over to diffuse the situation, but something in that sultry tone halted him.

"Safiya, I know you don't joke about your food, but calm down." The woman sitting by her laughed.

Darius observed the scene as the chief chef came out and

apologized profusely to both women. He then took her plate and hurried back to the kitchen. Darius took in both women. Since they were seated, he couldn't get a full view. However, the one he now knew as Safiya had him intrigued and his loins tight. The curiosity to see the face that went along with that voice had him sauntering towards their table.

"Good morning, ladies," Darius greeted.

Both ladies looked up at him, but only one of them showed signs of recognition.

"You are—" the other lady started.

He quickly cut her off. "Darius Gray, pleased to meet you." He nodded at the pair.

"Ummmm, you're more than Darius Gray. I have an interview with you later," Safiya's friend spoke again.

Darius nodded and smiled, his eyes resting on Safiya, who hadn't yet said a word. She had briefly acknowledged him with her eyes before refocusing on her food.

"I look forward to it Ms...."

She stretched out her hand "Assan. Layla Assan."

Darius shook her hand.

"And this rude one over here is Safiya Nadar." She nudged her friend with her elbow. Her friend growled back at her.

The sound sent an unfamiliar sensation up Darius's spine.

"Excuse her. Something about not getting her food right sets her off."

"Well, I hope the issue has been fixed to your satisfaction."

Safiya looked up at him. In that moment, the trip over to their table was worth it. The right words to describe her beauty eluded him. The wrong adjective would be a disservice.

"Yes, it has. Thank you," Safiya said, and immediately went back to scrolling through her phone and eating.

"I'm glad." Darius turned to Ms. Assan. "I'll see you in a couple of hours. You ladies enjoy your meal."

Darius walked away and went straight to guest services. He wanted to know if they were staying in the hotel or if they just came for breakfast. He had an interview with Ms. Assan soon and needed to know how cooperative he'd be based on what he needed her to do.

THREE

"Tell the pilot there's been a change of plans. We leave for Atlanta tomorrow night, not tonight."

A couple of hours later, Darius paced his office as he rattled off instructions to his assistant. Pleasure never came before business, but this time, he was willing to make a tiny exception.

"Call Mr. Chang in Hong Kong and tell him I have another obligation, so we'll have to push our meeting out. Tell Mr. Patrick he should head to Miami after he leaves San Diego. He has to represent me for the Realtors Annual Gala." Darius walked behind his desk and flipped through his iPad. "And lastly, call the florist. Instead of the usual white roses, send Grammy pink roses."

With the information he'd just gathered, he had to do some swift adjustments. His curiosity had been piqued and when that happened, he chased whatever it was until he got it. The mocha beauty currently staying in his hotel had his attention.

"Yes, Mr. Gray. Is there anything else?" Julia asked.

Darius leaned back in his leather seat and tented his index

fingers under his chin. A few seconds later, he looked up at Julia. "No, that will be all. Thank you."

Julia gave him her signature warm smile and walked toward the exit. Darius attempted to refocus on the day's activities, but try as he might, his mind wandered back to Safiya Nadar. In the moment he was in her presence, all the senses in his body came alive. He allowed his memory to recollect her features. Her mocha skin smelled like strawberries and coconut. Her lips were perfectly outlined with deep burgundy lipstick. As he watched her lips wrap around the fork, he almost let out a moan. Her hazel-brown eyes were shrouded by long black eyelashes. Her jet-black hair was straight and stopped right at her shoulders. He found it so sexy that she kept tucking loose strands behind her ears when she leaned into the plate in front of her. The black t-shirt she wore showed cleavage he'd love to bury his head in.

Over the years, women had come in and out of his life. Some as just bed partners, others as dates, but none could stake claim to him. After their time was up, he compensated them heavily, and they went their separate ways. He was no stranger to beauty. On his arms, he'd had models, actresses, white-collared professionals, you name it. But there was something about Safiya that pulled him in. If he had to move his flight several hours to find out what it was, that's exactly what was going to happen.

"SO, HOW DO YOU RELAX?" Ms. Assan asked.

"Relax? I have no idea what that is," Darius joked.

Ms. Assan had arrived in his office an hour ago for the interview and they were now finishing up. At least he hoped they were.

She had begun by asking him about his childhood. He never really shared his story in detail except the stuff the media already knew; he was an adopted orphan. He never shared the truth that he was abandoned before he became orphaned. The fact that his parents left him at a fire station like yesterday's trash and walked away was something he wasn't proud of. For years, the rejection made him hang his head in shame and fueled his rebellious phase. If he wasn't good enough for them, he didn't see how he could be good enough for anyone.

He'd continued that way until he met Jacqueline Gibson aka Ms. Jackie. That day he was in a store, stuffing essentials into his baggy pants. He bumped into her and everything fell to the floor. He was busted and furious at the same time. As he ran from the store, he cursed her as bad luck and hoped he'd never see the woman again. Fate had something different planned. A week later, she turned up in his orphanage to get some papers signed by the director. That was the beginning of his adoption journey. Darius winced at how much hassle and pain he had given her.

At the time, his goal was to shield himself from her love before she abandoned him like the other woman in his life had done. The reverse turned out to be the case though. She had cared for him unconditionally, making him a part of her family that just consisted of her mother. And when she died a few years later, he almost lost it, but Grammy, as he called his adopted grandmother, wouldn't let him. She put aside her own grief to make sure he was okay. She was his heart and he would move the world to give her anything she desired. Luckily, she hadn't asked him anything he couldn't provide.

"Mr. Gray?"

Darius blinked his eyes and returned his attention to the woman in front of him. "I apologize. You asked about relaxation, correct?"

"Yes. You're an astute billionaire, owning several chains of hotels and casinos around the globe. This year, you added team owner to your belt by acquiring the *Peach Heights* – the Atlanta Baseball team. I'm sure your schedule is extremely busy, but you know what they say, all work and no play..."

"For me, work is relaxing. I've come to find out an idle mind is a terrible thing. It can take me into dark places, so I like to remain occupied. However, I do find time to step away from it all, especially when I go back home to Atlanta."

"What do you like to do?"

"Let me start by saying not golf." Darius laughed and Ms. Assan joined him.

"There's a lake in my backyard and I love sitting there looking out into nature and meditating. I also like to work in my woodshed. Building unique fixtures."

"Oh wow, that's an interesting fact. Pieces you sell?"

"No, it's a hobby of mine and are for my eyes only."

Woodwork was something Jacqueline encouraged him to do to channel his anger. When she died, he stopped and resumed his rebellious behavior until Grammy had a heart-wrenching talk with him. He picked up the hobby again but now, the shed was where he worked and had private conversations with Jacqueline, alone.

"Got it." Ms. Assan looked at her watch. "We're at the end of our time. But I can't let you go without asking you the question on every single woman's mind."

Darius knew it was coming. She hadn't asked it and he dared hope she wouldn't, but here it was.

"We all know you're a very private man, but there has to be a girlfriend somewhere. Is there?"

Darius chuckled. "I'm still a single man. No significant other that I know of."

"Are you adverse to marriage?"

"Short answer...no."

"Long answer?"

"Women need attention and commitment, neither of which I have the capacity for presently."

"Well, at least you're honest about it and not leaving a trail of broken hearts." Ms. Assan smiled.

"Never that."

Several moments later, Darius walked back over to his desk while Ms. Assan packed up her camera and notepad. They'd wrapped up the interview, but she wanted a few pictures of his office and its view.

"Thank you again for talking to me. The interview should be out in next month's issue of the magazine."

"It was a pleasure." Darius extended his hand for a brief handshake. "I'd like to invite you and your friend to the grand opening of the hotel as my special guests tonight. As a rule, I never allow reporters in my private suite. However, I'll make an exception for you."

Just as he expected, Ms. Assan's mouth fell in shock. *Bingo, she took the bait.* He had quite a reputation over the years for being no-nonsense when it came to his privacy, so to invite a camera into his personal space was a major exclusive.

"What? Really?"

"Yes." Darius shoved his hands into his pockets. "Julia will give you the necessary information."

"Thank you so much, Mr. Gray." Ms. Assan made her way to the door and just as she was about to touch the doorknob, Darius called out.

"Ms. Assan."

She turned to face him.

"I do expect to see both of you tonight."

He saw the exact moment in her eyes when she understood

what he really wanted. To his surprise, a huge grin took over her face.

"You will," she responded and made her exit.

FOUR

"You cannot be serious."

Safiya cradled her face and took in a breath. She exhaled and glared at her friend as they walked through the upscale boutique.

"Will you stop being dramatic." Layla looked at her. "The interview went well, and the man invited us to be his guests. What's the big deal?" She lifted a dress from the rack and put it beneath her chin. She stepped in front of the mirror to inspect the outfit.

"The big deal is, you promised it would be a girls' trip. Come on, Lay, I'm not in the mood for a man," Safiya whined.

"A man is definitely in the mood for you," Layla snickered.

Safiya remained silent, a sign that she was serious and most likely frustrated. Layla got the message and turned to look at her. The stare-off lasted only a few second before Layla put the dress back and walked up to Safiya. She took her hand and they sat down on one of the benches.

"Remember that time in Middle School when your pet parrot died?"

Safiya creased her eyebrows, wondering what Slinky had to do with her not wanting to be at a loud party with a billionaire and his other rich friends.

"I hope there's a point to this."

"Stop being difficult and follow me here," Layla scolded.

Safiya nodded with a faint smile. Slinky was very dear to her. Her grandmother gave him to her right before she passed away. When the bird died, she was devastated.

"Remember you mourned that darn thing for weeks..."

"He was special."

"And so was Justin."

Safiya rolled her eyes.

"What I'm trying to say is that after a while, you got a dog and now Rex is like a member of the family."

"He *is* a member of the family." She loved her golden retriever.

"Exactly my point. You got over Slinky and were able to give Rex a chance and love again." Layla paused. "Yes, Justin messed up. Yes, you were hurt. But you must live your life. I'm not telling you to get married. What I am telling you is, have a good time tonight before we go back to our boring lives tomorrow."

Safiya sighed. "You have a whole fiancé. How would he feel?"

"I'll be there partially working. Also, I told Todd and as long as they don't touch or breathe on me, he's cool. You, on the other hand, have no restrictions. And I'm telling you now, Mr. Gray has a thing for you. Please don't be weird."

A few hours earlier, while Layla was conducting her interview, Safiya was lounging by the pool, taking in the Vegas sun while enjoying the company of her Kindle. As she sipped on a mimosa, she berated herself about not taking time off for self-care. She was getting to the erotic part of the book when Layla's loud squeal interrupted her. Several minutes later, Layla had run down how the interview went and told her about the extra pictures she could get tonight. But then there was a catch.

They had always had each other's back – doing anything for the other. That's just the kind of sisterhood they had, but Safiya didn't think she could pull this off. She hadn't been on any dates since Justin broke her heart and as she told Layla before, she had big short-term goals and men were nowhere in her immediate sights.

"Can you please get out of your head?"

"Uhhh...sorry."

"What had you so zoned out?"

"Just thinking about the future."

"There won't be any future if you don't start living for today."

"You know I'll go with you even if I don't want to."

"Yes, I know you will. But I'm asking more than that. I'm asking you to live a little. Don't be weird. Where's the woman I once knew? Daring, confident. Come on, Justin shouldn't have that much power."

In that moment, something snapped in Safiya. He had no power unless she gave it to him. All the lies and deceit came flooding through her like a wave that hit shore. She had pushed the hurt down so deep that she had begun to act like it wasn't so bad. But it was. She rode hard for that man and at the end of the day, he abandoned her in her time of need, and moved on to have a whole new family. That was it. Love was nowhere on the radar, but there was nothing that said she couldn't have a good time.

"What's that smile? A yes?" Layla asked.

"Yes."

Layla squealed and the two friends hugged. They stood up and walked through the store and picked up dresses they wanted to try out for the events of the evening. Since it was a grand opening and they were also relaxing in VIP for the night, they opted for classy and chic. As Safiya tried on the different dresses she took to the dressing room, her mind wandered to the man...Darius Gray.

After the breakfast fiasco and Layla told her who he was, she decided to Google him. Safiya knew from being with Justin that everything you read on the internet was not true. But there was never smoke without fire.

Darius Gray had the most alluring, chestnut colored eyes she'd ever seen. His smooth, hairless scalp, perfectly trimmed moustache and beard oozed dominance and authority. His face showed signs of a hard life that had been spruced up by money. From looking at him earlier, he probably stood at least six feet, five inches. There was still something about him that intrigued her. Especially when she saw the photo shoot he did for GQ.

The images of him flooded her mind and caused her body to tingle. He was cut to perfection, displaying a gorgeous six pack. His muscles rippled against one of the polo shirts he wore in another shot. The image that stuck with her most of all was his taunt ass in the last shoot. It looked like you could break something on it. He was exquisite.

Darius was six years older than her, and had numerous luxury hotels and resorts and other ventures. He came from a lowly background, but now lived in the opulent Johns Creek. Safiya sighed as that was a long way from her modest DeKalb County. What stuck out though was the abundance of information about his social life. He never seemed to keep one woman for long. She wouldn't exactly call him a playboy, as there was nothing about any kind of scandal with any of the women, and they were far and few in between. What was glaring was that none of them lived like her: normal. They were all actresses or models.

There was a knock on the dressing room door. "Girl, get out here. Let me see how the dress fit."

Safiya looked at the emerald gown she had on and smiled. She opened the door for her friend and stepped out.

Layla's mouth fell open. "They ain't ready, *rafiki*... nope they are not ready."

"You like it?"

"I love it! I can't wait until tonight."

"Let me see yours."

Layla lifted the black and white sequined dress. Safiya gave her a smile of approval. They already had their nails done at home, so all that was left was make-up and Layla did a mad face beat. Now all they had to do was enjoy the rest of their day and be ready for tonight.

As they paid for their dresses, Safiya thought about hers. It was a bit more daring than anything she would normally wear, but she was now determined to live a little. Even it was for just one night. The next day she'd be back home, to her boring job and her boring life. Besides, what happened in Vegas stayed in Vegas.

Mr. Gray wanted her company? Her company he would have.

FIVE

He was used to the opulence, the crowd and people vying for his attention. He was also used to people trying to fulfill his every desire. He was, after all, a very wealthy man, and not to be egotistical, but he was also aware of his charm and looks. But what Darius wasn't used to was being ignored by the person he wanted the most.

The ribbon cutting happened a couple of hours ago. After some speeches by him and key high-ranking members of the hotel's staff, dignitaries were taken on a tour of the hotel. After that, they retired to the massive dining room for a light lunch provided by the one and only Chef Perez he had flown in from Paris. Although he never got sidetracked when business was concerned, he couldn't keep his eyes off a certain Ms. Nadar.

When he saw her and Ms. Assan enter the lobby earlier, his breath literally caught in his throat. The dress she wore brought out the animal in him. It was a shade of green. He wasn't sure of the name, but the color against her sepia toned skin was magic. The dress stopped at her knees, showing her shapely legs and hugging her curves like a glove. She had on light make-up, but those lips. Those lips, lush and glossed, looked so soft. He longed to press his lips against them to test his assumption.

He was okay, until she walked across the room. Her exposed skin almost made him choke on his drink. The dress had a plunging back that stopped right above her waist and he could see the inscriptions of a tattoo across the base of her neck. The desire to trace his tongue over it was so strong, he had to put distance between them immediately. There was a time and place for everything.

But their time was now. Ms. Nadar had done everything she could to keep away from him. But now her time was up. Darius, Hakeem and some of his business associates and their significant others were in his private lounge above the hotel. He sat in the corner with Hakeem, nursing his drink.

"I've seen that look. So are you going to do something about it or mope all night?" Hakeem said interrupting his thoughts.

"Shut up, man."

Hakeem lifted his hands in surrender with a laugh. Darius never knew it was possible, but he was nervous about talking one on one with Safiya Nadar. Something about her told him she wasn't easily impressed. Lifting his glass, he threw back his drink, and grimaced at the burn of the liquor as it went down his throat. He set his empty glass down, and sauntered toward the women, who were laughing over drinks.

"Good evening, ladies, I hope you're having a nice time," Darius said.

"Ah! Mr. Gray—" Ms. Assan started.

"Call me Darius."

Safiya smiled and lifted her champagne flute in acknowledgement before taking a sip. *She isn't ignoring me. Progress.*

"Okay, Darius, this place is simply divine. I have no idea how people can afford to stay here for long periods of time. But then again, apparently a whole lot of people can."

Darius chuckled.

"Thank you. I'll be sure to pass your glowing compliments to my architect." Darius glanced at Safiya. "Ms. Nadar are you always this quiet?"

"I'm not quiet. Just observing."

"And what are your observations so far?"

"That there's a whole other world than the one I'm used to."

"How so?"

"Well, it's definitely not this."

"So tell me." Darius paused when he saw her hesitation. "That's if it's not too uncomfortable for you."

"It's not like the one you grew up in, for sure. This hotel is like something I think heaven would look like."

Darius laughed again, but didn't forget the insinuation that he'd always had it good. "You'd be surprised at how I grew up."

Darius glanced at Ms. Assan who smiled at him.

"Ms. Assan..."

"Please call me Layla and I'm giving you permission to call her Safiya."

Safiya rolled her eyes at her friend and laughed. Darius turned to her with a raised brow, non-verbally asking for her permission as well. She nodded and he turned toward Layla.

"I'll call over the hotel manager to walk you around to get some of the pictures I promised you." Darius looked around and summoned Mr. Wringer over.

"That would be fantastic." She patted her bag which Darius assumed had her camera. "While I'm gone, take care of my friend."

"You do know I'm standing right here." Safiya raised her hand.

Darius watched as Layla gave her friend a stoic look and returned her eyes to him. "You seem like a really nice man. But

I also know that if I make one wrong move, your security will tackle me like a ball player. I want you to know, though, that if anything happens to her, I'd gladly go to jail."

Darius was both stunned and pleased by her threat. He could already tell the dynamic of the friendship between the ladies. Normally quick on his toes, her words left him speechless, so he simply answered. "Noted."

Safiya shook her head and closed her mouth that had dropped open in shock.

Darius's hotel manager walked over. "Yes, Boss?"

"Ms. Assan here would like to take some pictures of the private lounge areas. Please show her around."

"Sure thing." He turned to Ms. Assan. "This way please."

Safiya followed them with her eyes until they disappeared around the corner. She then turned to Darius.

"I know you don't want to stand here by yourself. Please come with me. My area is over there. Then you can tell me all about how I grew up in a world so different from yours."

"You're not gonna let that go, are you?"

"Nope." Darius winked.

"So we might as well get started now."

A while later, Darius and Safiya were sitting on one of the plush couches in a secluded part of the club. She'd become more relaxed and he was enjoying her company. He still couldn't believe how strikingly beautiful she was. They'd talked a little politics, television shows – not that he really watched a lot of television – and sports. To his amazement, they shared some of the same interests. The more she spoke, the more he wanted to know. Why, he couldn't place, so for now he'd say she fascinated him.

"You've told me your favorite team, show, and political affiliation, but I still think there's so much more," Darius said.

Safiya took a sip of her drink. "Because there is, as I'm sure there is with you." She uncrossed her legs and then crossed them again. The rise of her dress had Darius's throat constricting. He had tried to ignore the pull between them all night, as he didn't want to scare her off. But the more comfortable they became with each other, the harder he found it to contain the desire that was growing within him.

"So why hotels?"

Darius thought about his reason and didn't know if he wanted to be that vulnerable with her.

"Let's make a deal. I provide an answer, and you grant me a personal question of my own."

"Can I reserve the right to decline to answer?"

"Yes, but you have to offer up something else."

"Offer? Don't you mean answer?"

"No, I mean offer." He winked at her.

Just as he expected, she hated to be challenged and took the bait. "Shoot."

"Okay, I was homeless for a period in my early teens. So, I guess subconsciously I wanted to own houses in excess. Homes that were like homes away from home."

"But why for the rich and not for the less privileged?"

Darius felt his anger rise at that question. Why people automatically assumed he didn't do anything for the less privileged always amazed him.

"Have you heard of Now Living?"

"Uhhh...yes. I love the work they do for the downtrodden. Is that you?" Safiya's eyes bugged out. She looked at him with remorse and astonishment.

Darius simply nodded.

"I'm so sorry for assuming. I should know better."

"That's okay. Let's just say you can make it up to me later." Darius paused and decided to pursue what she was saying. "Why should you know better?"

"I mean people make assumptions about me that aren't true."

"Like?"

"When I got my divorce…"

"You're divorced?"

"Yes," she whispered.

"How long now?" Darius wanted to ensure there wasn't a crazed ex running around somewhere.

He had lived his life scandal free and needed it to stay that way. One, he couldn't stomach scandals and two, he couldn't do anything that would affect his reputation, stock and eventually his money. Poverty was never ever going to be an option where he was concerned. This time, however, the mention of an ex brought out another feeling – possession.

"Over a year."

"I hope he's not lurking around somewhere trying to get you back."

Safiya raised her brows. "Why? Will you protect me?" She tilted her head back and laughed, showing her perfect, white teeth.

Her elongated neck begged for a kiss. When she noticed he wasn't sharing the moment, she calmed down.

"I'll do more than protect you if you let me." His voice was low.

She raised her hand and tugged her earlobe, something he noticed she did any time she was nervous.

"I didn't know that you had to wait for anyone to let you do anything."

"I usually don't, but you're different."

"Why? I'm sure you have women falling at your command."

"But I have a feeling, not you."

"You got that right." Safiya looked around the lounge. "This is all nice, but it isn't the real world."

He noticed her attempt to change the topic and indulged her. "Just because it's not your world doesn't mean it's not real."

"You do have a point. The more reason I'm not trying to get caught up in it."

Darius studied her. He made her nervous and he was conflicted about it. On one hand, it confirmed her attraction to him. While on the other, she was doing everything to fight it. All he wanted was for her to trust him enough to relax. He was used to women throwing themselves at him for what he had. The woman beside him couldn't care less and he was enjoying that.

"Tell you what? Let me make it your world for the night."

Safiya stood with an infuriated look on her face. Darius knew immediately that she had misconstrued what he meant to say. He stood. Despite her height, he still towered over her.

"No, no, I meant for you to allow me show you the town. The view of the city is exquisite at night and I'd love to show you around."

"Oh." Safiya used her hands to smooth down her dress that had risen with the haste in which she stood. "Ummmm.... let me go check on Layla."

"Ms. Assan is in good hands. I promise." Darius stepped closer to her, deliberately invading her space. Unlike before, she didn't back away. She was a far cry from the woman who didn't even look him in the eye at breakfast the previous day. He was grateful to whatever was responsible for the change. That and the liquid courage in her glass.

Safiya gave him a skeptical look. Darius chuckled when she took out her phone and called her friend. After a couple of "oh's", "that's nice", "sure", and "goodnights", Safiya hung up the phone and returned it to her purse.

"I told you she was fine. You ready?"

She nodded. "Lead the way tour guide. I have to be back early because my flight leaves pretty early in the morning."

"That's new. I've never been called that before."

"Well, Mr. Gray, there's always a first time for everything."

"Oh yes. Yes, there is."

SIX

"I can't believe it. Are you serious?" Safiya asked. She was barely able to hold her laughter in as she waited on Darius's answer.

His face was flushed. "Scout's honor." He raised his hand.

She swatted his hand. "You weren't even a scout."

He shrugged and laughed along with her. "You know what I mean."

For the past couple of hours, they'd been riding round the streets of Las Vegas in his stretch limousine. They shared drinks and stories about themselves that no one else knew. He had taken off his tie and jacket and rolled up his sleeves, while she was bare feet.

"Butt dialing her grandma has to be a classic." Safiya took another sip of her drink. Her tolerance meter was telling her she shouldn't, but she was enjoying herself. Darius had told her stories from his rebellious youth, even how he met his best friend, Hakeem Richardson and the rest of the gang; Brice and Aiden. This story about him and his teenage crush having sex, not knowing they had butt-dialed her grandmother took the cake.

"Okay, stop laughing at my pain, woman."

"Okay, okay...my bad."

Darius pulled her legs up and draped them across his knees. He began gently massaging her feet. Earlier, when she complained about them hurting, he had encouraged her to do away with her shoes. She hated heels. This was all Layla's idea, and they started to do what they always did; hurt her feet. At first the gesture seemed harmless, but now she wasn't so sure. Nevertheless, the will to repossess her feet eluded her as she let out a moan.

"Be careful, you won't want me to think you enjoy my foot rubs."

Safiya narrowed her eyes at him. The need to prove to Layla and herself that she still had what it took to attract any man had been on the rise all night. Before Justin, she was like Layla had said, daring and resourceful. So, just for tonight that's exactly what she'd be. After all, what happened in Vegas stayed here.

"Why Mr. Gray, supposing I do. What are you going to do about it?" She adjusted herself, propping herself up with her elbows.

"Supply your heart desires."

His eyes roamed her body, leaving a trail of fire in their path. Her breathing hitched, causing him to grin. He continued caressing her feet, then calves, slowly moving up to her thighs. The atmosphere around them was charged with lust, desires and, dare she say, greed. All night long, with his wit, charm and humor, he had slowly chipped away at the invisible wall she had put up. She actually liked him. The evening felt very inti-mate. Over and over, she chided herself that this was wrong, but then consoled herself that after tonight, she'd never see him again.

Darius caressed her jaw, then his fingers wrapped around her neck, pulling her flush into him. She straddled him with her hands flat on his rock-solid chest. They stayed locked in an intense gaze for a minute. It was as though Darius wanted her to register what was happening between them.

"May I?"

Safiya nodded.

"I need you to say the words, beautiful."

"Yes," she whispered.

The word was barely out when his lips hit hers. Like clay in the hands of a potter, her body melted and molded against his. Of their own accord, her arms wrapped themselves around his neck as her palms caressed his smooth head. His tongue invaded her mouth and tried to set up camp. Soon after, their tongues began to do battle as she held on for dear life. She had never been kissed that way before. He was on a mission to claim her soul. He nipped her lip and she moaned. His hands roamed her body and blood rushed to her head, making thinking impossible.

"Perfection," he whispered.

The tingling in her body made her weak. Now she understood the term, earth-shattering kiss. He gave her several light kisses along her face and neck. He gathered her into his lap while she came down from her high. She laid her head on his chest. Darius's fingers stroked her hair sending her straight into a sleep coma.

"MR. GRAY. MR. GRAY."

Darius felt nudging. He stretched his body and opened his

eyes. Standing before him was a fully dressed Safiya Nadar. He blinked to gather his bearings. They weren't in the Walden, rather in another one of his hotels in a different part of town. He returned his eyes to her. She lowered her eyes and stepped back. A move he found cute considering all the things he'd done to her body over the last several hours.

"Good morning, beautiful. And I think we're way past the formalities." He sat up against the headboard and folded his arms across his bare chest.

Safiya twisted her fingers together. "Ummm...Darius, I'd like to explain—"

Darius raised his hand to stop her. They'd been very reckless, but he still needed his ego intact. And her trying to tell him this was a mistake less than a couple of hours later wasn't the way to do it. Yes, it was a slip-up, but he was going to consider it the side effects of spur-of-the-moment Vegas nights.

"Can I at least freshen up before you start laying down the regrets?"

"Um, yeah sure."

Darius glanced at her again with a smile. Picking up the phone by the bedside, he made a quick call. Securing the sheet around his body, he walked toward her. He kissed her forehead and proceeded to the bathroom.

Darius stared at his reflection in the mirror. In the solitude of the room, he chided himself for being so careless. He'd always made sure he was cautious and strategic with everything he did. Getting drunk around the town with a stranger and ending up somewhere other than where he stayed was something he had never done. There was a uniqueness about Safiya, though. He couldn't shrug it off even if he wanted to.

He made up a plan to satisfy both his lust and curiosity; keep her around until she was out of his system. It would be a win-win. He'd offer to take care of her, and she'd be his companion. His lips turned up in a smile when they caught the hickey on his neck. Yes, she was one of a kind and he didn't want to let her go just yet. However, he had to think of something convincing enough to get her to stay.

Minutes later, Darius walked back into the bedroom. Safiya was no longer in her dress from yesterday, but a simple white tee and jeans he had the boutique downstairs bring up for her.

She was so preoccupied with something on her finger that she hadn't looked his way. Darius cleared his throat and she looked up at him.

"I see the clothes fit. I thought you'd prefer them to the dress you wore last night."

"Yes, thank you."

"Would you like to order breakfast?"

"Uhhh, no I really should be going back."

"Running away from me so soon?"

"Mr. Gray..."

The scowl on his face made her correct herself.

"Darius, this was fun. I have no regrets, Really, I don't, but I have to leave now."

"At least have breakfast with me first."

She looked at her watch.

"What time does your flight leave?" he asked.

"Soon."

"And you're going back to Atlanta, correct?"

"Yes."

"So, let's eat. You'll have ample time to make it." Even if he had to convince her to travel on his jet with him, he would.

She placed her hand on her hip and smirked. "Does anyone ever say no to you?"

"Not if I can help it. Could you please order us breakfast?" Darius wiggled his brows.

Safiya giggled. "Sure."

Darius walked back to the bag that held the clothes from the boutique and retrieved the brown khakis and a pink polo shirt. He quickly dressed as Safiya talked to someone on the phone. He presumed it was her family or Ms. Assan.

Soon after, there was a knock on the door. Darius opened the door to the waiter. The smell of eggs, waffles, sausage, ham, grits and coffee hit his nose, causing his stomach to rumble. Moments later, the pair had settled down to their food.

"So, did you have a good time in Vegas?"

"Yes. I had never been before, but I know for sure I can't live here. It's a little too fast paced for me." She raised her index finger. "But, I did meet a certain billionaire who showed me a nice time."

"Glad to be of service." Darius chuckled. "Supposing I told you I wanted to see you again?"

"This time I'd be firm on my 'no'." If she didn't have a flustered look on her face, Darius would've laughed.

"You hurt me. Am I that terrible?" He feigned pain.

"On the contrary. You're a decent human being, but like I've been telling you the past twenty-four hours, our worlds are very different." Safiya lifted her cup of coffee to her lips.

She stared down at her left hand with a puzzled look on her face. "Do you know why I have this soda ring thing on my finger?

Darius took her hand in his and studied it. It was the ring from the mouth of a soda can.

"I'm not sure, but I can't remember half of what happened yesterday. Maybe you tried to open a soda." Darius shrugged.

"Yeah maybe. I've been trying to take the darn thing off, but it hurts. When I get back to the room, I'll use some cocoa butter."

The rest of their breakfast was eaten with light chatter. They both talked about their other interests in the community and personal aspirations. Darius noticed that Safiya made him think a little deeper than he normally would. His whole focus in life was conquering the now and focusing on the next. That made him think about his deal in Paris coming up in the next couple of weeks.

Darius excused himself and walked over to the dresser to retrieve his phone. It was almost ten a.m. He had to return to the hotel and get on with the day. He glanced over at Safiya who was tucking a loose tress of her hair behind her ears. He winked at her and she bit her lip and lowered her head, trying to hide her blush. His mind wandered to their sexy escapade and he adjusted himself. His phone rang, interrupting his thoughts.

"Hey Hakeem, what's going on?" he answered the call.

"Is there anything you want to tell me?"

Darius frowned and removed the phone from his ear. He put the device back against his ear. "Who pissed in your Cheerios this morning?"

"A certain billionaire who's acting out of character."

"What has Brice done this time?" Darius asked.

The Richardson brothers, as they were known, were totally different in character. Hakeem was the more reserved one and Brice was the reckless one.

"Just turn on the TV man. We have to fix this because..."

Darius zoned out of the rest of the conversation. The frown on his face must have alerted Safiya. She stood and walked to him.

"What's wrong?"

"I'm about to find out." Darius looked around for the remote and couldn't find it. "Do you know where the remote is?"

Safiya did a quick search and found it behind the television. She handed it to him, and he powered on the television.

Darius placed the phone back to his ears. "What am I supposed to be looking for?"

Before Hakeem could speak, the headline splashed across the screen. *Billionaire Darius Gray is off the Market.* Darius's eyes bugged while Safiya let out a gasp. The presenter went on to say that he and an unidentified woman were seeing coming out of a chapel in the middle of the night after a quickie wedding by an Elvis impersonator. In the blurred footage, Safiya's head was down so no one could see her, but Darius was on full display. It went on to say that they were working on finding out who the woman was.

Safiya plopped down on the bed. Darius turned the television off and sat beside her. He took her hands in his. Neither of them said a word for several minutes. The memory of the previous day came flooding back to him. After their make-out session in the car, he'd ordered his driver to cruise around the strip while they soaked up the high. Sometime later, Safiya stood on the seat and stuck her head through the rooftop while the wind flowed through her hair. She encouraged him to join her and he did.

It was carefree and spontaneous. In that short time, that's exactly how she made him feel—lighthearted. They came across one of those chapels and she wanted to see what a real one looked like. Her wish was his command. He couldn't remember them getting hitched, but the reports claimed they did. He made a mental note to get Julia to obtain any records the chapel had.

"You still there?"

Darius heard Hakeem's voice come through the speaker. He hadn't hung up. He picked up the phone and told Hakeem to meet him in fifteen minutes in his suite. After hanging up, he called Julia, gave her some instructions and told her the same. He took in a breath, exhaled and faced Safiya.

"Please do something. We must get this annulled before they identify who I am. I can't do this. I can't." She was sobbing.

Darius knelt in front of her. He cupped her face in his hands. "I'll protect you. This will be annulled before the end of the day."

Her gaze bored into his eyes, probably searching for the truth of his words. He was extremely attracted to her, but he'd never kept a woman against her free will. And he wasn't going to start now. Besides, him wanting to see her again wasn't the same as wanting to be married to her – by a long shot. They were definitely on the same page. Annulment.

"I guess that answers the mystery of the soda ring on my finger," she whispered.

"I can't believe I was so cheap. You deserved a better ring." Darius joked, trying to make light of the situation.

Safiya nudged him playfully. He smirked. There was nothing light about the situation, but he couldn't stand to see her upset and panicked.

"You're so silly. But I'm serious, you'll take care of this? My dad and I live a very quiet life. I can't bring this spotlight to him. Not when he isn't feeling good."

"Scout's honor."

"Do I need to remind you again that you're not a scout?"

"Depends on how you want to remind me."

Ugh...move I can't take you seriously. That's how we landed in this mess in the first place."

SEVEN

"Just slow down a minute and think," Hakeem said.

Darius was growing frustrated with his friend's ridiculous idea. He buried his head in his hands and let out a growl. He had taken a quick shower and changed into some of his own clothes. He couldn't get in his second cup of coffee before Hakeem came barging in. Granted, he was his best friend and investment man, but what he was proposing was utterly ridiculous. Darius plopped down on the couch in the sitting area of his penthouse suite. He cradled his arms on his knees and leaned forward.

"I promised her that I'd get this thing annulled by tonight. The more I waste time with you, the possibility of that happening is slipping through my fingers."

"But listen to me. You're one of the very few billionaires that have been free of scandal. Your shareholders have come to rely on your sound judgement, meaning they and your investors trust you."

"And..."

"The world is still waiting on you to give a statement about this marriage. Now you want to give the statement and say it's a mistake?" Hakeem frowned. "You could lose your credibility; your stocks would plummet, and investors will pull out. It speaks a lot to how reckless you can potentially be."

"You and I know that I'm not reckless. It was a drunken mistake; one I plan to fix. More importantly, marriage is nowhere on my radar. So, no, I will not be forced into one because of what people would say," Darius emphasized.

"You and I are not the ones that lace your pockets. This could seriously affect your bottom line. Is it something you're willing to risk?"

Darius stood and walked over to the balcony. He opened the sliding door and walked out. His chest started to tighten. Logically, he knew that nothing the shareholders did would do any significant damage to his net worth. But fear was nagging at him. He vowed that he would never be poor again or be looked at as that orphan that wasn't of value to society. This wasn't the same thing, but it had the potential to be strikingly close.

Losing money or spoiling his name was a trigger for him, and Hakeem's words had begun playing mind games on him. But marriage? Even a fake one was nowhere in his cards. He was not averse to love...why was he even thinking about that word? This was purely lust. All the same, he wanted no parts of it on a permanent basis.

"Look man, it's not permanent. You like the chick—"

"Her name is Safiya." Darius snapped.

"You see, that proves my point. You like Safiya, so it's not that bad." Hakeem paused. "You said it yourself, you wanted her for a steady companion, so why not just ask her?"

"Wanting her for a steady companion and being married to her for convenience are two different things. I'm just setting myself up for..."

"For what? The possibility that you might actually fall?"

Darius clenched his jaw. "I think you have you and I confused. I'm not falling for anything. I'm just not trying to inconvenience myself or her."

"Well, you gotta figure it out. Is doing anything other than, at minimum, six months to a year of discomfort worth you potentially putting a dent in all that you've worked for?"

Darius frowned. Try as much as he could, he couldn't totally dismiss Hakeem's concerns. But why would she want to pretend to be married to him?

"Offer to pay her." Hakeem blurted out, as though he could read his thoughts. "Money can do anything, my friend. Persuade her by offering money. A cool million will do the trick."

Darius contemplated for several seconds. How could he tell her that because of his stocks, she should stay married to him for a while? The lady he had come to know in the last twenty-four hours would for sure tell him what he could do, and where he could go with his reputation and money. It wouldn't be pretty.

Darius toyed with both options. Do nothing and give her the annulment he promised her or be self-centered. The latter bothered him because it was all about his ego, but up until now, when it came to his reputation and money, that's exactly how he guarded it.

His phone buzzed in his pocket, breaking him away from his thoughts. It was his heart. He looked at his watch. He should've been on the jet by now, headed home to her.

"Hey, my favorite lady," Darius greeted his grandmother upon answering the phone.

"How are you doing, baby?" She paused. "But then again, I don't know how favorite I am if you couldn't call me first."

"Grammy, what are you talking about? You know I'm on my way back to you. We'll spend the whole week together."

"Don't you dare. That wife of yours deserves a proper honeymoon. When you get back, then come see me and then you can tell me why I had to hear it from the church instead of you."

Darius didn't even have the ability to formulate words to respond to her. *This can't be freaking happening.* He had gotten TMZ to pull the story earlier. Apparently, it wasn't done early enough to stop his grandmother's nosy friends from seeing it. He desperately wanted to tell her the truth, but she was still recovering from open heart surgery she'd had some weeks ago.

"Are you there, Darius? Did you hear me?"

"Uhhh, no Grammy. What did you say?"

"I said I'm happy you finally settled down. I want to see my great grandkids. You know I'm not getting younger. But I wasn't going to badger you about it. I knew you'd come around."

"Ummm, yes ma'am."

"So where are you going for the honeymoon? Do you know how long you'll be gone?" She fired questions at him. "Oh, never mind, take as long as you like, but bring my granddaughter-in-law back to me as soon as you get back," she instructed.

Darius was ready to respond when he heard coughing. The nurse he hired to take care of her could also be heard in the background. Moments later, she came to the phone.

"Mr. Gray, Ms. Elise needs to take her medication and rest now. Can she call you back?"

"Yes, sure. How is she doing?"

"She's doing great. I make sure to keep her stress and worry free. Soon she'll be out of the woods and back to her regular activities."

"How long will that take?"

"With the progress she's making, six to nine months tops."

"Okay, let me say bye to her." Seconds later his grand-mother was back on the phone. "I love you, Grammy."

"I love you too, baby, Take care of my granddaughter-in-law for me."

After they hung up, Darius remained silent. With that single phone call, the dynamics of his situation just changed. He had to convince Safiya. Now it was personal.

EIGHT

"I said come to Vegas and have a nice time." Layla fussed. "I said nothing about coming here and getting your behind married."

Safiya and Darius had returned to the Walden a little while ago. They left the other hotel through an exit she didn't even know hotels had. On getting here, they entered this one with the same secrecy. She always knew rich people did too much, but this was just extra. In this situation, though, she appreciated it.

When they arrived, two burly men met them. They didn't speak, but one carried her bag and the other carried his. Julia, his assistant was also there and was rattling things that Safiya couldn't keep up with. What she did hear – words like court, press and annul – satisfied her.

Darius didn't take her number, but told her that someone would be in touch. He brushed his lips lightly on her cheeks and wished her well. Safiya didn't want to admit it, but the gesture stung. Something had changed from when they were alone to when they were around his staff. She knew he couldn't be overly affectionate with her, but his coolness created a twinge in her heart.

"Lay, chill out. I told you Darius said it would be annulled before the day is over and the record sealed."

"Oh, so we're calling him Darius, now." Layla teased.

"Stop it. I'm stressed out enough." Safiya threw her clothes into her suitcase. They had to leave for the airport in the next hour.

"You wouldn't be stressed if when I tried to get you to have fun, you did." Layla walked to the dresser to pack up her hair products. "If you had fun on the regular like any normal twenty-nine-year-old, you wouldn't have gone all the way to the left when a little fun was dangled in front of you."

"Says the woman that bartered me off for some pictures."

"Sure did, but no one told you to give up the cookies. That was all you." Layla giggled. "I'm fine with that though, because despite all your fronting, you like that tall glass of cocoa."

Safiya tried but couldn't hide the heat that crept up into her cheeks. That man's body should be in a museum somewhere on display. When he was dressed, he was a thing to remember but naked, that physique should be studied in colleges.

"Oh Jeez, that look on your face!" Layla shook her head. "I'm glad he got you together. But again, did you have to marry the man?"

"I don't know why you're still carrying on. I should be the one panicking. But I'm not, because I know he'll fix this."

"No, you're not panicking because you're still under the trance of his charm." Layla placed her hand over her heart. "You gonna drive my pressure up."

"Stop being silly. I told you everything will be fine."

"And if it's not. Do you like him?"

"Like as a person, yes. Attracted even...yes. Do I want to be married to him? Hell nah. Do you know what kind of headache that would be? A real marriage to a billionaire? Not even a fake one. We barely know each other."

"But your lady bits know him." Layla winked.

Safiya waved her off. "Yeah and you can see what kind of asinine decisions came as a result."

The two friends laughed as they checked around the room to make sure they didn't forget anything. Putting their suitcases on the floor, they picked up their purses and made their way to the door. Safiya's eye widened at the two bodyguards she'd seen earlier, standing in front of her door.

"May I help you gentlemen?" Layla asked before Safiya could form the same question.

They glanced over at her. At least she assumed they did since their heads moved and their eyes were covered by dark shades. Safiya always found that dumb since there was no sun in a building. Once again, too much.

"Ms. Nadar, Mr. Gray would like to see you," one of them said.

"For what? We have a plane to catch."

"Those are our orders, Ms. Nadar."

"Well, you can tell your boss I have a plane to catch," Safiya said, fuming at the way Darius was summoning her. *Who does he think he is?*

"We can't allow you to leave."

"Can't?" Safiya seethed.

"Ms. Nadar, we're only doing our jobs. Mr. Gray requested your presence. If you just follow us, you'll make it easy on us all."

Safiya was about to say something else when Layla touched her arm. "Girl, I'm not trying to be on the news. Let's go see what the man wants, and we'll be on our way."

"He asked for just Ms. Nadar—"

"Well, that's where he messed up. Because she isn't going

anywhere without me," Layla responded. "So, what's it gonna be Hercules? You wanna go back and tell your boss she's not coming because you won't let me tag along?"

The two men looked at each other and shrugged. "Follow us."

"You're banned from giving out the cookies. You were generous one night and now we're being escorted to the upper room by Hercules and Mr. T over there," Layla said in a hushed tone.

Safiya would've found the joke hilarious, but her face was flush and the vein throbbing in her neck had her mind on one target. Darius Gray. No one summoned her. She didn't care how much money they had.

NINE

"Are you out of your mind? You want me to do what?!"

Safiya could almost feel the imaginary smoke being emitted from her ears. She stood on the opposite side of the chair and glared at the object of her rage. Seconds later, she lowered her eyes, disengaging from their stare-off. Although she could snap his neck right now, Darius was still the sexiest man she'd ever seen. *Get it together, Safiya. Focus!*

She and Layla were escorted to his suite several minutes ago. She met his friend, Hakeem. After she dug into him about summoning her, he apologized and politely asked Hakeem and Layla to give them some privacy. What she thought he wanted to say could never rival what he actually said.

"Safiya, I'll pay you two million dollars to stay married to me for nine months."

"Lower your voice, beautiful," he said calmly.

"Don't tell me to lower my voice. You're proposing to turn my life upside down so I can pretend to be your wife? Do you have any idea what you're asking me?"

"I do. And it's not my intention, but there are other variables to consider now. I can't make the annulment happen."

"Can't or won't?

"A little bit of both." He paused and walked towards her, she stepped back. He stopped and raised his hands in surrender. "Look, if I didn't really need you, I wouldn't ask."

"I have a life. Can you guarantee that it will go on without any changes while we're pretending?"

This was just crazy to her. One minute she was assuring Layla that he would be true to his word and ensure the annulment would go through. And the next, he's asking her to stay married to him for the next nine months. What about her dad? What about her job? Her quiet life? All of that would be interrupted just so he could please his grandmother. His grandmother was sick, and she felt bad. She wouldn't be human if she didn't, but why must her life change so that his could be good?

Since his grandmother had a heart condition, Safiya would not only have to pretend in public, but also in private. Darius was proposing that Safiya would move into the same mansion his grandmother lived in.

"No, your life will change drastically. You will be moved into my mansion. You can't go back to your job. As my wife, you'll have to head several charities, attend charity dinners and fundraisers, important events and, of course, travel with me as often as I require you to be there. But I promise you, the minute our contract is up, I won't keep you a moment longer.

"Wow! And your life, remains as it is. This is unfair. What will my dad say?"

"He can't think that it isn't real. That would do more harm than good. The only people that will know that this is an arrangement are Layla, Hakeem and my lawyer."

Safiya placed both hands on the back of the couch and

bowed her head. She wasn't sure she could do this. She wanted to make a better life for her dad and herself, but not like this. He had a ton of medical bills and she had school loans. She was making little to nothing in a job she hated. Nevertheless, was exchanging that for money worth what her life would become? Could she endure the scrutiny she'd be under? Not to mention the flock of women she was sure would come after her for snagging one of the most eligible billionaires in the country. She was deeply attracted to Darius, but in no way was she willing to put her heart on the line for him to potentially trample upon.

"You're a billionaire…"

"That I know."

"You can get anything you want in the world."

"Almost anything."

"I'm sure you can have any woman pretend to be married to you."

"I'm sure I can."

"So why me?"

"Because you're the one that my grandma saw."

"But she didn't see me. My head was bent."

"That's true, but she saw the color of your skin."

"So? You can get any other black woman to pretend to be your wife."

"None that I know are Safiya Nadar."

"Now you're just playing with me. Why me?"

Darius moved closer to her. She stepped back, but unlike before, he continued his approach until her back was against the wall. He leaned against her. Her breath hitched and her heart rate accelerated. His cologne made it impossible for her to breathe. Their eyes locked, as his fingers made a sensual and slow accent up her thigh. He lifted her and her legs immediately circled his waist. He captured her lips. Safiya groaned as his tongue invaded her mouth, ready for battle. Moments later, he set her lips free.

"I don't know any other Safiya, whose kisses drive me insane. I don't know any other Safiya, whose eyes have me ready to give her the world. I don't know any other Safiya whose raspy voice sends shivers down my spine. I don't know any other Safiya who makes me throw caution to the wind. Do you want me to go on?"

She shook her head, speechless. She was caught up in euphoria by his words and the feel of his hands caressing her back. She closed her eyes, and leaned her head back exposing her neck. He buried his head in the nook of her shoulder before setting her ablaze with light kisses.

Darius set her down. She looked up at him just in time to catch the smirk on his face. It jerked her back to reality. He had used her desires to his advantage. The right thing to do would be to push him away and stomp off. The will to do it, however, was missing. She liked him and he was willing to pay her. And she was sure she'd have some fun during the deal.

"Did that change your mind, beautiful?" His body was still flush against hers.

"You do know money and sex can't get you everything."

"Yes, I'm aware of that. If not, we would've been on our honeymoon by now and not wasting the past hour arguing."

"So, nine months, two million dollars and that's it?"

"Scout's honor."

Safiya rolled her eyes and pushed him away. "Jeez, I'm in trouble. There you go with that Scout's crap again."

Darius let his head fall back in laughter and pulled her close. He nipped her ear. "Behave woman. Don't push your husband away."

Safiya rolled her eyes. *Please, let me come out of this with my heart intact.*

THE NEXT DAY, after a painful interrogatory phone call with her dad – who was still not pleased - a draining talk with her best friend convincing her that she'd be okay; and the intense scrutiny of a lawyer, Safiya was finally on Darius's private jet headed to Tunisia in North Africa for their fake honeymoon. Not only had his grandmother insisted on it, but his lawyer, Layla and Hakeem had suggested that if they were going to do this, they might as well make it believable.

She was seated next to the windows as she scrolled through Instagram. Darius's lawyer released a short statement a few hours ago and already the press had dug up everything there was to know about her. Not only that, but she was now being compared to every woman he had ever dated. She rolled her eyes and continued to scroll through her feed. She hated the internet sometimes. She was so engrossed in reading the good and not so good posts that she didn't feel Darius standing by her side until her phone was being taken out of her hand.

"Stop reading that smut. The media will say whatever it takes to make people click on their links.

"So, they'll do anything for clout."

"Huh?"

"You have no idea where that line came from, do you?"

Darius shook his head, turned off her phone and slipped it into his front pocket. Safiya giggled at his confusion.

"Have you heard of Cardi B and Offset?"

Darius creased his brows. "Of course, I've heard of them."

Safiya narrowed her eyes. "But not that song?"

"No. Not really a fan."

"I am. The line is off their "Clout." song. Basically—"

"Safi baby, I know what clout is. I'm not that removed."

"Okay, just checking," she chuckled. "Can't believe you

don't know the song though. It was so popular. Hmm, I guess I'll let you slide."

"Don't tease me, woman. Because you know exactly what I wanna slide in."

"Get your mind out of the gutter." Safiya giggled and turned her head so she could look out the window. Needing a break from his intense stare. His eyes, if she stared at them too long, she'd find herself trapped in a trance. She hoped that at the end of this she wouldn't find her heart trapped in limbo, because despite their attraction to each other, he had paid her, and she had accepted. She had to remember that.

The pair settled in for the seventeen-hour flight. They had casual conversation over their meal, played cards, talked some more, and watched a couple of movies before settling in for the night.

Safiya woke up to a kiss on her forehead "We're here, beautiful."

She stretched her body, it seemed like she only went to sleep a minute ago. Not wanting to share her stale breath with him, she made her way to the bathroom.

"No kiss?" His deep chuckled tailed her.

Moments later, they deplaned at Djerba Zarzis airport and were whisked away by a long, black car with tinted windows. Darius placed his hand on her thigh as they rode through the small, quaint town. Being from the eastern part of Africa, she had learned about the other regions of Africa. Her dad made sure of that. She had never however been anywhere in North Africa. She was so excited about being able to see some of it in person.

They were spending the next three weeks in Djerba, the largest island in North Africa, which was in the Gulf of Gabes. According to Darius, he bought a villa in Houmt El Souk, which was the main city on the island about a year and a half ago.

"So, how did you find this place?" Safiya asked.

"I came here once with a business partner. I knew instantly I wanted to own property here. In America and almost all of Europe, I'm known as Mr. Gray. When I come here, I'm just Darius," he said. "And sometimes I need to be that."

"I'm honored you decided to share this place with me."

He responded by squeezing her thigh. Safiya turned her body slightly to get a good view of the scenery.

"I know it's going to be a lot when we get back. So, I figured this will be a good place to be without all the chaos."

"I appreciate it." The only problem was that with only the two of them and little or no staff, she wasn't sure how she'd be able to avoid him. Which she had come to realize was something she must do.

Once they arrived at the guarded residence, Darius gave her a tour of the place. The ground level of the two-story villa had a full kitchen, a patio, pool, an office and a total of five bedrooms, each with a balcony and an adjoining bathroom. Half of what he was telling her about the history of the place, was lost on the opulence of the villa.

Even if he didn't want others to know who he was, I'm sure this house will give them an idea.

Moments later, they made their way up the stairs and came to a halt in front of a room down the hall. Darius opened the door, allowing enough space for her to enter. It was huge, probably the size of her one-bedroom studio apartment. The décor was crème, pink and grey. With such feminine colors, she immediately wondered how many women he'd brought here. She walked over to the balcony and opened the double doors. The view and the sunshine hitting her face was heaven. The air seemed to be saturated with the smell of the Sahara Desert mixed with waters of the Mediterranean Seas. She took in a deep breath and exhaled.

"This will be your room. I'd rather you stay with me, but I understand this may all be too much, so I'm willing to give you options," Darius said, after he'd tucked her bags neatly away.

"Willing? Oh, how kind of you sir," Safiya snickered.

Darius shook his head at her. "My room is at the other end of the hall. Make yourself at home and I'll come check on you later."

Left by herself, Safiya checked out her room. The details were outstanding, the bed linen was certainly 100% silk. The pink and grey tiles in the bathroom were so intricately put together, she wondered how long it took and the patience to see it through. She took out her phone and called her dad and Layla to let them know she'd arrived safely. A few seconds later, still sitting on the bed, Safiya yawned. It was Tuesday evening and in just seventy-two hours, her life had completely changed.

She decided to take a shower so she could relax on the king-sized bed, even though it looked too good to lay on. As she went into the bathroom, she remembered she had nothing to wear. She had packed extra light for Vegas, and never made it home.

She went in search of her bag in the closet. Her mouth gaped and her eyes widened at the sight before her. Quickly gathering herself, she walked into the expansive space. There was every piece of clothing a woman could need – jeans, dresses, shorts, skirts, blouses, formal wear – you name it. There were also belts, bags, hats, purses, sneakers and heels. Safiya's mouth hung open in awe. There was a note on the island located in the middle of the closet. Her hands shook as she walked over to retrieve it.

I hope everything is to your liking.
See you later

DG

When did he have time to do this? Safiya's mind travelled back to the phone calls Darius had made right after she signed the contract two days ago. She overheard him mention Tunis, but assumed he was telling someone to get the house ready. Not buy up the whole mall. Safiya picked out a cute loungewear set, took a quick shower and hopped into bed for what she thought would be a quick nap.

TEN

Darius opened the cabinet and got out two plates. He dished out *ojja*. It was a traditional breakfast he tasted a while ago and had become very fond of. It was basically eggs poached in a deliciously spicy tomato sauce mixed with spicy lamb sausage and local spices. He sliced a fresh baguette and set it on the side. He hoped she'd like the staple Tunisian breakfast, if not he could easily whip up an omelet. He walked over to the boiling hot water and poured it into a tea pot over mint tea.

The three days since their arrival in Houmt El Souk were spent in the villa. Safiya introduced him to Nollywood movies on Netflix. The Nigerian movie industry, which to his surprise was the third largest movie industry in the world, behind Hollywood and Bollywood. She was adamant about him not checking his phone or any of his gadgets. In her words, they needed to get with the business of getting to know one another so they could convince his Grammy that the marriage was legit. The last thing he wanted to do was rattle her even further, so he complied.

Relaxation.

It was a strange feeling since he didn't really believe in the concept. He had work to do, deals to close. Time and circumstances were constantly changing, so he made it a point to use his judiciously.

Darius was sorely mistaken when he'd thought that since they were indoors, they'd spend most of their time reacquainting their bodies. Safiya vetoed that, along with them sharing a bed. When he gave her a separate room, he didn't really believe she'd use it. Today, he was working on changing that. True, this was a phony marriage, but there was nothing fake about the way his body craved hers.

Setting their food in the middle of the island, he turned to the refrigerator for the juice, then poured her a cup of tea. He smiled when he remembered the first morning they woke up and she frantically searched for a coffee pot. He didn't drink it, so had no use for it. Safiya he noticed couldn't do without it. Darius rectified that within the hour. Today however, she lost in their game of scrabble the day before, so she was drinking tea.

"A man who knows his way around the kitchen. I like it."

Darius turned and was stunned at the sight before him. Her hair was in a messy bun on her head, her face was bare, and she had on the shirt he discarded on the couch last evening. The shirt stopped halfway down her thighs, displaying her toned legs. He'd never seen anything sexier.

"You do know that coming in here like that will have you hemmed up against the wall."

"I'd like to think you can show restraint and at least feed me first." She winked.

Darius smirked. "Be careful, beautiful. Here, sit. I made you breakfast."

Safiya walked closer to the island and the first thing she did was lift the cup of tea and take in the aroma. "Smells good. I guess I'll be a good sport." She took a sip from the cup.

Darius sat opposite her. Safiya took his hand as she had done with every meal and blessed the food.

"What's this?" She picked up her spoon.

"You don't know?" he asked.

"Why should I? Please don't tell me you are one of those?"

That quickly, Darius saw her smile disappear, replaced with tight eyes and a head cocked to the side.

"One of who?" He had an idea what she might mean but was buying time to come up with an explanation that would get his foot out of his mouth.

"Those that think because I'm from the Continent it means I should know everything African."

"I'm educated enough to know that's not the case. But I admit sometimes our unintended bias rears its head. My apologies." He reached over and placed his hand over hers.

"None, necessary besides, you're right. Just how I assumed you don't have problems because you are rich, or you should know Cardi B and Offset's song because you are Black American."

"We have to be more aware and be willing to offer grace." Darius didn't mean for them to get so deep so early so he quickly ended that line of conversation by explaining the meal he made. He watched her pick up her spoon for a taste.

"Good, but where's the pepper?"

"You see I tried not to assume—"

"You're not assuming. Those are facts, Africans love spice."

Both of them shared a laugh as she walked to the cupboard to retrieve the paprika and add it to her bowl. He remembered the day Hakeem's girlfriend, Mariama, who was Senegalese prepared them some yassa chicken, and they had to drink a ton of milk to get that spice off their tongue.

A few minutes later, Safiya spoke. "Okay, I know you're tired of being cooped up all day watching movies. So, I was looking online and there are a lot of things for us to do. Are you up for it?"

Before he could respond, she spoke again. "Oh, I forgot you don't have security with you. Can you go out?"

Darius smiled at her flustered expression. "Relax beautiful, I do have security. You just can't see them. However, with or without them, we can explore the town. What do you have in mind?"

In response, Safiya clapped her hands, jumped off the stool and ran from the kitchen. Darius smiled at her goofiness. He'd stayed in this home only once. That was when one of the companies whose Board he sat on, invited all its board members to participate in a ceremony which took place in one of the mausoleums at Borj El Kebir castle. All he did then was attend the festivities, agreed to host an after-party, and flew back to Atlanta the following day.

Moments later, she came back with her iPad in her hand, scrolling through what he assumed was some tourist site.

"Today is Thursday so we can go to the one of the souk markets. Did you know we can take a ride from here to Camp Yadis Ksar Ghilane? Or we can explore the Yasmine Shopping Center, there is a gourmet coffee house. You know I wanna check that out. The museums, did you know it was around the Ajim port they shot some Star Wars scenes? Obi-Wan Kenobi's house is here. The one in the original movie...here...in Tunisia. Layla would kill me if I don't take pictures. She's a huge fan." Safiya rattled off.

Before Darius could respond, she started talking again. "There's even an ancient castle here—"

"Borj El Kebir. Yes, now that I know." Darius looked at her in amazement and admiration. Over the past couple of days, this carefree attitude had become his kryptonite. Every woman he had ever dated was as serious as he was. But with Safiya, it was different. He would've attributed it to their six-year age difference, but he had also seen the serious side of her. The part that wasn't moved by him and his money and deeply passionate about her ambition in life. The side that put her father's needs ahead of her own. The one who wanted to know about the ugly parts of his life as well as what made it pretty now.

Her laughter brought him out of this trance. "So, tell me, what else do you know?"

"I know that in this island, Djerba, according to legend used to be the land of lotus eaters where Odysseus was stranded on hos voyage," he said.

Safiya raised her brow. "You're talking Greek mythology?"

"Yep."

"Well, that I know nothing about. This island however from the little I saw online is gorgeous. Now let's see if reality matches up." She tore a piece of her baguette and scooped her ojja.

He lifter his tea to his lips. "I'm sure it does, but I'll let you tell me."

She chuckled, covering her mouth with her hand. His heart twanged. The uncomfortable feeling intensified the more he remained in her presence. His chest tightened at the fleeting thought that what he felt was past lust. But what was the feeling past lust, because it couldn't be love? He barely knew her, but his adopted mother's words entered his mind. *Time doesn't matter. When cupid hits you, it just does.*

Darius blinked his eyes to rid himself of the useless senti-ment. Cupid was not hitting him. They had come to that agree-ment a while ago. It was Cupid's stupid arrow that made his mother blind to the red flags of love until it was too late. After these three weeks and another two weeks in Atlanta, he'd dive into work so deep that Cupid's arrow wouldn't even be able to find him.

"Are you listening to me?"

"I'm all yours, Beautiful. We can do anything you want."

Darius stood and took their empty plates to the sink. He discarded the scraps and filled the sink with soap. That was another thing Safiya got him to do, wash his own dishes. He hadn't done that in ages. His hands were immersed in the soapy water when he felt her warms hands creep under his shirt. She massaged his abdomen and he bit his lip, holding in his pleasure.

"Anything?" her raspy voice sent a tingling up his spine.

Darius turned, leaned against the sink, and encased her in his arms. He pulled her against his hard body. Narrowing his eyes at her full breasts, Darius bent his head and took her mouth with his. He tried to swallow her whole with his passion. Their tongues entwined, stroking each other to a feverish pitch, a clear indication that for three days, he hadn't felt the softness of her lips. Breaking away from their kiss, Darius hoisted her up on the island and stood between her legs. Safiya stared at him with pure desire that matched his.

"As much as I want to let you have your way with me, if we start, we won't be going anywhere today." Darius leaned his forehead against hers.

Smiling, Safiya ran her hand over his head. "Okay, husband. But you owe me."

Darius cupped one of her breasts and squeezed. "Your wish is my command, wife. Now go get dressed. I need to make a few calls."

SEVERAL HOURS LATER, Safiya sat between Darius's legs as they sailed the open seas. Darius stroked her cheek as she rested her head on his chest. She had the perfect day planned. Except when they found out that Yadis Ksar Ghilane was a luxurious camp that offered tents in the oasis of the Sahara Desert. He promised to bring her back so they could spend a couple of nights and go camel back riding. Safiya quickly changed course and they took a trip to the castle, shopped in the souk market, visited the museum and finally they ate lunch in a private secluded booth at Restaurant Dar Hassine. She gave him the attractions, he made it happen. The last part of the day however was put together by him. When she talked of Ajim earlier, he didn't want to tell her he had a yacht docked there. After they visited and took pictures at the Star Wars house, he brought her here. Her reaction was worth the surprise.

"This view is fantastic."

Darius tried to contain her hair that was flying in his face. "Yes, it is." She had tied her hair up in a ponytail before, but he had insisted she let it down.

"I still can't believe you own a yacht here that you barely use. I went on a vacation tour in Florida once and we were told that just parking the boat, set owners back like twenty grand a day."

"You went on this vacation, alone, right?"

"Out of all I said, that's what you picked up on." Safiya giggled. "Don't you think we're a little late in the game for you to be thinking or worrying about whether I have a significant other?"

"Who says I'm worried? Even if you did, it became insignificant the minute you entered the limo with me."

Safiya turned her head to the side to look up at him. "You're joking, right?"

"I never joke when it comes to you. I was going to pursue you regardless." He kissed her hair. "Fate made my job a whole lot easier by you marrying me."

"Don't you mean a drunken night?

"Not really. I wanted you and I wasn't ready to give you up just yet." When he said it out loud, it did sound less than romantic.

"Oh." Her low whisper confirmed his thoughts.

Darius could feel the atmosphere shift. He didn't mean to make her sad, but he would always be truthful with her. He wanted to make sure they were on the same page, so she wouldn't end up hurt when their time was up. They sat in silence for a while before they were interrupted by one of the attendants, who brought them the food and drinks they had ordered. They ate in silence for a few minutes before they began to chat on safer topics like her job and plans. He let her in on his upcoming deals and travel plans after they arrived Atlanta.

Hours later, they were back at the house, showered and retired on the bed. His bed. He lay his head on Safiya's lap and looked into her eyes. She was watching reruns of *Martin*.

"I didn't mean to upset you earlier," he said.

She picked up the remote and paused her show. She looked down at him. "You didn't upset me as much as you brought me back to reality."

"Meaning?"

Safiya shrugged. "In the days I've been here with you, away from reality, I kinda got caught up that this really was a thing. I'm here to do a job, after which, you'll pay me for my services."

Although he was now sure they were on the same page, to hear her say it out loud was like a sucker punch to his gut. Before he could voice his opinion, she spoke again.

"But that doesn't mean we can't satisfy our bodies. And if I remember correctly, Mr. Gray, you owe me."

Safiya lowered her head and captured his lips. Raw passion took over and whatever he had wanted to say moved to the back of his mind. This conversation was far from over, but in the moment, talk was the last thing on his mind.

ELEVEN

Safiya looked out the window and took in the familiar sights and sounds of downtown Atlanta. The driver Darius insisted on her having was taking her to the restaurant where she was meeting Layla for lunch.

The last eight months were like a blur. Who knew the life of the rich and famous was so busy? The three weeks she and Darius had spent in the Tunisia seemed like light years away. While in Djerba, they had gotten closer and the cares of the world seemed to be a distant thing.

After the awkward conversation they'd had the first week, Safiya's resolve to live in the moment but guard her heart became greater. Before their return, Darius had bought her the most expensive ring set he could find. Very quickly, she had gotten settled into her new abode. Just like in Djerba, everything a woman could need and desired was set up in the bedroom she now shared with Darius.

Over the course of the first couple of weeks, they'd visited her father. Just as he did on the phone, he expressed his displeasure and suspicion of their hasty nuptials. To her surprise,

Darius spent time trying to convince him otherwise. They went out fishing and golfing, but what totally got her dad to calm down was when he was treated to owner suite privileges at the Atlanta Heights game. It also helped that Darius was genuinely attracted to her, so his hands never stayed to himself.

His grandmother was an easier sell. She had her own smaller house on the property, but as Safiya soon learned, she popped in wherever she felt like it and when it was least expected. Safiya was now fond of the little older lady, but she knew the woman watched her like a hawk. It was undeniable that the older woman was thrilled her grandson was now married. Safiya still doubted that she believed Darius's story that he decided to keep their relationship a secret, hence the suddenness of their marriage. Since she was being paid two million dollars, Safiya took it upon herself to convince her. Her thoughts went back to the dinner they had on the second night they arrived home.

"Ah, young love, tell me again. How did you two meet?" Darius's grandmother had a huge smile on her face as she asked the question Safiya was sure they had answered up to three times already.

Safiya felt her piercing eyes rip through her soul. Was she just messing with her or did she know the truth? Safiya smiled and glanced over at Darius who wiped the corner of his mouth with a napkin and placed his hand over hers.

"Grammy, we've told this story more than enough times now. Safiya and I met during a business meeting, but decided we didn't want the media in our business. When the time was right, we both agreed we were ready to take the next step."

"Oh, right that's it." His grandmother took her eyes off her grandson and turned her way. "Well, Safiya welcome to the family."

"Thank you, Mrs. Gibson."

"No, around here I'm Grammy." For the first time in the last forty-eight hours since she'd met the woman, her smile was warm and genuine.

"I want to get to know my granddaughter in-law better, so I'll move back into my old room."

For the six months that followed, Grammy kept her eyes on them like a hawk. Well, her mostly, because Darius resumed business travels a month after their fake honeymoon. He made sure he wasn't gone for more than a week at a time, but he was still gone. Safiya, on the other hand, quit her job and was assigned an assistant who helped her get acclimated to her new duties as the billionaire's wife.

THE WAITER BROUGHT over their cheesecakes and placed them on the table. For the past couple of hours, she and Layla caught up over lunch. The friends still talked on the phone almost every day, but hadn't seen each other for a while.

"While I loved you feeding me and what not, I also know something is on your mind. Can you tell me what it is while I work on this cheesecake?" Layla lifted a piece of her dessert to her mouth.

"Why does something have to be wrong for me to see my friend?"

"I didn't say something had to be wrong for you to see me. I'm saying something is bothering you... now."

Something was wrong, something she hadn't told anybody because she still couldn't believe it was real. She'd taken all the necessary precautions.

"I'm pregnant," Safiya blurted out.

Layla remained silent. She lifted her lemonade to her

mouth and took a loud sip. Her dramatics were driving Safiya insane.

"Please say something."

"What I have to say, you've heard before, but you and your fake husband are the most prideful people I've ever met. So, I'll say what I know you want to hear."

"And what's that?"

"I know where you can get an abortion." Layla shrugged.

Safiya frowned. "What?! Stop joking around."

"I'm not."

"You're serious?" Safiya hissed. "Come on Lay, this is serious business. I don't know how it happened, but I think in all the—"

"I'll tell you what happened. Love. Look, I know this thing started off as a sham, but even a blind man on the street can see that you and Darius love each other. You can act, but not that well. Social media has you and him as hashtag couple goals. The way he looks at you in public, the way you can't keep your hands off him. You guys have stopped deceiving the public long ago. The only people you're deceiving are yourselves."

"Okay, okay. I admit it. I love him. Gosh, how can I not? But I will not force him to love me or beg him to let me stay – baby or no baby." Safiya took a sip of her drink.

It was true that sometimes she forgot that they were in a fake marriage. The way he treated her, she was sure he forgot, too. However, he had made no mention of feeling anything deeper for her or wanting her to stay. The last thing she was going to do was tell him about the baby and be a charity case. A man like Darius would never let her take the baby away, so he would force her to stay with him out of obligation and that would kill her more than anything.

"Darius is different. I don't know what it is, but in the last several weeks, he's become distant. We still share the same bed and make love, but something is missing. I did ask him what was wrong, and as usual, he said nothing. Then I told him that I was going to start looking for a house to move into once our deal was up. Do you know what he said?"

Layla shook her head.

"He said he'll get Julia to help me. I love him, but I won't be a fool for him. But now this baby complicates things." Safiya bowed her head. "But I can't kill it." She rubbed her flat belly.

"How far along are you?"

"Eight weeks."

"You've been to a doctor already? How did you manage that, being Mrs. Gray and all?"

"It wasn't easy, but money is a powerful thing," Safiya said wearily. "It must have happened when we went to Europe two months ago."

"Look, my friend, you're happy. You didn't plan this life, but you've been blessed with it. Good thing the man is not stuck up either. Plus, he is all types of cocoa-shake fine."

"Watch it," Safiya warned playfully.

Layla waved her off. "Whatever...don't nobody want your man. What I'm saying is, don't make any hasty decisions without at least talking to him. Sit him down and tell him how you feel. Most of all, tell him about the baby. There's no need assuming and then walking out of a great life you could've had."

Safiya took in her friend's words. Darius was due back from Milan tonight. She would plan something special and then tell him in the morning over breakfast.

"Okay, even though I have three more weeks until the contract is up, I won't be able to stay there and face him if he dismisses me."

"And the money? You'll miss out on two million dollars?"

"He gave me the check last month. I haven't cashed it.

However, he also opened an account for me, and I've been taking care of any other things from there." Safiya paused. "I don't know Lay. All I know is now."

"Please be smart about this."

Safiya nodded and the two women went back to enjoying the remaining part of their afternoon, which also included some retail therapy.

TWELVE

Darius's flight arrived a couple of hours ahead of schedule. He'd come home to a quiet house. He searched for Safiya but didn't see her anywhere. One of the housekeepers informed him she'd gone out for lunch. His first instinct had been to call her, but lately he had found himself in self-preservation mode. She was with him just for the money and sex, nothing else. He had to keep reminding himself. That part was made pretty clear when she told him she would start looking for a place.

Granted, he hadn't said the words, but couldn't she feel that he loved her by his actions? Well, his actions before she let that sentence come out of her mouth. He shouldn't have let himself get carried away by the breath of fresh air she brought him, or the fact that she provided the piece of sunshine that had been missing since his adoptive mother died. He always knew love was a weak emotion and he had allowed himself to fall and the joke was now on him.

He was in the den watching a repeat episode of *Ozark*, a show she had introduced him to. Yes, he was a glutton for punishment. His phone rang. He let out a breath and picked it up. Not wanting to hold it to his ear or put in his ear pods, he put the phone on speaker.

"Hey Hakeem," he answered.

"Hey man, I know you just got back from your trip, but I was calling to tell you about this new property in Australia. I think it would be a good investment."

Darius contemplated. He just got home and wanted to spend some time with Safiya before they said their goodbyes. But then again, he was doubting his ability to be present as she walked away.

"Tell me about it."

Briefly Hakeem talked him through the history of the hotel franchise they were potentially going after, the pros, cons, and how long it would take before he saw a return on his investment. Darius decided it was worth a shot.

"Good man, I'll prepare everything," Hakeem said. "So, we haven't talked in a while about you. How are you doing?"

"I'm good. And we talk almost every week."

"You know what I'm referring to you. You and Safiya. I saw Vanessa try to slither her way into your VIP lounge two nights ago. What was she doing there? Are you and Safiya okay?"

Darius took a deep breath and decided to ignore the Vanessa part of Hakeem's statement. She was in Milan when he was there celebrating with some business associates. She tried to immerse herself into the party in his VIP suite, but he quickly shut that down.

"It's been good, but it has to come to an end, right?" Despair laced his words.

"Not everything. I've never seen you this happy or carefree, so what's stopping you from making her yours, permanently? Her dad and Grammy seem to be happy with the union." A beat passed between them. "You guys are happy. That's if you'd stop avoiding the truth."

"It's not that simple..."

"Yeah, that's because you choose to complicate it." He took a breath. "Look man, I know this started because we needed the shareholders to maintain their faith in you. You've done that. So, what seems to be the problem?"

"I don't think she feels the same and I won't expose myself only to be rejected."

"Now you sound like a coward. I know this is a touchy subject for you, but regardless of what you think, Ms. Jackie loved and was happy. What ended up happening to her isn't her fault but that jerk."

Darius's nostrils flared. It was a touchy subject for him and that was why love was an emotion he'd never allowed himself to feel. He finally messed up, but he was going to fix it.

He'd been living with Ms. Jackie and Grammy for about two years when she got a boyfriend. At first sight, Darius hated him; something about him seemed off. He couldn't place it, but about eighteen months into the relationship, the man's violent tendencies started to show. One day during dinner, he got upset and slapped his mother, and she hit her head on the table. She was taken to the hospital and was diagnosed with a concussion. Somehow, they missed that she was bleeding internally, and she died some days later. If she wasn't so much in love, she wouldn't have had blinders on and would've seen her so called boyfriend for who he really was. A monster.

"I don't know man. I just don't know," Darius said. "Send me the packet for the Australia thing so I can review it and give you my final decision."

He disconnected the call and lifted his legs onto the settee. He twirled the drink in his hand and he mulled over the last several months. Safiya had opened his eyes to life, not just checking things off his list, but living it. He loved coming home to her in his bed. Her dark long thick hair pilled across his pillow was always a sight to behold. She wanted to wear a bonnet, he bought satin pillows instead. She wasn't only a beautiful and very adventurous and satisfying wife and lover, she was kind, caring and compassionate.

He had never seen his staff laugh so much since he hired them. There was an airiness to the house that she brought with her and they were all better for it. Even his grandmother had a glow having someone to talk to. She'd made his house a home. All of her made him happy, and he realized that it was more than a euphoric feeling of something new. He loved her.

The idea of loving her and making this a permanent arrangement didn't sound bad, but he didn't have the courage to believe she felt the same way about him. He refused to let down the last piece of guard that surrounded his heart, especially when she hadn't said anything to even give him a tiny hint she felt the same. He wasn't ready to put what was left of his heart on the line. If she rejected him, he wasn't sure he could bear it. He'd been let down by the first woman in his life – his biological mother. He wasn't ready to be let down again.

* * *

"YOU GUYS ARE HAPPY. *That's if you'd stop avoiding the truth."*

"It's not that simple..."

"Yeah, that's because you choose to complicate it. Look man, I know this started because we needed the shareholders to maintain their faith in you. You've done that. So, what seems to be the problem?"

Safiya backed away from the den's door not waiting to hear Darius response. She made a beeline to the bedroom. She couldn't stop the tears from falling. On her way back to the estate, her phone wouldn't stop buzzing. She checked it out and discovered she got several Instagram notifications. She loved the app; it was about the only social media platform she knew she probably couldn't live without. She'd gotten tagged on several photos showing Darius and Vanessa in conversation in Milan. Not only was Vanessa potentially a thing, but to hear that the reason he asked her to stay married to him was for some stupid shares. Some shares? She felt stupid and betrayed. All this while, she thought it was because of his recovering grandmother but he used her as a pawn for his business. He was a billionaire for goodness sake. What could the shareholders have ever done to him that he needed to come in and turn her life upside down?

Some months ago, she would've brushed it off. But the way things were with them now, she wasn't so sure. Or was it this baby that was making her insecure? Safiya got to meet Vanessa several weeks after their nuptials. That day she wanted to surprise Darius with lunch in his downtown office. The person who ended up being surprised was her. On Darius's previous instruction, Safiya was never to be stopped from entering his office. She still however, as a courtesy, respected protocol.

That day, as she approached his door, she could hear a female voice that was far from calm. Safiya entered and Darius made the introductions. After Vanessa left, he promised her that she wasn't that important and so would never be someone she'd have to worry about. Now she wasn't so sure.

Safiya plopped down on the sofa in the sitting area of the bedroom. She cradled her head with her hands. She felt her heart shatter for the second time in about two years. During this marriage, she had undoubtedly gained things along the way. But then again, what she had no knowledge of in the first place, she couldn't miss. Now he made her get used to all this, and she was just a pawn in a cause that didn't make any sense. The more she tried to contain her tears, the more they fell. This wasn't her; she was never this emotional. Safiya placed her hand on her tummy and rubbed, her emotions conflicted. Her heart swelled with love at the being they'd created. But also angry at herself and the situation.

For minutes, she sat in silence pondering her next course of action. He had lied to her. What else had he lied about? Was it over with Vanessa or was he good at covering it up? In the last eight months of being in his world, she knew for a fact money could keep anything hidden. At least for a while.

Safiya didn't know how long she sat playing out different scenarios in her head. The plan to do something special for Darius suddenly left a bad taste in her mouth. She would never be one of those women that kept their child away from its father. She was too close to hers to ever deprive another of the feeling. But she needed to get away from here. Even for just a while.

Trust. Could she still trust him? What did they have without it? Her eyes travelled to the picture of them that hung above the dresser. The joy...that couldn't all be a lie. She knew they needed to talk but, in this moment, she didn't even have the strength.

With her game face back on, she stood up and opened the door. Darius stood there, mid-knock. No matter how hurt and angry she was with him, her body yearned for him.

"Hi, beautiful. I didn't know you were back." He moved closer to her and placed a kiss on her lips. As was the case lately, it lacked the passion it once held. It felt like he had taken back pieces of him he'd given her.

"Oh, I came in some hours ago. How was your trip?" She struggled to keep her voice clear and light.

"Boring, but very productive."

"At least it was productive." Safiya mustered up a faint smile

"I guess so. Have you found the building you want to rent yet?" He asked, loosening his belt, walking to the bathroom, and starting the shower.

She followed. "Yeah, there's one in Atlantic Station that would be perfect." Her eyes roamed his body as each piece of clothing came off.

"Awesome," Darius yelled from the under shower.

Safiya sat on the sink and they proceeded to discuss what Safiya would consider safe topics while he showered.

Several minutes later, Darius held her close in bed. It felt like she was floating on cloud nine. As always. He ran his fingers through her hair, listening as she discussed her dad and plans for her business. She loved this man. Deeply. Did he love her? Did he want a child? Over the past couple of months, he'd taught her to demand more. But what if that more was something she couldn't have? How much different would life be if their foundation wasn't built on lies? Being with him like this made her want to woman-up and confess how she felt about him, inquire about what she'd overheard. She opened her mouth to spill her guts when he spoke.

"I have to make a short trip tomorrow."

"But you just got back," her tone was accusatory.

He kissed her temple. "I know but I have to go to DC. I should be back in three days."

She remained silent.

"You could come with me if you like."

Safiya thought about it. Everything she wanted to say flew out the window. He was leaving so soon. He never did that. Was he trying to tell her this arrangement had turned back to business as usual? Her earlier resolve returned. This would be the perfect time for her to leave without all the emotions. Even if she did go to DC, she'd still return to face her problems. It was better to make this as painless as possible.

"No, that's okay. Since its just three days. I'll be fine."

Safiya needed answers to her questions and some clarification before she told him how she felt. With him leaving again, that wasn't going to happen soon. Just in case she didn't like his answers, she needed to be ready.

Darius cuddled her close, placing warm kisses on her nape. Their passion escalated. His hands roamed her body at a feverish pace. A tear formed in the corner of her eye at the impending loss of his warmth. He rolled her over and made love to her all night long.

THIRTEEN

"I never figured you to be a coward."

It was approaching noon when Safiya and Layla walked into the building that would be the future home of Kupendeza Scents. She ignored her friend who stomped behind her, trying to assert her point. Safiya smiled, pleasantly surprised at the progress that was being made. The mixing room was finished, and the display section was coming together nicely. The registers she'd ordered were still in their casing because the contractor had to redo the sales area again.

After she and Darius got married, he couldn't stay away from her for so long, and she travelled with him almost everywhere. Being with him, representing him in events and sitting on boards didn't give her much time to get started on her dream, but now she was seeing it come to life and her joy knew no bounds.

"Safiya! I think you're going about this the wrong way," Layla said.

Safiya placed her hand on her hip and turned to face her

brooding friend. "Look Lay, you aren't the one that has to deal with a broken heart. I do—"

"I get that. What I don't understand is, why you couldn't have a simple conversation with him and clear everything up?"

Safiya was tempted to let the debate end there, but she knew the rest of her Saturday would be hounded with questions.

"He lied to me. The whole reason I thought we were doing this was a lie."

"But the whole thing started off as a lie."

"That's not the point. The fact is if I knew this was about some silly shares, I wouldn't have agreed."

"The lies you tell." Layla rolled her eyes. "You want me to believe you would have turned down two million dollars?" A furrow lay between the lines of Layla's brows.

Safiya shifted from one foot to the other. She needed to use the restroom. This baby growing inside her wasn't even a full three months and was already controlling her body function. "Well, you're right, but I also know you understand what I mean. Besides, I did want to talk to him. But like he's been doing for the last couple of months, he ran away. And you know I'm not going to chase after any man."

Safiya noticed the moment the unspoken challenge left Layla's eyes. She was grateful for that because she really wanted to enjoy this moment. "Tell me what you think?"

Her mouth twitched on the verge of a smile. "I'm so proud of you, Safiya."

"Aww, thank you *rafiki*. I really should be thanking you. If you hadn't dragged me along..."

"I just want you to be happy. I saw what your breakup with Justin did to you." Layla looped her hand in Safiya's.

"I am happy. Besides, he's just another man."

"The lies you tell. He's a wealthy, fine man. If I wasn't

happy with Todd, I'd give his friend Hakeem some play." Both friends laughed.

"Hate to break it to you, but Darius told me he and his one true love broke up in college and ever since then, he hasn't taken any woman seriously. And you know I can't let my friend go out like that."

"That's why I love you, *rafiki*." Layla paused. "Now finish showing me this place so you can feed me. Since you're the one with the money and all."

In palpable silence, the women strolled around the ground floor, which was the sales and display area, then took the elevator to the second floor where the storage and mixing areas were.

A few notes and a call to the contractor later, the women where in the car to one of their favorite stores. They discussed Layla's upcoming wedding and things they'd buy for the baby. Safiya pulled out her phone to check in with her dad. He was at a baseball game. It was something he did often since Darius got him season tickets. The car pulled up to prime parking space by the side of the store. Safiya placed her hand on the door handle when she felt Layla tugging her back slightly.

"Hold on, Safi. I'll say this only once and I promise I won't bring it up again, but I'll always be there for you with whatever you decide to do. You moving out of your home is a coward move, especially when you didn't have a conversation with him. You and I grew up with one parent each and we vowed that would never be the case of our children. It's just not you."

"I agree, but I needed a breather, so I left. I didn't totally move out. Also, I would've talked to him if he came back two days ago like he said he would. That man has been gone another week. We talk every night, but our conversation is so strained. I'm not trying to force him to be where he doesn't want to be." Safiya rubbed her stomach. "Maybe this is his way of detaching, but I tell you this, this baby won't grow up without two parents because of my feelings. I'll tell him about the child soon. I'm not one to use a baby as a pawn. If Darius decides to be there, fine."

"Okay, that's all I can ask for," Layla said, stepping out of the car. "I'm so surprised your dad hasn't said anything yet about you not being with his beloved Darius. Where's his grandma? She hasn't noticed you left?"

"Grammy is on a retreat with her church, so, she's not in town. And I'm surprised about my dad too. You know how he was when I told him we got married."

Layla gave her a knowing look and they walked toward the store.

LATER THAT EVENING, Safiya had changed into comfortable loungewear and was seated on top of the island in her dad's kitchen. He had prepared his famous boneless barbeque. Earlier, she and Layla had parted ways after spending money on things Safiya now felt were totally ridiculous. There was no telling what she was having, but Layla had coaxed her into buying unisex baby clothes. It way too early to be shopping and despite everything, she wanted her baby's father by her side. She fully expected for her friend to be by her side, but today, she really wanted her man – her husband.

With rising frustration from the second unanswered call, Safiya opened the Safari icon on her phone and typed Darius's name in Google. This is what her life had turned into, stalking her husband on the internet in case he turned up with Vanessa. Her eyes scanned the links. Nothing recent. She tossed the phone and walked up to her dad.

Safiya placed her hands on his shoulders and looked while

he brushed the meat with his secret sauce. *"lijē,"* he said with a smile.

"Hey, Papa, I see you still got it."

"Yep and I'll never lose it."

She grinned and he twisted his head to kiss the back of her hand. He returned to what he was doing, and she leaned against the sink next to him, observing. He had single handedly taken care of her after her mother died. No matter what was going on, he'd been there for her. He always said he promised her mother when she was on her sick bed. Safiya knew for a fact that if they had remained in Ethiopia, he would've remarried and probably bore a son due to family pressure. Minutes later, she watched him put the meat on the indoor grill. He turned to her and adjusted his glasses on his nose. Her body stung from the judgement she sensed. In the seven days she'd been staying at his house, he had let her be, but in this moment she knew that reprieve was over. Layla just had to go and talk him up.

"I know you know what I'm about to say." Her dad traced the brim of his shot glass with his thumb. "What are you still doing here?"

Safiya gave a wave. "Daddy, I did tell you that I came to spend time with you."

"When I married your mother, the love of my life, there was no way she was sleeping anywhere without me. I was skeptical on this rushed marriage with Darius, especially after the last jerk." He pulled out the stool near the island and sat.

"Dad, Darius is out of town, so I decided to spend a little time with you. Are you saying you've not enjoyed my company?"

"No, I'm saying that you could've come during the day and still gone back home."

"We live on the other side of town and there was no way I

was driving that long." Safiya moved to the fridge and removed the potato salad they had prepared earlier. She felt her dad's eyes follow her, but she avoided them.

"You are grown, and I won't get into your business. You're always welcomed here, but if you have problems with your husband, my expectation is you try and work it out before seeking cover."

Safiya wanted to come clean with her father. Tell him what was really going on. He would be the best one to talk to from a male's perspective. But she couldn't disappoint him again. She did when she married Justin. That man made a fool out of her, making her and her dad the laughingstock of their circle. How could she now tell him that for the past several months, she'd been in a marriage of convenience? With one of the most sought-after billionaires in Atlanta. It was still bad that their arrangement was coming to an end and she would be a divorcee twice over, but at least she had a few more weeks before that happened.

She slid past him and placed a kiss on his forehead. "We're fine dad. Now can you please check on the barbeque? I'm starving."

An uncertain smile spread across his face as he studied her for cracks. She remained unfazed. Soon after, father and daughter set the table and sat to eat. Over the meal, she updated him on the progress the contractors were making, and he informed her of a new lady friend he met at the library a while ago. Safiya's mom had been dead now for twenty years and in that time, her dad never dated anyone that she knew of. It was time for him to be happy again. His eyes twinkled when he spoke of his lady friend, so she figured she must have made an impact on him.

After the dishes were washed and the kitchen cleaned, her father took his nightly cup of Tetley tea and headed upstairs for his room. Ever since she could remember, that had been his routine. Safiya double checked the doors and headed for her old room, located in the lower level of the house. Despite her pleas, he'd refused to move from this house when she asked him to some months ago.

There was a light rap on the door. Her eyes went to the clock. It read 9:05 PM. She checked for her phone, but remembered she hadn't picked it up since she tossed it earlier. The knock came again but it was louder this time. With calculated steps, she reached the door, looked through the peephole and her heart jumped. She leaned her back against the door. The knock came again, startling her. Quickly coming to terms with the fact that she couldn't let him stand outside all night and curious as to what he was doing here, she opened the door.

"Are you seeing him?" Darius seethed, waving what looked like a magazine in his hand. Her eyes followed it for a moment, then she gazed at him. His eyes were darkened with rage. What the heck did he have to be angry about?

FOURTEEN

"What's wrong with you and who are you talking about?" she asked. Instead of giving an answer, Darius brushed past her into the house. Safiya closed the door and turned to face him. He was pacing like a wild animal in a cage. His mouth moved with what she assumed to be expletives, but he never voiced them.

He stopped and observed her as she stood by the wall with both arms folded across her chest.

"Why are you here and not in our home? Did you need somewhere where you could go undetected?" he growled.

She placed her hands on her hips. "First, I need you to respect my dad's house and lower your voice. We can go into my room and talk like adults. And home? Ha! That place hasn't been a home for a couple of months now."

"Which way?" Darius asked.

Safiya turned and went to her bedroom. His light footsteps indicated that he'd fallen in line. She entered and turned to face him standing with his hands balled. He closed the door. He still had the scowl on his face that had greeted her earlier.

Her eyes roamed over him. This was the most inopportune time, but she couldn't contain her love or attraction toward him. He was the sexiest man she'd seen. Her body ached as she recalled the last time he was in control of it. They needed a vacation for how much work they put into guaranteeing the other's satisfaction. Instead, he left before she woke up and now, they were here fighting.

"Now answer my question," his voice boomed, bringing her out of her revere.

"Your question makes no sense. Who are you talking about?"

Darius moved closer to her and placed the paper he held earlier on her vanity and shoved his finger at a picture on the front page. "Him!"

Safiya looked at the paper. It was a sleazy tabloid, one she hadn't heard of before, but what was most shocking was they photoshopped a photo of her and Justin from years ago and made up a ridiculous headline about Darius Gray not being able to keep his wife. She looked back up to her husband. If he didn't look like he was about to blow, she'd laugh. Upon further thought, it occurred to her. Why was he so angry? Did he want her? Well, of course he wanted her. The chemistry between them was never an issue. It was the heart.

"It took this to bring you home?"

"I've been working."

"You were working when I met you."

"Safiya now is not a good time to play with me. Answer my question."

"You're the master of games and your question is absurd."

"Safiya, don't—"

"Besides what does it matter if I am seeing him?"

Darius's eyes sent daggers through her. He walked closer.

"It matters because you belong to me and I told you in the beginning; I don't share."

Cold shivers danced along her spine. She was turned on by his possessiveness, but enraged at the same time. What gave him that right when he was living foul himself?

"Under false pretenses."

"What the heck is that supposed to mean?"

"You lied to me."

"I've never lied to you...now—"

"Give it a rest. I'm not seeing him. That's an old picture. If you weren't so busy avoiding me, you would know what I've been up to," she said. She could see the unspoken relief in his eyes. She rolled her eyes. All this was about his bruised ego. "Now you got your answer, you can leave."

"Not without you."

"I'm not going anywhere with you. We have three more weeks before the contract ends. I'll just stay here."

"That wasn't the deal."

"Consider this an amendment." At this point, the questions she had for him didn't even matter. For a moment, she was under the illusion that he came here to fight for them. He just wanted to make sure appearances were kept. Probably to make sure his name didn't get muddied.

"I don't do amendments. Either we go home, or I sleep here with you tonight. Whatever sound bites your dad gets are totally up to you." Darius sat on the bed and began to take off his shoes."

"Why are you here, Darius?" The fight in her had left.

"Because you are." His tone was nonchalant.

"You're being a jerk?"

"I hate you feel that way. But when it comes to you, I'm irrational." Darius took his shirt out of his pants and leaned back against her pillows. "And don't ask me to apologize for it."

Safiya shook her head and sat on the opposite side of the bed. The two of them remained in silence until Safiya decided to lay everything out in the open.

"Darius, I came here to think and you're not making it easy."

"About?"

She sighed. "You. Us. Me. I need to get my thoughts together."

The bed creaked and soon after Darius was kneeling in front of her. Despite her melancholy, a wave of excitement made her heart leap. His head briefly rested in her lap. Then he looked up at her. She looked into his eyes, which now seemed softer. The hunger in them was undeniable. They roamed her body as though it was a treasure map. He lifted his hand to her face, and she snapped out of her trance. She had to protect her heart. Sex was never their problem and she had to remember that and not mistake this for more than it was.

"You lied to me."

"You mentioned that. When?" The sincerity in his question tugged at her heart.

"When we woke up in the hotel, you promised to get the marriage annulled. Then you changed your mind and came up with this contract. Why?"

Darius stood, sat next to her and lifted her to his lap. She prayed he didn't lie to her now. She didn't know whether they had a future together, but if he lied to her, the probability was closer to none.

"When I was a young boy, my mother died. I had no idea who my father was, and I guess there were no relatives because I ended up in an orphanage. My childhood was extremely hard. As fate would have it, I met a woman in my early teens who loved me through everything, took me in and changed my life. Until hers was cut short. In my mind, her death meant the comfort I'd come to know was going to be taken away from me again. The way she died also closed off a part of me. Now two women I loved and depended on were taken away from me, by love."

Safiya's hands that were on her lap itched to pull him in for a hug, but he needed to say this. She needed to hear it. It was the only chance they had.

"My biological mother was taken away because of a broken heart. My dad passed before I was born. When I was growing up, she'd say things that made me know she pined over him. He was the love of her life. Sometimes I think she worked herself to the bone just to be away from me. I'm told I'm his carbon copy. I knew she loved me, but I could also tell I brought her pain. My adoptive mother was taken away because she stood up for me against the man she loved. Love gets people killed. From then on, two things drove me; avoiding love and making money."

"I'm so sorry to hear that, but it still doesn't answer my question."

"From the moment I laid eyes on you, I wanted you. It's that simple. But Hakeem did persuade me to stay married to you by reminding me that I hadn't had a scandal to my name and quickly getting an annulment could equate to bad publicity, which would affect my stock. But then Grammy solidified the decision."

Safiya shot to her feet. Somehow the fact that he needed her to prove his character made her feel dirty. She shouldn't, as she was getting something out of the deal. If she wanted, she could buy all the soap in the world to wash herself clean. She knew it was silly, but she had to admit that the only reason she was angry now was that she loved him. Things were different.

Darius eyes followed her as she paced.

"Why didn't you tell me?"

"It wasn't necessary." He searched her eyes. "Does it matter?"

"It shouldn't, but it does..."

He closed the distance between them. "Why?"

Safiya open her mouth to respond, instead she stumbled back as a wave of nausea hit her, sending her scrambling for the adjoining bathroom. She flung her head over the toilet seat and let the contents of her stomach spill. She felt the gentle grip Darius had on her hair to keep it out of her face. He rubbed her back in a circular motion. She hated him seeing her like this, but nothing was as she liked when it came to this life growing in her. After a couple more elongated dry heaves, she wiped her mouth with the back of her hand and proceeded to the sink.

"I can't smell that bad." He joked, leaving the bathroom.

She brushed her teeth and dabbed her face with cold water. Darius came back in with her nightwear. She stretched her hand to take the clothes from him and he dismissed her. "Move, woman. Let me take care of you." Safiya leaned against the sink as Darius carefully undressed her and redressed her in her night wear.

"Are you ill?"

"No, it must be something I ate."

"Okay. I can always call Dr. McNair and he can fit us in."

"That won't be necessary." *Because I know what's going on with me. You and your child are stressing me out.*

Darius picked her up and placed her on the bed, and got in with her. Safiya wanted nothing more but to rest in his arms, but knew she couldn't. She wiggled to get free, but he held her tighter and caressed her hair.

"When I saw that paper, I was in rage, but when I went home and you weren't there, I went crazy. All sensibility left me. I'll admit I have issues with love and dependency, but in those moments, I came to the quick resolution that I had to take a chance and see if you feel an inkling of what I do."

"And what do you feel?"

With bated breath, Safiya waited on his response. She could feel his breath on her nape and the thumping of his heart beating against her back.

"I love you, Safiya Nadar Gray. I love you. I know this contract ends soon, but we must figure something out. My existence will cease to have meaning without you in it."

Her rib cage expanded with each syllable he spoke. Her brain scrambled to find the right words. This was what she wanted, but there was still something nagging at her. Vanessa and the fact that he hadn't asked that they stay married. Figure something out – what did that mean?

"What about Vanessa? She seemed to have all your attention."

Darius's head jerked up. "I don't care about anybody's attention but yours. Besides where did Vanessa come into play?"

"When I saw her with you in *The Socialite Magazine*."

Darius's brows furrowed. "You shouldn't believe everything you read."

Safiya raised her brow and pointed to the magazine he brought in earlier.

"Touché, but I did say when it comes to you, I'm irrational." In the next few moments, he explained the Vanessa situation to her. As he got to the end, she couldn't contain her smile.

Safiya straddled him and his hands went around her waist. "I love you, too. So much. But explain this 'we gotta figure something out statement'."

Darius brushed his lips against hers. "It means for the rest of my life, I want to wake up, roll over and kiss the love of my life good morning."

"Hmmm, that can be arranged. But am I giving you back your last name?" She struggled to stifle her smile.

A scowl appeared across his face. "Not on your life. I'd never had a dream come true until I met you."

"Not even when you made your first billion?"

"That pales in comparison to the way you make me feel." His lips caressed her neck and roamed her body.

Safiya stretched her neck to give him better access. "When...we started this, I thought it was gonna be...a huge mistake." She moaned.

"Woman, are you done talking? I have other things that need my attention." He squeezed her bottom.

"Quit it. Not under my dad's roof."

"I gave you the option to leave with me, but you didn't take it." He captured her lips with his. His tongue invaded her mouth, sensually caressing it with love.

"Darius, wait, I have something else to tell you..."

"Tell me later, I told you I have things to do." He rolled her over and began to lift her night dress, relegating her next words to the back of her mind.

For the next couple of hours, Darius made love to her body in ways she never knew was possible. It was a good thing her father's room was on the other side of the house. Her body tingled from the aftermath. She shifted to get up. Her bladder was about to overflow. He squeezed tighter holding her in place.

"Where are you going?"

"Your child is sitting on my bladder," she tossed out. Through the sliver of the streetlights entering the room, she saw his eyelids fly open. She grinned at his expression.

"My what? When did you find out? Why didn't you tell me?" With each question, his hand moved over her stomach and his eyes bounced between it and her face.

"Your child, some weeks ago. I was going to, in fact I tried to some hours ago."

His lip came crashing down on hers. Moments later, he set her free and cupped her face. "I promise to do my best to make myself worthy. Thank you."

"You already are...but I really need to pee now." She scurried from the bed and headed to the bathroom.

"Hey," Darius called out. She turned to him. "We might have been a spur of the moment thing, but that warm Vegas night was the beginning of the best nights of my life."

She blew him a kiss. "You promise?"

"Scout's honor," he raised two fingers.

Safiya rolled her eyes and pushed the door open. "Oh jeez, here we go."

THE END

EPILOGUE

Thirteen Months Later,

For a lavish wedding in the beautiful Saint Joseph's Catholic Church in Houmt El Souk, Safiya and Darius's celebration had been beautiful. With their adorable six-month-old daughter, Nia, sleeping peacefully, Safiya gazed into the magnificence of the stars above. She lifted her wine flute and took a sip, sighing deeply as the liquid made its way down her throat. She closed her eyes and leaned back into the lounge chair near the pool of their Jones Creek Mansion.

The memories of Darius's spectacular proposal two weeks after he found out she was pregnant still made her tingle all over. They'd been at a final championship game for the *Peach Heights*. Right before half time, he slipped away. Before she knew it, a stage rose from the middle of the field with Darius standing on it and a boy's scout group behind him. After the sweetest serenade of words, baring his soul before thousands, the boys lifted placards to their chest that formed the words, 'Will You Marry Me, Again?' Tears had rushed down her face and she hadn't noticed the microphone that had been placed by her side.

The whirlwind of events between that day and their wedding were a blur. She hadn't wanted to walk down the aisle with a protruding stomach, so she wanted to wait after she gave birth. Darius cancelled the idea immediately; he gave her ten days and that was it. Since money talked, it took seven. She was surprised at how many of his closest friends attended on such short notice.

"That smile on your face better be about me."

Startled, Safiya opened her eyes and took in her husband. He'd changed into his swimming trunks and held in his hand a platter of cheese, grapes and assorted fruits.

"Always baby," she responded. Even she could hear the lust that laced her tone.

He set down the tray, picked up a bunch of grapes and sauntered over to her. He held her throat lightly and placed the fruit above her mouth. She bit off two, so did he and quickly bent to capture her lips, his hand gently applying pressure to her throat. Their tongues tangoed, both enjoying the juice from the grape. He released her when it became apparent, they had to breathe.

"Come take a swim with me Mrs. Gray." He stretched out his hand.

She placed her hand in his. "Your wish is my command."

"Hmmm, really now." Darius swooped her up and walked toward the pool. "Don't punk out when I cash in on that comment." He winked at her.

Safiya smiled back, thankful for spontaneous Vegas Nights.

SECOND SHOT

Billionaire Pact Book 2

FIFTEEN

Early Spring 2011.

HIS BODY SLID BEHIND HERS, trapping her between the railing and himself. Her pulse began to race as it did when he was near. They stood that way for a few minutes, taking in the serene view. Brushing his hand against her hair, Hakeem Richardson broke the comfortable silence.

"What do you want to do on our last night of the cruise?"

Mariama Niang leaned her back into her boyfriend of two years with her eyes still on the open seas. The magnificence of the view captivated her each time she came onto the deck. It was the last night of their brief getaway and she wanted it to be special. She turned to face him. Standing on the tip of her toes, she cupped his face and kissed him.

"Baby, I know you probably want to spend time with your boys. So, do that and we'll go dancing later. I heard it's Calypso night."

Hakeem smiled down at her and cupped her buttocks with

one hand to draw her closer. "Have I told you how much I love you lately?"

"Hmm, let me check. Yes. Yes, I believe you have. When we woke up, in the shower, at breakfast…"

"You're mocking my undying love, woman?"

"How dare I? To do that would be to mock myself because I love you just as much."

"Good, because you have no other choice. You're stuck with me." He pecked her forehead and took her hand in his. Hakeem walked them to their lounge chair on the deck. He sat down and made her straddle him.

They were surrounded by different people from all walks of life who like them, were enjoying vacationing in multiple countries via the open seas. Despite the noise around them, Hakeem looked into her eyes. She saw the love that equated hers. Some would say it was too soon and they were still kinda young, with her being twenty-four and he, twenty-seven, but they knew, there couldn't be another person out here for them. They were the loves of each other's lives.

He's often told her that never in a million years would he have thought that he'd be fortunate enough to have her in his life. Truth be told, she was the one that was blessed. Love wasn't something she was good at until he came her way. She still remembered the day like it was yesterday. They literally bumped into each other in the graduate school administration's office. He was finishing up necessary paperwork to ensure he graduated. She was completing her registration to get started. After the initial apologies, they engaged in idle chatter while they waited on their appointments. After this cruise, he was moving to New York to start a new job. She'd graduate in six months and the plan was for her to join him.

With a lazy smile, Hakeem lifted his hand to her signature braids. He moved them to expose the crook of her neck.

Burying his head in it, he inhaled. It was one of his favorite spots. According to him, the citrus mango scent of her body lotion sent his senses into a tailspin. He brushed kisses against her exposed skin as his hands roamed her back. Moments later, his lips connected with hers. At first it was sensual, but as the intensity increased, Mariama pushed against him. It was now or never.

"Baby, there are people out here," she whispered, her breath labored. And as usual, his lips turned up in a smirk. He loved the effect he had on her.

"RiRi baby, you should know by now that when it comes to you, I don't care who's near. You are mine. I can touch you whenever."

"Be that as it may, we're in public. Behave yourself." She looked around. "Where's your crew anyway?"

"Trying to get rid of me?" His onyx eyes held a hint of amusement.

She traced the outline of his low-cut hair and tugged on his full beard. Leaving him no choice but to move his face closer to hers. She pecked his lips. "I tried that years ago and it didn't work, so I'm stuck with you," she winked.

He laughed. "I see you need me to re-teach you last night's lesson. You know, the one about sharp tongues and the inability to follow through."

She leaned her forehead against his. "Baby, you can teach me any lesson you like."

"For Pete's sake, will you guys get a room?"

The lovers disengaged. Mariama tried to stand, but Hakeem's arm locked firm around her waist, keeping her in place. He did allow her to turn around, so she was in his lap and facing the intrusive voice that belonged to Hakeem's brother Briceson Richardson, fondly called Brice.

"Mind your business, bro," Hakeem chided.

"I would if you guys didn't have yours out for display." Brice took the seat next to them. "RiRi…"

"Mari," Hakeem corrected.

Brice raised his hands in surrender and Mariama rolled her eyes. Her man hated for anyone to call her by the nickname reserved for her family and now him. One day, he heard her talking to her aunt who kept calling her that. From that day on, he adopted the name and forbade anyone else in their circle from using it. It was either Mari or Mariama. He was so extra, in her opinion.

"Mari, I don't want to see you anywhere on campus crying because this guy has moved," Brice warned.

"There won't be room for any of that. Six months will be over soon, and she'll be so focused on her finals and thesis," Hakeem responded. He kissed her back.

"That's right, babe. Besides, Brice, you'll be too busy with your harem of women to notice."

She and Brice took some classes together and were set to graduate at the same time. No one would mistake that he and Hakeem weren't brothers. They shared the same features; 6'3, although Brice was probably an inch shorter. A cut physique that was a result of dedicated gym hours and a proper diet. Chocolate smooth skin, low cut hair and a well-groomed beard.

"Family comes first, so I'll cut through them to make sure you're okay," he winked.

She furrowed her brows. "Don't you want what I and your brother have?"

"That would be a no," Brice answered.

As far as she had known the brothers, he was the goofier and more outgoing of the two. His specialty was playing the field. In fact, all of them, which included Darius Gray, Hakeem's best friend, did. Which was why it took so long to see that Hakeem was a little different. He didn't change women as much, but Darius and Brice had a different woman on their arm every time she saw them. The only constant was Imani Sharif, Brice's best friend.

"'Keem, the guys and I are going to the court then the bar. You coming?"

Mariama looked at him and nodded. "Go have fun, babe. I have plenty to occupy myself and I can also get a head start on packing."

Hakeem tapped her thigh and they stood. He snaked his arm around her waist and kissed her forehead. "All right, be good and don't be the reason I go to jail on foreign land."

"Huh?"

"Act like you're taken."

Mariama shook her head and stalked off. "You're something else."

"Yeah, something serious." Mariama heard him yell behind her.

She grinned, remembering the time she hadn't taken him seriously. They'd broken up over a silly argument. He had tried to reach her, and she'd been ignoring his calls all week. Then it so happened that when he did see her, a guy from her class was helping her on a project. Hakeem was furious. That was when she knew for certain her baby was no punk. His reaction was totally uncalled for, but it was sweet. He was possessive, but not overbearingly so.

SEVERAL HOURS LATER, Hakeem, Darius and Brice sat at one of the bars located on the ship. This was the first vacation they'd taken together. The years of their brotherhood and friendship had been filled with hardship, struggle, and pain. Things only became brighter after they got scholarships to go to college. They attended college together and eventually graduate school. This cruise was a celebration for Hakeem and Darius graduating.

Hakeem lifted his drink to his lips, aware of the two pairs of eyes on him, waiting for his answer.

"I don't know." He gave a truthful response.

"What do you mean you don't know? You do know that this cruise ends tomorrow morning? At the dock, you and Mari will go your separate ways. Her back to DC and you, New York," Darius said.

"Yes," Hakeem whispered.

"And you're saying you don't know if you can do the distance?" Brice asked.

Hakeem looked around the bar, his eyes connecting with everything and nothing at the same time. After shooting hoops with the fellas earlier, he'd gone for a swim. He needed it to take his mind off the conversation he and the guys had on the court. They questioned his readiness to settle down when he hadn't done half of the things they'd made a pact to do.

It was no secret that he was the only one in a committed relationship. They loved Mariama, but at the same time expressed concerns of love clouding his judgement. Hakeem knew it wasn't with malicious intent. The three of them had a brotherhood that started from the orphanage and spanned two decades. His father bailed when he was four and Brice was two. Their mother worked tirelessly to make ends meet but, in the end, died from overextension and not seeking the proper medical attention. The brothers were sent to the orphanage when their mother passed, and no family member stepped up. They met Darius there and they'd all been like brothers since.

"'Keem man, you know we're just looking out. We went through a lot growing up and made a pact to do what we needed to do to make a legacy, not just for ourselves, but our future children. Key word being 'future'," Darius said.

"Yeah. You talked about doing so many things, but with Mari moving to New York with you, will you be able to? You have this great new job, but remember the billionaire pact?" Brice asked with concern.

"Mari is good for you. It's better for you to come clean with her than for you to try and juggle everything, neglecting and hurting her in the process," Darius advised.

"Dating in school is way different from both of you living together when you guys basically have nothing," Brice said.

"I love her, man. I can't see my life meaning anything without her," Hakeem said.

"Who says you have to be without her? What we're saying is you guys need to slow things down a bit so you can focus on your goals." Darius picked up his drink and took a sip.

"You do want to provide a better life for her, right?" Brice asked. He looked at him with hidden meaning behind the question – their parents.

The bartender approached them and refilled their drinks. Hakeem used the opportunity to think. He didn't want to let Mariama go, even if it wasn't completely, but he was realizing it was best to slow things down. What good would it be to her if he tied her down now when he had hardly any money in his bank account and thousands of dollars in student loans from grad school?

He never wanted to end up like his father, whom his mother said struggled to provide because they got together so young and had kids. His ego was bruised, and he couldn't take staying, so he bailed. Neither did Hakeem want Mariama to end up like his mother, frustrated and tired.

Mariama was from an immigrant middle-class Senegalese family, but once they moved in together, he would take over all financial responsibility. Seeing what his mother went through, he was determined that no woman of his would ever go through the same. They talked and had a plan, but now he was beginning to think that they were hasty and removed from reality. He would never stop loving Mariama, but after their date tonight, he'd tell her they needed to slow things down. Just until he was secure on his feet and able to provide for them the way he should. The instability of a new job while she was going to be searching for one would put a strain on their relationship.

He didn't want to hurt her, but he had to do what was best for them. Hopefully, she would see things his way.

SIXTEEN

Seven Years Later

I THINK *we need to slow down. Instead of moving to New York, find something in DC and when the time is right, we'll be back together.*

Six years later, those words still stung and shattered Mariama Niang's heart as though Hakeem had just uttered them. The last day on that cruise had been the worst day of her life. How did all their plans blow up to smithereens over money? She knew it was a major hang up for him, considering how he and his brother grew up. But they talked, had plans, and were going to make them work. But one drink with the guys and suddenly he had cold feet. She never blamed his friends. They owed her nothing. The fracturing of her heart lay solely at the feet of Hakeem Richardson.

Leaning against the island in her kitchen, Mariama stirred the contents of her favorite mug. The yellow and grey décor was warm and calm, matching her mood. It was the early hours of the morning and this was the time she took to reflect upon the day, meditate and recite her daily affirmations. Four years ago, her parents retired and moved to Miami. Although she'd attended grad school in DC, her parents lived in Stone Mountain, Georgia where they migrated to with her and her older brother when she was ten. They left their home in Dakar, Senegal in search of a better life. Right after college her brother returned to Dakar to better their home country, but she decided to stay in the US with her parents. Their childhood home lay dormant since their retirement until Mariama decided to make stateside her home again.

She took her tea, walked over to the bay window in the corner of the kitchen. Sitting, she gazed out of the window at the well-manicured lawn. It was early morning but still dark, as the sun hadn't made its way over the horizon. Leaning back against the wall, she pushed a loc of hair back from her face. Even after all these years, having her hair in a protective style was still her default. But with maturity and new responsibility, she wore it differently. Now she had them in faux locs, which she'd come to love.

Hakeem used to love tugging on them. She smiled when she remembered his one attempt to oil her scalp with castor oil. Those intimate moments and times were what made it hard for her to understand his one eighty on their plans. After all these years, she still had questions. It was those same times that made her try and reach out to him for three months after he dumped her. She thought he'd have a change of heart. She also had something to tell him. Their love wasn't for naught. It had produced something so pure. But after several unanswered or unreturned calls, she decided to brave it and travel to New York. What she saw crushed her. Soon after, with a one-way ticket to Manchester in the United Kingdom, she left the US and moved in with her aunt. She eliminated all ways anyone apart from her parents could reach her. There, she picked up the pieces of her heart and got herself together. There was more at stake. More in the form of a milk chocolate, brown-eyed, five-year-old piece of deliciousness. Her son. *Their son.* Hakeem James Richardson, Jr. was her heart in human form. Every breath and everything she did was for him.

Mariama knew Hakeem was now a big-time billionaire. Go figure. Since moving back to the States, she couldn't escape his new status which was plastered on the cover of all of the top business magazines. Year after year, she told herself that she would reach out to him and tell him about HR, but year after year, she chickened out. HR was now asking questions on when the man she had shown him in pictures and referred to as his dad, would make an appearance. She was so scared that HR would think him up but the saving grace she had was that they were in Atlanta and the last she knew, he still lived in New York.

She looked up at the clock on the wall. It was time to get prepared for her day. Thinking of Hakeem first thing in the morning was always a bad idea, but a habit she couldn't let go of. Dwelling on their failed fairy-tale would have her curled up in bed, wishing she could escape the world.

"Mummy, where are you?"

Mariama smiled. That was her reminder that there was no escaping. Her son deserved better than a mother that was a coward.

"I'm coming, baby." Mariama rinsed her cup and placed it in the sink. She exited the kitchen and made her way up the stairs.

"Mummy, I'm not a baby." He folded his arms across his chest.

Just like his father.

Mariama placed her hand on his head. She made a mental

note to stop by the barber shop to get his hair braided and shaped up. She kneeled before him.

"Of course, you're not. Now what do you say?"

HR hugged her. "Good morning, Mummy."

"Good morning. Did you sleep well?"

He nodded.

"Good. Okay, let's go say our prayers, get ready for the day so we can have breakfast and be off."

"Fruit Loops?" he squealed.

"Yes, Fruit Loops." Mariama smiled. "Now come on, so we won't be late." She stretched out her hand which he took, and they headed to his room.

***

"ABBY, please get Rachael on the phone again," Mariama said. She had dropped her son off at school and was currently at her Buckhead office, but nothing was going according to plan.

Once she moved back to the US, her mother came to stay with her to help with HR. She used a chunk of her savings to renovate the three-bedroom house to her taste and kept the remainder for her future office space. Her brother who was doing very well, also sent her some money to make her transition easier. In her earlier days in the UK, with a Masters in Management and a baby on the way, she had to support herself. She began with virtual assistant work, but with her dedication and performance, it took little or no time for her to build a loyal customer base. Earning her an excess of two thousand dollars a month on Upwork, a freelance site.

It was something that became a passion and still gave her time to take care of her son. After a couple of years, Mariama set up her own company, Coup de Main, a professional, executive assistant agency. She trained and outsourced temporary executive assistants to top notch executives who needed them. All her operations were online until she decided to set up a physical office. It was turning a profit, but she had eyes on expanding outside Atlanta. For that, she needed more clients. That was the reason for her current agitation.

"Ms. Niang, I've tried. She's not answering," Abby, her assistant, responded.

"Is there anyone else we can get?"

"Not unless it's online."

Mariama placed her hands on her hips and paced. She shook her head. Lemoore Southern LLC, a top-notch food and beverage company, was her biggest client and had a six-month contract. This week, they had some big wigs coming into town and today, of all days, Rachael, one of her girls, decided to pull a disappearing act.

"No, they want a physical body." Mariama walked behind her desk and stuffed her iPad in her bag. "All other domestics are on assignment; Rachael is MIA and my one backup called in sick. I'm going to have to do this myself."

"Umm, are you for real?" Abby asked.

Mariama looked over her shoulder as she made her way to the front of the office. She creased her brow. "Yes, why?"

"In the two years I have been working for you, I've never seen you take on an assignment."

"That's because I didn't have to. But Lemoore is our biggest client and if we want recommendations, our service has to be impeccable."

"I'm so inspired right now," Abby said.

Mariama chuckled. "Coup de Main is my baby. And don't forget, before I sat behind that glass door to train others, I did this myself." She paused. "I'll be out for the rest of the day. I should be back tomorrow. Please try Rachael again. I hope nothing has happened to her."

"Will do, Boss Lady."

Minutes later, Mariama stepped into the elevator to the parking garage under the twenty-story building. She had less than thirty minutes to reach Lemoore and settle in for the board meeting they had. With her sunshades on and the melodies of Heather Headley's "Sista Girl" booming through her speakers, she pulled out of the parking lot and merged with traffic to her destination.

Several minutes later, Mariama set her bag down under the chair she had been assigned in the big conference room. She had broken most traffic laws to get here, but she was on time with minutes to spare. After stepping into the ladies' room to gather herself, she went up to the third floor, received her instructions and proceeded in the direction of the boardroom. She found out she would spend the majority of the morning taking notes and assisting where needed.

Soon after, the door opened, and five men and three women stepped in. Mariama showed them the light refreshments that were set up in the corner. Bill Lemoore was the Chief Executive Officer. His assistant left the company a week ago and because of a pending reorganization, the company didn't want to hire any permanent staff.

"I'm glad you made it, Mariama," Mr. Lemoore said.

He and Mariama were well acquainted from other professional circles around Atlanta, but business still came first.

"My girl couldn't make it today, but I wouldn't let you down."

"I get the boss herself. What more could I ask for?"

Mariama smiled. They conversed briefly about the agenda for the day. He ushered her around the room introducing her to the rest of the staff. Seconds later, Bill stood at the head of the table and cleared his throat to gain the room's attention.

"Good morning, ladies and gentlemen. As you know, an

investor made a large investment in the company last week. While our leadership won't change, this week the key members of our new parent company will be visiting and touring the facility."

Mariama had her head bent as she took down everything he was saying. He went on to reiterate the benefits to the company and what could potentially change for the staff to increase productivity and efficiencies. Other department heads spoke and gave updates to prepare for the visitors. An hour later, they broke for a quick, ten-minute break. When they reassembled, the lady Mariama now knew as Mrs. Newsome, Head of Operations, stood.

"I've just been informed the party for Richardson investments has arrived. They should be with us shortly," she said.

Richardson investments? Mariama's heart quickened at an exponential rate. She placed her hand over her chest and took in a deep breath. *No, it can't be.*

Granted, she didn't follow Hakeem's business dealings, but what was he doing with a food company? *No, it's not him.*

Well, even if it was, he was the head honcho in charge. Of course, he had better things to do than tour one of the facilities he owned. Mariama focused her attention on her notes as she willed herself to remain in control. She had to keep believing that Hakeem Richardson wasn't a part of the party they were waiting on. That was the only way she'd get through the day in one piece.

She was still stuck in her head when the conference room door opened. The hair on the back of her neck stood up, goose bumps appeared on her arms and her heart rate began to rise. She lifted her lids and her eyes landed on the man she could admit she still loved but hated at the same time – Hakeem Richardson. The only thing that surprised her was that in his eyes, she saw a rage that mirrored hers.

What the heck does he have to be mad about? He dumped me!

She had to get out of here, even if for only a few moments. Mariama walked to Mr. Lemoore. "I'll be right back. I need to visit the ladies' room."

Bill nodded. "Sure, we'll start once you get back."

Mariama bolted for the door. As she thought, Hakeem made a move to follow. When she heard Mr. Lemoore call out his name, she sighed in relief and headed down the hall.

SEVENTEEN

Shock, desire...unadulterated rage. Those were the emotions that coursed through Hakeem Richardson's body when his eyes locked with Mariama's. If someone had told him when he woke up in his Upper New York apartment that today, he'd see the woman that had eluded him for seven years, he never would've believed it. Before he had time to react, she bolted. Now that she was back and the meeting had started, she had done everything in her power to avoid eye contact with him. He'd play her little game, but she wasn't leaving here without talking to him.

Considering what happened the last time they were together, she had every right to be angry with him. But he'd realized his mistake. He had tried to make amends. He went back to get her. Not immediately, but he did, but it was as though she had dropped off the face of the earth and she took his heart with her. He had suggested they slow things down. He said nothing about her bailing.

He adjusted his tie and half listened as Mr. Lemoore presented to his team the changes they had been asked to make. He wasn't supposed to be here. The only time he came to one of the companies he invested in was when his share was more than fifty percent and during initial negotiations. After that, his head of acquisitions did the rest. The only reason he came was to make up for missing the initial negotiations. And he wanted to see his eight-month-old goddaughter, Nia Gray. He hadn't seen her since her christening when she was just eight weeks. He'd warned Darius and his wife, Safiya, beforehand that he wasn't going to be an inactive godparent. Especially since he hadn't been so lucky as to have a child. The one woman he ever wanted to have one with was sitting across the room from him – cool, calm and smiling at everyone but him.

Three hours and an excruciating tour of three warehouses later, Hakeem clenched his teeth. The only thing that kept him in check was the fact that she was at work. Why was she working here? After all these years, was she an executive assistant? Had she been in Atlanta all this time? These were questions he burned to ask her, but she'd been shrewd in avoiding him all day. Hakeem was preoccupied with members of his team, but kept his peripheral vision on Mariama. She was packing up and taking last minute instructions from Bill Lemoore. Throughout the day, it was obvious that Bill was smitten with her and that was another reason for Hakeem's frustration.

"Excuse me," Hakeem said. He side-stepped the people talking to him and headed out of the door after her. He didn't call out to her immediately. He took the time to observe the sway of her hips which had gotten a tad bit wider. Her buttocks filled out the red skirt she wore. All day he wanted to tell her to button her top button to conceal her cleavage, but he knew he no longer had that right. Her locs were wrapped in a low pony-tail and landed just on top the small of her back. The clicking of her black stilettoes brought him out of his lustful gaze.

"Mariama."

She kept on walking.

His heart quickened. "RiRi."

She stopped just before the doors that led to the elevators, but didn't turn to face him. He took calculated steps toward her. He kept his hands in his pockets to keep from touching her. A beat passed between them before she took in a breath, exhaled, and turned to face him.

Hakeem looked into her hazel eyes and everything he had planned to say all morning disappeared. She pursed her lips and raised her brow.

"Don't call me that. It's Mari, Mariama or Ms. Niang." Her tone had a slight edge to it. She seemed offended, or rather disgusted by his presence. It was strange to feel this energy from her. Her apparent discomfort made him uneasy, but that all disappeared when he realized her name was still Ms. Niang.

"Why?"

"Just don't. Now, Mr. Richardson, is there anything I can do for you because I have somewhere to be."

His brows furrowed. They were lovers, best friends, soul mates and now he was Mr. Richardson? Anger boiled in his gut.

"We're in the hallway. I do business with these people. Either you say why you called me or let me be on my way," she whispered.

"We need to talk." His assertive tone was back as he gained his composure. He had always admired Mariama's strength and independence, but unfortunately, they would have to take a back seat.

"We have nothing to talk about." She pressed the button for the parking garage.

"Mariama. Please don't make me come looking for you. You owe me a conversation."

"I owe you nothing." The elevator opened and she stepped in.

Hakeem did the same. Fire burned through his body at the way she was dismissing him. She rolled her eyes at him and stood in the corner. He pressed the "Stop" button to jam the elevator between floors. Taking out his phone, he sent a quick text to his assistant to meet him downstairs.

"What is wrong with you?" Her look of disdain almost made him chuckle.

Hakeem walked toward her. He used his hands to trap her in the corner. He leaned over her five-foot five frame. "You want to know what's wrong with me."

She nodded as her chest rose and fell.

He should be mad. He was mad, but she was still the sexiest woman he'd ever seen, especially when she was furious with him.

"I'm annoyed that you could go the whole day and act like I was just another client. I'm upset that you can act like I never meant anything to you. That you're not the least bit interested in talking to me. How can you act like I don't know intimately every beautiful inch of your body?"

Mariama didn't flinch. Instead she locked eyes with him and said, "Number one, you are another client, just not mine. Number two, keyword 'meant', past tense. Number three, no I'm not interested in talking to you. And finally, I hope you got a good memory, because you'll never have that privilege again."

Hakeem raised his brow. A sarcastic chuckle escaped his lips. He pushed away from her. "I can't believe this."

"Oh, my bad. Did you expect me to lay down at your feet, Mr. Richardson?" The indifference in her tone cut him deep.

He leaned back in the adjacent corner. He wasn't going to get anywhere like this. Hakeem pulled his anger and sense of entitlement together. He looked up at her and for a second, he saw her eyes soften toward him.

"Hakeem, you broke up what we had. Why are you so angry that I gave you exactly what you wanted?"

"I asked to slow things down, not for you to freaking bail on me."

"We were young, but I didn't have time for childish games. And I didn't think you did either. One minute, we're planning a future, the next you want to slow down. Code for 'you wanted to do you.' Like a fool, I waited for you. All my texts and calls all went unanswered. Was I supposed to keep waiting for you?"

"You're right. I'm sorry." Hakeem sighed. "I did come looking for you."

She cocked her head to the side. "Well, you know what they say. You snooze, you lose." She glanced at her watch. "If you don't mind, I have to get going."

Hakeem hung his head and pushed the button setting the elevator in motion again. In tension filled silence, they rode down to the parking garage. He was surprised when her key fob unlocked a Pathfinder. She used to fear trucks. What didn't surprise him was the fact that it was grey with red accents - her favorite colors. She opened the driver's door and placed her bag on the passenger's seat and got in.

He smiled when she took off her shoes and replaced them with slippers. She never wore heels to drive. Despite her coldness which he deserved, he was relieved to know that not everything had changed.

Mariama still didn't say anything to him as she reached for the handle of the door. He stopped her. She was in such a hurry to get away from him that she hadn't put on her seat belt.

"Allow me," he whispered.

He leaned in. The action put him in close proximity with her. The sweet scent of mango citrus brought back memories of yesteryears. He could feel her holding her breath. The desire to feel her lips against his burned within him. He turned his face to catch the fire that flashed in her eyes. For the first time that day, he rejoiced inwardly. Before she replaced the emotion with her façade, he had a chance to see recognition of the connection they once shared.

'Hakeem buckled her in and stood. He was about to close the door when his eye caught something lying on the backseat. A toy Spiderman. His heart stopped. He felt like he had just been punched in the gut. He never got to meet her brother but knew he wasn't married yet. So, she didn't have nieces or nephews.

"Bye, Hakeem," she said.

"See you soon, RiRi," he responded.

Hakeem shoved his hands into his pockets and clenched his jaw as she drove away. His eyes followed the car until it was out of sight. Mariama knew him well enough to know this wasn't the last she'd see of him. If he was determined to get her back before, he was on a war path now. She not only bailed on him, but she had a kid with another man. He didn't see a ring on her finger, but supposing the kid's father was waiting for the right time. Now that he had found her, this planet couldn't contain him and any man who thought he was going to be her husband.

With his resources, Hakeem could find out everything about her in minutes. But Mariama wasn't like these other women out there. A dossier wouldn't give him the result he needed. He'd have to use his power another way. He pulled out his cell phone as he walked to the elevator.

"Hey Carl, tell Mr. Lemoore to wait for me in his office. I need to speak with him briefly," Hakeem told his assistant.

"On it, boss. The driver is also out front to take us back to the air strip when you're ready to leave."

"There's been a change of plans." He gave Carl further instructions on his way back up to the tenth floor.

Seven years ago, Hakeem made the biggest error of his life. True, he had done everything he set out to. At thirty-five, he was a billionaire. Over the years, he'd aggressively pursued the dollar in investments—his and others—takeovers, hedge funds, name it. He was never without sexual partners when he wanted them, but his heart was empty.

For the first time in years, he wasn't walking around with a hole in his chest. He'd found his lifeline. He probably didn't deserve her, but the selfish part of him didn't care. Mariama Niang was his. He had a second chance. There was no way he was messing it up.

EIGHTEEN

"I think that man was sent to this earth to play with my sanity," Mariama told Brianna. "I mean, just as I was finally getting everything together, he pops up and dares to be angry at me. Me Bri? Me?"

Later that evening, Mariama paced between the island and the oven with her iPod earbuds in her ears. When she was stressed, she baked, and right now she had already come up with a red velvet, a pound, and a Bundt cake. When she baked like this, she never ate them all, she either took them to her office for her staff to enjoy or the local fire station.

"Mari, I love you, but it's two a.m. here. I've listened to you fuss for the past thirty minutes. Can I talk now, or do you want to keep going?"

Brianna Nelson was her aunt's neighbor's daughter. When Mariama relocated to the UK, Brianna had recently moved back in with her parents. Something about an engagement gone wrong. The two women who were close in age bonded over Kleenex, ice cream and sad love songs. They had been best friends ever since. Brianna still lived in the UK, but was now married and expecting her first child.

"It's not fair Bri, he broke my heart." Mariama checked the kitchen timer and sat down by the bay window.

"I know, but life isn't fair. You've worked too darn hard to crumple into mush now. Don't let Hakeem's presence take away the fruits of your labor. Where is my bad ass friend? I know you're having a moment and it's okay too."

Mariama smiled. "You're right."

"I'm always right," Brianna said. "From what you've told me about this man over the years, he is relentless. So, we both know that this fantasy you have in your head about him quietly crawling back under the rock he came from will not happen."

"Ugh..."

"Yeah, ugh is right. Instead of breaking down, you need to figure out a way to handle him...and fast."

"From the way he looked at me, I know what he wants and I can't give it to him."

"What's that?"

"He wants to explain. I'm not going to give him the satisfaction of making himself feel better."

"Well, you might want to."

"Whose side are you on anyway?"

"Yours, so I'm telling you the truth. Or have you forgotten you have the man's son and haven't told him?"

Mariama covered her face with her palm. She was lucky because earlier, her sitter asked her if she could keep HR's booster seat in the school's front office. The booster seat she owned was in the car she had at the mechanics. That was close, because if Hakeem had seen it, for sure, he wouldn't have let her go without a few more questions.

"You know why I haven't told him," she sighed.

"Knowing why doesn't make it right my friend." A beat of

silence passed between them before Brianna continued. "Be prepared, that man is going to be royally vexed when you do tell him. So, you should let him explain now because when it's time for you to explain, you're going to need him to have some good memories...recent ones."

"I so hate you. For real," Mariama said.

"Yeah, sure you do. Just like you told me when I was dragging Kenny through the ringer and back for my ex's issues; I'm telling you the same thing," Brianna said. "You've been in the US for three years now. The plan was to look for him and tell him. I know you did try on many occasions, but the bottom line is, you didn't."

"Okay, okay, I called you to vent and make me feel better, but now I feel like trash." Mariama stood and walked back to the island. She started cleaning up the mess she'd made in the kitchen.

"You're not trash. You're the sweetest, most generous and kindest person I know, but you did a bad thing," Brianna said. "And I let you fuss for thirty minutes straight to get it all out, but I love us because we always tell each other the painful truth. What kind of friend would I be if I let you think you're out here winning when you're not?"

Mariama sighed. Brianna was right. She always was. When HR was one, she did try to call Hakeem from the UK, but his number no longer worked. She knew there were so many other ways she could contact him, but the truth – her truth – was that she wasn't strong enough to do it. She knew he would have insisted they get back together, and it would've killed her that a baby would be the reason instead of the connection they had. Hakeem did teach her a valuable lesson. It was dangerous to love someone, anyone, as much as she loved him. The only person worthy of that kind of love was her son.

"Okay, I hear you. HR leaves in the morning for Miami with my mom—"

"When did your mom get in?'

"Girl, she was here when I got back. She has zero time for me. All she wanted was her grandson."

"Does she know about Hakeem's reappearance?"

"Yes, and she gave me a sermon about it."

"See, I'm not the only one. Summer Break, right? So he'll be gone for some weeks?"

"Yes. It'll give me ample time to contact Hakeem and arrange a sit down to tell him."

Brianna cackled.

"What's so funny?"

"You. The fact that I seem to know Hakeem better than you. He'll be in your face by sunrise."

"Don't wish that on me. I need to get my baby safely away from the city because his daddy will be on a rampage when I tell him." Unintentionally, her lips turned up in a smile. Memories of how Hakeem would lose his mind over all that concerned her flooded her mind. She'd found it sexy. She always felt safe and protected with him. That was until he rocked her equilibrium with his stinging words.

"Are you smiling? You like that craziness, huh? You need help."

Mariama put the last cake in the warmer and cut off the lights in the kitchen. She listened as Brianna described the house that they were planning to buy. Mariama was so happy for her friend.

"Hold on Bri, I got a text coming through. Don't hang up," Mariama said.

She picked up her phone and frowned. *No, no, I can't handle them at the same time.* She sighed.

"What's wrong?" Brianna asked.

"My life..."

"Can you be more specific?"

"Anthony is in town."

Brianna's laughter started as soft giggles, then graduated into full blown hilarity. For someone who was just complaining about it being the wee hours of the morning, she was enjoying her pain and suffering a little too much.

"I thought you were sleepy?"

"I was. All your drama has me wide awake now. Even Kenny had to come to the kitchen to check on me." She paused. "In fact, I need to ask him how we can get this new TV station."

"Huh? What TV station?"

"Mari TV. Your life is a soap opera."

"On that note, good night, or I guess for you good morning."

"Come on, Mari, don't hang up. This is getting good." She laughed. "Anthony..."

Her friend was still laughing when Mariama hung up the phone. She made her way up the stairs. Without making a sound, she checked on her mother who was asleep. Right after, she walked into HR's room. The room had a Spiderman theme to it. She kissed his forehead and caressed his cheek. A tear ran down hers. She wiped it away and tucked his Spiderman comforter securely around him.

"I love you HR and I'm so sorry," she whispered.

Closing his door behind her, she strode down the hall to her room. After a long shower, Mariama slipped into bed. She laid on her back, crossed her arms over her chest and stared at the celling. She said a silent prayer for help. She needed all she could get.

HAKEEM ROLLED his glass between his hands and looked out into the distance. It was a little past ten p.m. and he was still at his friend, Darius Gray's home.

"I'm surprised you're in town, but I'm glad man," Hakeem said.

"Who you telling? Me too, we can't have you doing anything irrational," Darius responded.

After he left Mr. Lemoore several hours ago, Hakeem checked in to his regular penthouse suite at the Westin. Then he called Darius to tell him that he was in town and on his way to see Nia and Safiya. He was happy that Darius was home and not in Chicago as he thought he'd be. Apparently, Julia, Darius's assistant, got things mixed up and he had to attend some golf charity event in the morning as a favor to a business partner he met a while ago.

Earlier, Hakeem had dinner with the whole family and played with his goddaughter before she and her mom retired for the night. The men retreated to Darius's expansive lounge area, with burning fire pits and a bar, at the backyard. Darius mixed some drinks for them while Hakeem filled him in on the latest developments.

"I can tell she's bent on driving me insane. The way she looked through me. You wouldn't believe she'd ever been my RiRi," Hakeem said, his tone somber.

"Look, man. I'm still trying to get over the fact that you just happened to walk in a meeting and boom, Mari. I wanna ask you so many questions but from what you've told me, you have no answers."

"That's because she won't even talk to me."

"What did you expect? This is Mari we're talking about. You had to go pick the mean girl." Darius laughed.

They'd always teased her about being mean. She really wasn't, she just took no mess from anyone. Her confidence was a trait they all admired and always told him he was indeed lucky to have her on his side. He used to be the only person that could bend her a little. But not this RiRi.

Hakeem shook his head. "And I love her."

"That's not news. You've loved her forever and we all regret getting into your head all those years ago. Question is, what are you going to do about it?"

Hakeem turned to face Darius. He furrowed his eyebrows at him. "What do you mean, what am I going to do? I'm going to get her back."

"Unless you're going to kidnap her and become a fugitive on the run, you actually need a strategy."

Hakeem tugged on his full beard. He was a ruthless investor and businessman. He handled situations with poise and calculation, but the one person who could unravel him was Mariama Niang. Darius was right, he did need a plan, but none came to mind. All he knew was she owned her own company with an office located in Buckhead. He had an address but with it being Friday, he knew she wouldn't be working until Monday.

He did manage to get her home address and phone number, but he didn't want to set her off by popping up. He had every intention of doing that in her office on Monday, but what was he going to do with himself for two whole days? He didn't want to go back to New York without talking to her.

"Might not be a bad plan since she won't willingly talk to me."

"Please tell me you're joking. And when does anyone have to let you do anything?" Darius chuckled. "Do I need to call Brice for an intervention?"

"You weren't laughing when you got back home and Safiya was gone," Hakeem said.

"True, difference is, Safiya and I didn't have the history you and Mari do."

Several beats of silence passed between them. Hakeem knew all the ways to get the old Mariama to talk to him. The one he met earlier, the one who looked at him with disdain, was different. He deserved it, but she owed him a conversation. Mariama was as stubborn as she was beautiful, and that was saying a lot.

"I think she has a kid…"

"How do you know this? I thought you didn't do a dossier on her?"

"I didn't. But when I walked her to her car, I saw a toy."

"There could be many explanations for that."

Hakeem set his glass down and looked at his friend with one eyebrow raised. "Really?"

"Come on, 'Keem. I watched you beat yourself up every day about Mari leaving. You got her back. Well, you don't, but you know what I'm saying. Even if she does have a kid, they are a package deal. So, all you need to be concerned about is figuring out a way to get her to talk to you."

Hakeem nodded his head. A kid, he could handle. Some other man, he couldn't. "I need to get going man. Safiya's going to kill me for keeping you out this late."

Darius laughed. Hakeem was so happy for his friend. He had finally found what money couldn't buy. True love from a woman he called his queen. A little over two years ago, he was this shrewd billionaire who had little time for a love connection. Now, he was a happily married man and a doting father who still made money, but it just didn't matter as much.

"Why not come with me tomorrow?" Darius asked.

"Nah, you know I don't do those things. I'd rather just write a check."

"Yeah, I know you don't, but a change would be good. Get

your mind off Mariama." Darius raised his hands in surrender at the look Hakeem gave him. "I know it's not easy, but it'll give you something to do while you wait on Monday, since you don't want to pop up at her home."

Hakeem shrugged. He didn't feel like going, but the hours he was away from her were chipping away at his resolve. Maybe he did need something to occupy his time.

"Sure man, whatever. Come pick me up from the Westin downtown."

Several minutes later, Hakeem was driving down the road with one mission on his mind. Getting Mariama Niang back.

NINETEEN

Mariama cruised down the I-20 Atlanta freeway back toward her house. She'd dropped her son and mother off at the airport and was finally kid-free for a while. It was summer break, but her bills didn't know a thing about that, so she had some particularly important proposals to write and deals to close. The Lemoore contract was going great, as were the other smaller businesses she had as clients, locally and virtually. However, with her goal of opening offices in other parts of the country, she needed a few more big names with longer contract tenures.

In her sight now was Spartan Enterprises. They were a European-based company making three American cities their international base, Atlanta, New York, and Chicago. Anthony had introduced her to the CEO a while back and she soft pitched her interest. Now it was becoming a reality, but she had to put up a convincing bid. Although he liked to think otherwise, Anthony Roberts and she were just friends. Really good friends, and she didn't want people thinking it was because of him that she got anything.

Several minutes later, she pulled into her driveway and

headed inside. She had exactly two hours before Anthony would be here to take her on their date. Or rather, before he needed her to be candy on his arm. It was harmless and she could make a friend happy, so why not?

Mariama met Anthony during her last year in Manchester. She had attended a function with Brianna and her parents and Anthony happened to be there as well. He had done a good job of keeping a low profile. If she had known then that he was a wealthy man, she wouldn't have allowed Brianna to pressure her into giving him her number, and she would've run in the opposite direction.

Hakeem deciding to forgo all their plans for the dollar left a bad taste in her mouth. She was done with rich men. She wanted a provider when she eventually decided to get married, but she didn't want one who was driven solely by the need to make money. There were far more important things in the world than that. Anthony had asked her out on a date for three months straight before she gave in. Over that period, they spent a lot of time on the phone getting to know one another. Slowly and surely, he warmed his way into her heart, but not in a romantic sense. That space was unavailable.

They went out a couple of times, movies, art shows, sailing, but she always stressed she wasn't in the market for anything more. He said he understood, but over time his pursuit intensified. It was a good thing she left the UK when she did. Since then, they kept in touch. Whenever he came to the US, he'd let her know in advance, but this popping up was strange, even for him. When she talked to him earlier, he said the trip wasn't planned but she wasn't so sure.

Mariama had no idea where Hakeem was and that bothered her. She knew him well enough to know he had something up his sleeve. He was never a patient man. So, for him to find her now and be silent for the past twenty-four hours rattled her.

Walking into her closet to choose an outfit, her chest tightened. What if Hakeem had done a background check on her? He knew her license plate number and knowing him, where she worked and lived. Did he know she had a son? Would he take HR from her?

She sat on the bench in her closet and took in a deep breath. She exhaled. The thought of HR not being in her life was scary. Just thinking that could happen could kill her. On Monday morning, she was going to look for Hakeem and talk to him.

Yeah, Monday. She stood and went over to her shoe boxes. Armed with a plan, she picked out what she wanted to wear. There was no way she could deal with two wealthy, egotistical men at once. Anthony had nowhere as much money as Hakeem. But she didn't need a testosterone contest on her hands. So, the plan was, get one out of the country before dealing with the other.

MARIAMA FELL in step with Anthony as they headed inside the country club. He had told her to dress casually. He didn't tell her that they were going to schmooze with the rich and famous. Trust me, trust me he said. Now she wished she hadn't. His idea of going out always included somewhere quiet – not this. As they walked and greeted people, Mariama could see that this was the quintessential "who's who" in the modern world of business. Some people she recognized from magazines and some she didn't.

"This is my close friend, Mariama." Anthony's words drew her focus away from the painting she was looking at.

"Hi, it's nice to meet you." Mariama smiled as she took the older man's hand.

"It's my pleasure, young lady." The man took her hand and kissed the back of it.

Mariama looked over at Anthony and he winked at her. He knew her well enough to know that she was going to ask him what the deal was with him placing a qualifier before the word "friend." The word close had so many implied meanings and he knew that. He had been doing things all morning that were out of character. She had ignored him touching the small of her back and caressing her face, but now it was time to have a serious talk.

"Would you please excuse us?" Mariama asked.

The man nodded and Mariama grabbed Anthony's hand. When they got to a secluded corner of the room, she turned to him. "What was that about Tony? What's going on?"

"What? Me calling you close? We are close, so what's the problem?" He smirked.

"Stop being obtuse. You know exactly what I mean. You've been acting strange and I want to know why."

He shoved his hands into his khakis and stared down at her. "I'm tired of waiting Mari. I want to be with you, and you've known this. I care for you and HR, so why do you keep pushing me away?"

Talk about timing.

Mariama rubbed her hand up and down her arm. "Tony, come on. We've talked about this."

"Yes, and I still don't understand your point. We're good together. Everyone we've met since we got here seems to think so." He took a stride toward her, entering her personal space.

Mariama took a step back but ended up with her back against the wall. Anthony was a very handsome man who stood about three inches taller than her. Despite the invasion of her personal space, she was doing good keeping her composure. Especially since she hadn't had sex in years.

"Let's not discuss this now. This charity golf luncheon is business for you. You should do what rich people like you do at these things." Mariama winked, causing him to chuckle.

"Still resourceful in getting yourself out of any conversation. But you're right. I need to go and mingle and since I have the most beautiful lady on my arm, I might be able to close some deals."

Mariama swatted his arm. "I can't believe you'd use me like that."

"And I can't believe you won't be mine. But here we are." Anthony stepped away.

The two shared a laugh when her phone buzzed. Mariama reached into the pockets of her khaki miniskirt and took it out. It was a text from an unknown number.

Get him out of your face, now.

In a frantic haste, Mariama looked around the room. There was only one person who would dare talk to her like that. But he didn't come to these kinds of things.

Seconds later, she let out a breath she didn't even know she was holding. Nothing seemed out of the ordinary. She shrugged. She was being paranoid. It was probably a wrong number.

"You ready?" Anthony asked when he turned back toward her.

"Umm.... yes. I'm ready to see you kick some golf butt." Mariama took his outstretched hand.

"That's my girl. Darius Gray doesn't stand a chance."

Mariama stumbled. Anthony caught her fall. "Are you okay?"

She tried to calm down the beating of her heart. Darius was here. That meant Hakeem was, too. She was single and wasn't doing anything wrong. With Hakeem however, everything was complicated. This was the weekend, and she didn't want to have to deal with anything but having a nice time and facing her issues on Monday.

"Yes, I'm fine. I need a drink of water."

"Okay. I'll be right back. But then I want you to stay under the shade while I go out there. I shouldn't be long," Anthony said.

He walked away and seconds later was back with a bottle of water. He kissed her forehead and went out to the course after she convinced him she was fine. Mariama laid her head back in the chair and closed her eyes. What was she going to do? She could order an Uber and explain to Anthony she had to go home. But that would make her a coward. This was her city, her home. She felt stupid allowing Hakeem to come in from New York and make her feel like she couldn't come out. Immediately, she opened her eyes and stood. She secured her bag across her body, tossed the empty water bottle in the recycle bin, and turned toward the course so she could see Anthony play.

"Going somewhere?" His deep voice halted her in her tracks.

Mariama closed her eyes and mentally willed for any magic trick that could make her disappear and reappear in the comforts of her home. She shook her head, sighed, and turned. She took in his appearance – dark blue khaki shorts, light pink polo shirt with the collar standing and as usual, he looked like he' just visited a barber.

"Hakeem, what are you doing here?"

"The more important question is, why are you here with Roberts and who is he to you?"

Mariama's eyes widened. "You are kidding me, right?"

Hakeem walked toward her. The scent of his cologne and his smoldering gaze almost tempted her to step back. But she was tired of all these men approaching her like she was a prey.

Mariama held her head up high and stood her ground. When he was inches away from her, she immediately begun to reevaluate her decision-making skills.

"No, I'm not. Now answer the question." Hakeem's seductive voice was laced with disapproval.

"It's been years, but I am still the same woman. You don't scare me."

"I'm not trying to scare you. I'm trying to get you to talk to me. You don't want to, but you have time to laugh and go on dates?"

"Are you jealous?" Mariama asked coolly. "You do know that you lost that right many years ago."

"Jealousy would be to imply that I want, or I'm envious of what someone else has." He stepped closer to her. "You, RiRi, are mine."

"I'm not yours."

"You're angry with me. You possibly want to strangle me. All that you deserve to do, but you'll always be mine."

"Yeah, me and all the others." Mariama regretted the words immediately when they left her mouth. She didn't want him to think she kept up with his sex-life. Even though the truth of the matter was, she did. For a while at least, then she let him go.

He caressed her face with the back of his hand. "None of them could compare to you. You had something they could never have."

Mariama rolled her eyes. "Oh, yeah and what's that?"

He took her hand and placed it across his heart. "This. You've always had my heart."

Mariama couldn't help the shiver that ran down her spine. Hakeem lowered his head and brushed his lips lightly against her. A few moments later, she jerked away. She wasn't falling for that again.

"And look where it brought us. As far as I'm concerned, they can have it."

Hakeem's face flashed with anger. "I deserve that."

"You deserve a lot of things."

"And I know that. The quicker we have the conversation, the earlier we can get to you giving me what I deserve and then we can go back to loving."

"You really think my heart is some toy? One you pick up and drop whenever you feel like it?"

"No baby, I don't, but I'm grasping for straws here. Please, I'm begging. One conversation."

"I'll think about it. And after that, you'll drop this me being yours thing."

"Let's have the conversation first."

"'Keem..."

"Make no mistake, RiRi. My mission is to become a part of your life. Don't make me promise you something I can't deliver."

"I heard Darius was here. How is he?" she asked, grasping for a safer topic.

"Good. You ask of him, but don't care about me?"

"I see you're good. Getting on my nerves...I see that hasn't changed."

Hakeem laughed. He reached for her hand. They both engaged in a silent stare off. She was telling herself not to get caught up again, while reciting how she was going to tell him they had a son. Mariama knew getting her back was top on his agenda, she wondered what it would be if he knew she was a package deal.

"I should get going." Mariama said.

"Why? Roberts can do without you for a few more minutes." The coldness in his voice had returned.

"Don't start. I came here with him and it's rude."

"What is he to you?" His voice boomed.

"None of your business. And you need to lower your voice," she whispered harshly, smiling at the couple who happened to be walking by.

"He lives in the UK. I don't get the connection."

"Do you know how ignorant you sound?" She placed her hand on her hip.

"Don't be rude. You know what I mean."

"He's a friend."

"I'm not stupid. I can see that with him all up in your face. I mean, what kind of friend?" Hakeem lowered his voice, but the harshness in his words didn't guise his frustration.

Mariama felt like a standing contradiction. She was baffled at his audacity, but found it so endearing that he was feeling threatened about his assumed position in her life.

"If I give you your conversation, will you let this go so I can leave?"

"Leave with him?"

"Yes, I came with him."

"You mean you let him come to your house?"

They engaged in an intense stare down. Mariama blew air from her lips. His tantrum was driving her insane. She opened her mouth to speak when someone cleared their throat behind her.

Hakeem looked up with a smirk. Mariama turned around and saw Anthony who had a deep scowl on his face, and Darius who had a knowing smile.

Oh great. Just great.

TWENTY

"Hold on a sec, Brice," Hakeem said.

He thumbed his iPad and connected with Carl. "Tell me something good, Carl."

"Unfortunately, sir, it's not good. This event has been pushed back two times to accommodate your schedule and you promised this time that you would be there."

Hakeem ran his hand over his head and leaned back into the leather seat in the back of the hired car. He never liked to push his weight around, especially if it wasn't necessary. His personal life might be in shambles, but he still had a business to run. Fire blazed through his veins as the events of the past seventy hours came flooding through his mind. He was acting irrational and he had to get it together.

"Okay Carl, tell the pilot to meet me here in a couple of hours. I'll leave from Atlanta."

"Sounds good. Do you need me to go to your apartment and have Priscilla pack a suitcase for you?"

Carl had been his assistant for over three years. When he caught his last female assistant in his office naked late at night, he decided never to hire a woman to work so closely with. He knew she wasn't representative of the whole species, but the last thing he needed was to be hit with a sexual harassment lawsuit or have a scorned woman on his hands. One thing he never joked about was his business. Not only his investments, but those of his partners, silent and otherwise were at stake.

"No, thanks. I'll get whatever I need when I get there. As for the housekeeper, I'll call her so she can take a couple of days off. You, I'll see later."

Hakeem disconnected the call and picked up his cell phone. "Hey Brice, you still there?"

"Yeah, bro. I was talking to Imani. She's going to make me mess her up," Brice said.

"I'm not touching that with a ten-foot pole," he replied.

Imani was his brother's best friend since high school. They'd been there for each other through everything, but somehow couldn't get themselves together to commit to one another. Everyone in their circle knew they loved each other, but they swore they didn't. Hakeem wasn't the one to say anything. He couldn't even get his own life together.

"I'm letting you know in case I need bail money."

Hakeem laughed. His brother was a silent partner in most of his investments and although he had a college degree, he refused to use it. Modeling seemed to bring him joy, so that's what he did. The fact that he would need money for anything when he was also a billionaire was funny. He never talked about his net worth, so people assumed he wasn't.

"Yeah, right."

"Okay, so let me get this straight. In one weekend you find our Mari, she rejects your sorry apology repeatedly, she walks out on you, gets in the car with another man, then hides from you all yesterday and refused to answer any of your calls."

Hakeem winced at Brice's recollection of events, but that

was exactly what happened. But all that was being corrected today. She must have forgotten who he was. He never played fair when it came to her.

"You and Darius are just going to absolve yourselves from contributing to my bad decision years ago?" Hakeem joked. He knew they weren't' to blame, and the final decision lay with him. He'd dealt with and was still dealing with the consequences.

"We were drunk and only expressing our concerns. No one told you to break Mari's heart. You know how mean she is." Brice laughed.

"We're here, sir," the driver said, bringing the car to a halt.

Hakeem looked outside the window. They were in a parking lot in the busy Buckhead business district. He looked up at the building he now knew contained Coup de Main on the seventh floor. Yes, she had avoided him the previous day, but she wouldn't let anything stop her business, so she was going to have to see him.

"Thanks, I'll be right back." Hakeem said. He got out of the car and walked to the front of the building. He entered and went straight for the elevator. 'I gotta go, but I'll be in touch."

"Okay, good luck. Piece of advice—"

"From you?" Hakeem smiled.

"Yes, from me. Not having a steady woman doesn't mean I don't know how to make women fall for me." Brice sounded offended.

Hakeem pressed the button to summon the elevator.

"Show her you. This is Mari we're dealing with. All that 'I am billionaire do what I say' junk won't work because she knew you way before then. Show her the person she fell in love with."

"Got it, lil brother. I'll talk to you later. And thanks."

Hakeem entered the elevator and pressed the button for the seventh floor.

Minutes later, he walked into the suite that housed Mariama's office. The decor wasn't too flashy, but he could tell the personal touches that were solely Mariama's. The white flowers in the corner, the paintings and quotes on the wall all oozed Mariama – confident, strong, bold and daring.

"May I help you?" the lady at the reception desk asked.

"Yes, I'm here to see Mariama."

Skepticism adorned her face.

"Ms. Niang," he corrected himself. "I'm here to see Ms. Niang."

"Oh, do you have an appointment?" She moved her mouse and clicked several times before looking up at him.

"No, but I'm pretty sure she'll see me." Hakeem looked at his watch. He had exactly forty-five minutes to accomplish his mission since he had a flight to catch. What he came to do exactly eluded him, but seeing Mariama was paramount.

"She's finishing up a meeting. May I have your name? I'll see if she can squeeze you in."

He smiled. "It's Mr. Richardson. Just tell her Hakeem." He walked toward the middle of the room as the lady went in the direction of what he assumed was Mariama's office.

SEVERAL MOMENTS LATER, Hakeem was being escorted down the hall. She stood behind her desk with her hands on her hips. She had her earbuds in, talking to someone. She looked up at him, holding up her index finger indicating she needed a minute. Her receptionist dutifully closed the door and left.

Hakeem scanned her office. The first thing he looked for

was personal photos, but there were none. If she did have a kid, he was sure there was no way she wouldn't have a picture. He planned on asking her, but he needed to get her alone first for a simple conversation.

He sauntered to the two chairs in front of her desk and pulled one out. He unbuttoned his suit jacket, sat and crossed his ankle over his knee. He took the time to study her. Her locs were swooped across her right shoulder. She had on a blue wrap dress that fit her body to perfection.

"Ok, great, thank you. I'll send the proposal over immediately." She paused. "Yes, I understand, and I look forward to the partnership." She ended the call and studied him for a few seconds.

"Hakeem? What are you doing here?"

"I thought that would be obvious. To see you."

"I'm working, 'Keem. Are you here to tell me what I can and can't do or who I can be seen with?" she sassed and sat in her large, leather chair.

The reminder of the events of the last two days ago had him tightening his fists. He reined in the rise of his temper, remembering her walking away from him with Roberts. From the beginning of time, he'd always felt possessive of Mariama, and the feeling didn't dissipate with time.

"No, I'm here for business."

She narrowed her eyes at him.

He smiled. "Come on RiRi, it's still me."

"I told you not to call me that. And I know it's you. That's why I'm suspicious. Humor me."

Hakeem chuckled. She was so beautiful to him. Since their breakup, he'd kicked himself every day for losing her. "I need your services." Hakeem made sure to keep his expression blank. Mariama always had a way of seeing right through him.

She was silent for a moment. "Really, Hakeem? You're a

walking, whole money bag. I'm sure you have a full team with extras. Why would you need my services?"

"Does my money bother you?" It was partially the reason for their demise. What if she could never be with him because of it?

"No, you do. What are you up to?"

"I do have a team, but they're all tied up and I have this commitment that needs my attention overseas. I need a temporary assistant."

"And you're telling me none of them could move things around for the boss?"

"They can if I ask them too, but what sense would that make, when I'm here and you have a functional, executive assistant temp service?" Hakeem shrugged.

She was slower with her comebacks which could only mean she was considering it.

"I book clients by appointment..." She tapped her keyboard for the next few moments and clicked a few screens.

He assumed she was looking for someone to assign to him. He let her do her thing, but he knew he wouldn't accept anybody but her.

"Hakeem, I don't have anyone. Not anyone that has a passport and would be ready to go in...how long?" She continued to type without glancing in his direction.

"In thirty minutes and for a week." He stood, put his hands in his pockets and walked to the middle of the room.

She looked up at him briefly. "Where?"

"Abidjan." He shrugged.

Her eyes bugged. "Abidjan as in Côte d'Ivoire, Abidjan?"

"You forgot in West Africa, yes. The one and the same?" Hakeem chuckled at her surprise and holding herself from wanting to know more.

She kept her eyes fixed on him for a couple of seconds

before returning her eyes to the screen in front of her. "I don't have anyone, Hakeem. You're gonna to have to get one of your people to go with you."

Hakeem strode back to the front of her desk. He placed both palms on it and leaned in. "You still do this, right?"

"Y—yes, but I can't go with you." She shook her head gently.

"Why?" Hakeem raised his brow.

Mariama's eyes wandered around the room, avoiding his.

He cupped his ear. "I can't hear you?"

"Be—because…," she stuttered.

He straightened and folded his arms across his chest, issuing a nonverbal dare.

"You can't afford my personal services."

Hakeem grinned. "If Lemoore could afford you, I'm quite sure I can. I own the man's company. Also, you speak fluent French, I'll need a translator."

"Didn't you plan for that before?"

"I did, but you're way better."

"I can't just up and leave the country—" She got out of her chair and headed for the small fridge in her office.

"What's holding you? You used to love to travel." He observed her flustered state and decided it was time to go in for the kill. "Are you scared of me, RiRi? I never would have pegged you for a coward."

His remark put a frown on her face. He hated to be the one to put it there, but he had to remember the end game.

"Now, you know better than that." She rolled her eyes at him.

"Prove it." He knew she could never resist a challenge.

She stared at him for a moment and walked behind her desk. With her eyes still fixed on him, she picked up the phone. Still staring at him, she spoke. She instructed her assistant to pull up a standard contract and amend it to accommodate his overseas request and the time frame.

"You do know the price won't be standard." Mariama pointed her well-manicured fingers at him.

"Of course." He nodded.

"And I don't know what you're planning, but I don't fraternize with my clients."

He winked and saluted her. "Got it."

Minutes later, Abby entered the office with the contract. Mariama looked over it and signed. Hakeem merely gave it a glance before signing the document.

"I already know I'm going to regret this." She packed up.

"It'll be my duty to make sure you don't."

TWENTY-ONE

Mariama rolled her eyes for the umpteenth time as Brianna busted out in laughter. She walked from her closet to the bedroom, throwing clothes into her suitcase. Minutes earlier, she'd gotten off a Facetime call with her parents informing them of her trip. Her whole world felt right again when she saw the smile on her baby's face, as he excitedly told her about his escapades so far.

"Can you stop laughing now?" Mariama asked, now regretting calling her friend.

Brianna giggled some more. "Okay, I'm done. But I got to say it one more time. How did you walk into that trap with your eyes open?"

"Simple, money and he challenged me. You know I'm trying to expand and although business is good, I need some more big names. And the man insinuated I was a coward."

"You do know he did that on purpose?"

"Now I do." Mariama zipped her suitcase and rolled it out of her bedroom. She'd insisted she'd meet Hakeem at the airstrip in an hour. Thankfully, he agreed, but it wouldn't be

Hakeem without him issuing the threat of coming to get her if she was a minute late. There was no way she could have him in her home without telling him about HR first. The whole house was littered with toys and pictures.

"Real talk?"

"Yeah, sure." Mariama set the alarm and walked out to the car that Hakeem had bring her home. The driver took her luggage and opened the door for her to get in.

"This is an opportunity for you both to lay it bare. I know you're working and all that stuff, but you need to tell him about HR. He needs to be mad at you, and then you guys can eventually become a family." Brianna paused, presumably waiting for her to counter, but she had nothing.

Mariama was tired of carrying this monkey on her back, so she agreed with everything her friend said. She knew what she did—keeping his son away—was despicable and she had to take responsibility for that. Anthony figured out Hakeem was HR's father immediately when he saw them together. They had a long talk and Anthony told her he'd step back until she got that situation under control. She knew that once Hakeem saw HR, he'd figure it out too and she didn't want it to happen that way.

"You're right. I'll tell him and let the chips fall where they may."

"I know you still love him, so I hope they fall in your favor. I love you girl and have fun."

"Love you, too." Mariama ended the call, leaned back and closed her eyes.

SEVERAL HOURS LATER, Mariama, Hakeem and another guy she was introduced to as Carl were airborne and on their way to Abidjan, Côte d'Ivoire. She'd never let her excitement show but she was thrilled about being able to see the West African city. She'd been back home to Senegal to see her brother on a few occasions, she had even been to Ghana and Nigeria but that was about it. She wasn't even sure how Hakeem got her a Visa but even before his money, he'd always been resourceful. At first, she'd been suspicious of Hakeem's motives, but he had switched into business mode once they boarded his jet. Once the flight was at the appropriate altitude, the hostess brought them a light lunch. Then they sat around a table in the middle of the plane to go over his schedule which included a three-day conference, a tour of some facility, exhibit, and a gala. Once everything was laid out, they retreated to their private corners.

"Come with me."

Hakeem's seductive voice interrupted her. She had been so engrossed in the romance novel she was reading that she didn't hear him approach. He stretched out his hand towards her. She glanced at it, then met his eyes without taking his hand.

"Where are we going?" She had never been on a jet before but wondered how big this thing was if they were going places on it.

"Can you just trust me? I've been on my best behavior."

"Yeah, for a whole two hours of an eleven-hour flight." She took his hand and he helped her up. He ushered her down the aisle, they passed Carl, who was sleeping, and entered another compartment.

Mariama's eye widened. *This thing is huge.* The door slid shut behind them as he led them to lounging sofas. The place was equipped with the largest TV she had ever seen, a mini kitchen, a bar and a huge bed. The initials *MNR* were engraved on everything. She had been meaning to ask what it meant when she saw it on the body of the aircraft earlier, but was afraid of the answer.

"Why are we in a bedroom, 'Keem?" She asked. They had agreed to talk, but she didn't know if she could trust herself to do it in here with him.

He remained silent and ushered her to one of the lounge chairs. He then proceeded to fix them some drinks. Handing her hers, he sat down next to her.

"I wanted us to talk in private. You don't fraternize with clients. I remember." He gave her a weary smile.

Mariama didn't know how to take this Hakeem. Cocky, possessive, sometimes arrogant, loving and passionate Hakeem she could handle. But the Hakeem in front of her seemed unsure of himself.

"'Keem..."

"I had just graduated and start a new job in a new city. I was so sure about us, then I wasn't. Not because we didn't love each other. But I panicked wondering if love would be enough. At that moment, I didn't know what the future held, yea we made plans and I was afraid of history repeating itself."

"'Keem—"

He held up his hand to her. "Let me get this out, okay?"

She nodded.

"My mom was young when she married my dad. It was love that brought them together, but his inability to sustain the family drove him away causing her to struggle until her dying day. He left us when I was four, but as I grew older, I saw my mom work herself to exhaustion to provide for us. Working two jobs, including a meat factory, in the freezer section. She developed this cough one day but because of us, refused to take time off. It continued until one day, she collapsed and ended up dying of pneumonia. If only he had stayed. If only she had help...

"From that day, my goal was to become somebody. I wanted to work hard and make money to leave a legacy for my children and help women, like my mother. In fact, the foundation I have is in her name. The problem came when I doubted my ability to do that and be the man, I should be to you at the same time. Supposing I failed? I was afraid that eventually, we'd end up like them. I couldn't put you through that. I was terrified, I didn't want to lose you, but I didn't want to string you along, so I suggested we slow down." He cradled his forearms on his thighs and bent his head.

Mariama stood. He was too close to her. Her heart thudded against her chest while the tears freely flowed. Before her eyes, her strong and secure Hakeem had turned into a boy who hurt for his mother's pain. She sobbed because she was so angry at him for not telling her this so they could talk through it and reassure one another. She cried for all the years that were wasted and her son missing out on the presence of a father. Now would be a good time to tell him about HR. She opened her mouth, but fear and regret kept her mute. He sauntered towards her and wiped the tears from her face.

"I'm so sorry, Mariama. If I could go back to that day, I would, and I'd do it all over again." He cupped her face.

"Hold on." Even she could hear her words carried no weight.

Hakeem lowered his head and her lips, puckered on their own accord. His lips crashed against hers, igniting every neuron in her body. She moaned and her lips parted. He slid his tongue into her mouth and hers tangoed with it. Her fingers made their way to his hair. She drew him closer. She needed him. All her carefully erected walls were crumbling to mush. He was an essential part of her, and the years and anger couldn't erase that fact. However, she needed to stop this, as there was so much left unsaid between them.

He leaned his forehead against her. Considering their height difference, she was sure his back was screaming. "I love you, RiRi. You are the air I breathe. The day I saw you again it was like I let out a breath I'd been holding on to for years," He whispered, peppering light kisses down her neck.

"Hakeem, wait, hold on..." He wasn't playing fair.

"Oh I remember, you don't fraternize with clients." He let her go, turned and walked out of the enclosed space.

"What? Huh?" She fought to regain her bearings and make sense of what he was talking about.

He returned seconds later with a paper in his hand. "Baby, I love you but you're fired." He tore up what she could now see was the contract they had signed.

"Huh? Who'll help you?"

"That's what Carl is for. Didn't I introduce you two?" He tossed the torn document in the trash.

"You said he was an associate." She crossed her arms over her chest.

"Oh, he is. A senior executive associate for Richardson Investments and my PA." He returned to her and picked her up. Her arms wrapped around his neck. He sat with her in his lap.

"I knew you had something up your sleeves."

"I was desperate, and you were killing me. I had to think fast." He kissed the tip of her nose. "Do you forgive me?"

"Hakeem, it's not that simple. You hurt me."

"I know. I'm sorry."

She sighed. "There's so much more we have to discuss."

"I know and we will. Just give me a second shot. I promise to spend the rest of my life making it up to you."

You might not feel that way after what I have to tell you.

She knew she should just blurt it out and get it over with. But the words clung to her tongue like rustic metal. They would end up fighting, he would turn the plane around, and he would forgo this multi-million dollar deal he was headed to wrap up. *I don't want to rock the boat*, she rationalized.

"I have to ask you something," Hakeem said.

Her chest tightened. Had he found out her secret? He couldn't have if he was still holding on to her body like she'd disappear.

"Okay," she whispered.

"Do you have a kid?"

"Yes. A son," she replied. For a quick minute she could've sworn his eyes darkened in rage. "'Keem—"

"Is his father in his life or yours?"

Mariama lowered her head. "No."

He lifted her chin with his index finger. "I don't care about the details. We can figure it out later. I know that you are a package deal and if you let me, I'm ready to fill those shoes for you and him."

In that moment, she hated herself. She never hid who Hakeem was from HR, but Hakeem had no idea who HR was and was willing to step up because he came from her. She nodded and sobbed. Hakeem carried her to the bed and laid her down. He took off her shoes and his and got in behind her. He cuddled her close to him. She was back in her familiar place – his arms. Even if it was for a short while.

THREE DAYS LATER, Mariama poured herself a glass of orange juice and returned to the table that had papers spread all over it. They were staying at the prestigious Radisson Blu Hotel in Port-Bouët on the shore of the Ebrie Lagoon. The local driver of the car service that picked them up from the private airstrip informed them that the lagoon, for almost all its length, was separated from the Atlantic Ocean by only a narrow strip. The views from the suite that Hakeem reserved for her were spectacular.

Before this trip, she thought rich people had someone on call for everything jumping at their beck and call while they kicked back and enjoyed time off. It surprised her though how much Hakeem worked. The last two nights, Mariama had had fallen asleep in Hakeem's room. After his activities for the day, he retired with her to his suite, but didn't rest. To occupy herself, she did a little work of her own, then watched a movie while he went through emails, signed off on various items and talked to his teams located in different time zones. Every morning, however, she woke up in her own bed. Despite his pleas and flirtation, she made it clear they weren't sharing a bed.

Her routine was the same. She got up, said her prayers, took care of her hygiene, got dressed, and then proceeded to breakfast and the conference. By midday, she called to check on HR and her parents, then her office.

"Sorry about that, Carl. I'm back." She picked up her phone and wedged it between her ear and shoulder. All morning, she'd been looking for her earbuds but couldn't find them.

"No problem Ms. Niang," he replied.

"Please, I've told you to call me Mariama or Mari."

"I'm sorry I can't do that."

She rolled her eyes because she knew Hakeem was probably behind it. She also knew she'd be fighting a losing battle.

"Fine." Her eyes darted to the bedside clock. They had a couple of hours to spare before they headed to the last day of the conference which was scheduled to begin by noon.

In his spare time, Carl showed her new technology and apps that would make her and girls' jobs so much easier. She listened attentively as Carl walked her through another tutorial. Moments later, there was a knock on the door.

"Ugh, hold on Carl. I'm so sorry." Mariama walked to the

door.

She opened it to find Hakeem, who was still in his loungewear with a devilish grin spread across his face.

"Good morning, my love," he said.

"Morning. I see you're a bit relaxed today," she responded as he walked her backwards into the room.

He shut the door with his feet and pulled her against him. With one hand around her waist, he used the other to grab a handful of her hair, keeping her head in place. He kissed her with so much passion that he took her breath away—literally. Despite the euphoric moment, she remembered she had someone on the phone.

"As much as I enjoy your kisses, I'm working. We talked about this."

"No, you talked, informing me you'll still do the job I paid you for, even though I fired you. And I, as any good man would do, listened." He winked.

"What am I going to do with you?"

"You'll figure something out." He attempted to kiss her again.

Mariama wiggled out of his embrace. "I have someone on the phone."

He furrowed his eyebrows and walked toward the table where her MacBook and phone were. She contemplated calming the fire she saw rising in him but changed her mind. He picked up the phone and saw the name on the screen.

"Hello, Carl. Goodbye, Carl." He hung up the phone and turned to her. "You love to see me crazy over you."

She shrugged. "Yeah, it's kinda sexy."

Hakeem narrowed his eyes. The intensity in his stare sent shivers up and down her spine. He strode toward her. Mariama's feet were planted in position. He tugged her forward. "Where were we?"

She placed both hands flat against his muscular chest. "You were going to your room to get ready and I was going to do the same."

"Hmm, I don't quite recall it that way."

Mariama chuckled. "Today is the last day of the conference. We then have three more days to enjoy ourselves before we go back." She dreaded having to face reality. Somehow in the time they had left, she had to find time to tell him about his son. One thing she was now sure of was that he was avoiding reality too. Not once had he asked any questions about her child, except to inquire if she'd spoken to him and how he was doing. He didn't even take calls from his brother and friend. It was as though he was intent on them being in their own little bubble and reconnecting before they had to face the world. The plan was all right by her, as it also bought her some time.

"I can't wait to show you off at the gala tonight."

"That reminds me, I didn't pack for that, so I have to stop somewhere to get something appropriate."

"It's all taken care of my love."

"Aww, how sweet. Thank you." She stood on the tips of her toes and brushed her lips against his.

"I know you can do better than that," he challenged.

She removed his hand from her waist and nudged him toward the door. "Yes, I can but we have to get ready. It's going to be a busy day."

"You're a bossy little woman. You know that?"

She opened the door. "Not bossy, assertive. Now get."

He chuckled and leaned toward her ear. "We are going to finish this later." He stepped out.

"I'm counting on it." She shut the door and leaned her back against it. She was playing with fire and she was sure her heart in the process.

TWENTY-TWO

Hakeem walked to Mariama's door. Business was almost over, and he planned to enjoy the remaining days they had getting reacquainted. By the time they left Abidjan, there wouldn't be any doubt on exactly where they stood with one another. He had all their activities planned and this was his chance to remind Mariama of the love they shared and still had for each other. Although she hadn't said the words, she had shown him in the past couple of days there was something still there.

Once the main conference ended some hours ago, he gave Carl the option of leaving for home on the next available flight. An offer he gladly accepted.

Hakeem knocked. He heard her unhook the chain, but he wasn't ready for what he saw. His heart swelled with admiration and gratitude that she was all his.

Mariama was a vision to behold, an image of perfection in the red, off-shoulder dress that adorned her body. When he saw the dress some days ago, he knew it would be perfect, but the way it clung to her shapely body was better than perfection. Her exposed skin glowed. Her hair flowed down her back and her well-manicured toes were on full display in the open-toe stilettos she wore. The sight of her temporarily made him want to cancel their plans for the night.

Mariama cleared her throat. "I'm guessing you like what you see."

He smiled. "I love what I see. You look beautiful, RiRi." He leaned in and kissed her cheek.

"You don't look too bad yourself. Dashing as always."

Hakeem reached out his hand. "You ready?"

She placed her small hand in his. "Lead the way."

Hakeem led her to the elevators for a quick ride down to the lobby and into the car that was waiting. Mariama was rattling off something about the events of the last couple of days and how she could improve upon her services. He, on the other hand, was cementing the resolve he had when it came to winning her back and being the best father, he could to her son. He'd be the first to admit that when she confirmed she did have a son, he wanted to kill something. The fact that she had procreated with someone else drove him insane. He knew it was selfish of him to think she would've put her life on hold for him, but the thought alone blurred his vision with rage. So he decided to push it to the back burner for now. They'd deal with it when they returned stateside.

Hours later, Hakeem's arm was snaked around Mariama's waist. Her palm rested securely on his chest while the other found a home in his free hand. They swayed back and forth to the soft music playing in the background. Speeches had been made, dinner had been served and the event was winding down. They'd spent the evening networking with other participants and talking and reconnecting.

"You have no idea how much I've missed you."

Mariama tiptoed and pecked his lips. "Probably as much as I've missed you."

Hakeem groaned. He still found it difficult to believe that just a week ago, Mariama hated his guts. Now she seemed to be back to the woman he knew and loved. He gazed into her eyes. "Did you have a good time tonight?"

"Yes, I did. Thought it'd be another stuffy end-of-conference gala, but it wasn't."

Hakeem chuckled. "We have the next couple of days to do anything you want, and I have just the perfect place to do it."

"Yay! I can't wait."

MARIAMA SAT out on the balcony of Hakeem's Presidential Suite staring up at the night sky, wearing a simple crop tank and a pair of shorts. Below the city flowed in its relaxed way, tranquil and calm. For the past couple of nights, she had enjoyed being a passive observer. The lagoon breeze sent a slight shiver up her arm. She tugged on the blanket that covered her legs and picked up another handful of plantain chips from the bowl on her lap. She moved her body slightly to the melody of "Photograph "by Ed Sheeran.

"Baby, red or white?"

Mariama turned her head slightly and smiled up at the person she had kept in the pocket of her own ripped jeans. Hakeem awakened the desire and trepidation within her.

"Red."

"Got it. I'll be right back."

The night after the gala, Hakeem had extended their stay a couple more nights. After calling her parents and checking on her son and business, she agreed. They had made his suite their own private paradise. True to his word, the few past days had been simply amazing. They'd visited PlaYce- Marcory, a magnificent shopping center. Then they took a tour of the

Plateau, Hakeem said the place reminded him of New York with its big city feel and mix pot of different cultures. Funny because in the restaurant where they stopped for lunch, their waiter called it the Manhattan of Africa. They had spent hours on a paid walking tour and a canoe ride. She particularly enjoyed the helicopter tour. Mariama giggled to herself when she remembered how deathly scared Hakeem had been during the canoe ride because of its size. But he loved her, so he braved the adventure for her. The best day so far was when they visited the St. Paul's Cathedral. The way the structure and design was done made it look like the cross was being pulled towards the lagoon. Hand in hand and terrified, she and Hakeem climbed the tower to the outstretched hands of the cross. The view was indescribable.

Other days they lazed around the suite, got a private spa session, ate, made love, and worked on urgent business matters they couldn't put off. Every other night they cooked dinner together in the kitchen. It was something they did before their split and it brought back nostalgic memories.

Hakeem spared no expense on her and surprisingly he also bought gifts for her parents and HR. Guilt sliced through her at his gesture. She knew she was for sure going to hell because she hadn't been able to tell him. She told herself that it was because they were in a foreign country and she wanted to be in familiar territory.

"Here you go, baby."

"Thanks."

His voice pulled her from her reverie. She tilted her head to look up at him, taking the drink from him. Hakeem lifted the blanket and snuggled in behind her. He placed his hands on her thighs and she leaned back against him. For a few moments, they sat in palpable silence, their hearts beating in sync, enjoying the calm night. Mariama took a sip of her drink and exhaled a deep sigh of satisfaction. His selection was perfect. Chuckling softly, Hakeem brushed his lips against her neck, finding the sensitive spot behind her ear that made her shiver.

"I refuse to be apart from you again RiRi," he whispered, his breath low and tingling against her skin. "Promise me that when we get back, you'll commit to figuring something out."

Her chest had a familiar ache to it. Does she rock the boat now or wait until throwing her in the lagoon won't be an option? She knew he'd never do that, and it was her guilt playing tricks on her mind. Hakeem continued his onslaught on her skin. Mariama couldn't tell whether it was the wine or him, but she felt as though she was floating and wasn't able to string together a complete thought. She clung to his arms that circled her waist.

"Promise me."

Shuddering, she panted. "I...can't" She didn't want to make any promises until she laid all her cards on the table. "Hakeem, I...have..." she tried to continue, but he apparently wasn't happy with her response because before she knew it, she was being lifted and turned around to face him. He cradled her face between his hands. His forehead leaned against hers, his cool breath sending tiny tremors of heat through her pores.

"I'm so sorry, babe. I wish I could turn back the hands of time, but I can't. Please give me the chance to make it up to you. To take care of your son. Give me a chance to make this right. Don't tell me no."

She hated that he was pleading with her when right now, she was wrong. Mariama broke free. She needed to be of clear mind to tell him what remained clogged in her throat. Her heart raced. His face was covered with a frown. She loved him and wanted all three of them to be a family, but was she willing to pack up her life for him? Suppose she packed up, moved and they crashed and burned again? The first time she hadn't seen it coming so there was no way she could be prepared for the signs. He was different from the Hakeem she once knew; his lifestyle was different. Would she be able to survive? How would it affect HR? Co-parenting from the beginning is totally different from getting together then breaking up. She wouldn't have the answers to any of her questions unless she got her secret out in the open.

"'Keem, I—"

The shrill of her phone paused her speech. Her chest tightened in panic. It was the ring tone assigned to her mother. Mariama had given clear instructions for her parents not to call her while she was here. She would do all the calling. For her mother to call, something was wrong. Eyes wide, she looked at Hakeem. He stood up, walked to the side table, and picked up the phone. His action sent her into motion. She took the phone out of his hand and answered the call.

"Hello, Ma?"

Mariama's eyes enlarged with each word her mother uttered. Moments later, she hung up the phone with tears flowing from her eyes. She looked up at Hakeem who closed the distance between them.

"What's wrong, baby?"

"We have to go home now. There's been an accident."

TWENTY-THREE

Mariama turned to Hakeem. They'd touched down in Florida thirty minutes ago and were headed to Lake Memorial. She'd been updated by her father that HR was out of surgery and resting. His arm had to have a small screw put in it, and now it was in a cast. He was slowly getting over the concussion and was expected to make a full recovery. Now, it was time to face the music.

Her betrayal was sure to cut Hakeem deep, but there was no way she could let him walk into the hospital and be blindsided. The last twenty-four hours had been a blur. All that occupied her mind was getting to Florida. Hakeem had been so comforting. He just held her. He didn't force her to talk or anything. After they got that phone call, he sprang into action.

"You okay?" He asked.

"Ummm...no I'm not, but I need to tell you something."

He caressed her face with the back of his hand. His eyes were filled with pure love. Her chest tightened at the sight.

"I love you more than anything," she said.

"I know baby and I love you too," he replied.

Tears ran down her cheeks. "Please don't ever forget it, okay?"

"What's going on?" Concern was written all over his face.

"Remember I told you that I tried to call you several times after I left the country…"

"I remember, but that's in the past. I made a terrible mistake and you reacted the only way you knew how." He thumbed away her tear.

She wasn't worthy of this love he was giving her. "Yeah, I know but there is another reason why I left."

Hakeem's brows furrowed. He opened his mouth to speak, but was interrupted by the driver.

"We're here."

She looked out of the window and took in a deep breath, then let it out. *Here goes nothing.*

"We'll talk about this later. Let's go see how your son is doing." Hakeem opened the door and helped her out. With his hand around her waist, he escorted her into the hospital. They walked up to the desk and just as she was about to ask questions, she saw her mother approaching them, her father in tow. Mariama reintroduced them to Hakeem. They had been always cordial to him when he followed her home once or twice for the holidays all those years ago.

"Why are you guys out here in the waiting room instead of in his room?" Mariama asked.

"They had to take him for more tests," her father answered.

"More tests…is he okay?" Mariama asked as Hakeem rubbed her back.

"Yes, they say they would come and get us the minute he returns to his room."

Mariama nodded and turned to Hakeem. "I need to talk to you. It's important."

Hakeem nodded and they walked over to a secluded corner. Mariama wringed her hands.

"RiRi, you know you can tell me anything. What's wrong?"

"I was so mad at you Hakeem and so hurt—"

"And I'll keep—"

She raised her hands to him, her eyes pleading, "Let me get this out." She let out a heavy sigh. "I was so mad at you, but I did try to reach out. Then I was hurt when that woman answered your phone and I wanted you to hurt the way you hurt me. I've tried to tell you for the past couple of days that—"

"The family of Hakeem James Richardson, Junior?"

Before her eyes, Hakeem's eyes darkened. It appeared he couldn't breathe as his breath came in short pants. He stared at her in disbelief and slowly turned around to the older looking doctor who seemed to have come out of nowhere. Mariama began to move, and Hakeem followed. As the doctor provided them with an update, Mariama could feel Hakeem's stare boring a hole into her side.

"The tests came back normal, so I see no reason why he can't leave tomorrow morning." The doctor gave them some instructions then walked away.

"We'll go and check on him, so you guys can talk." Her mother took her father's hand and they strode in the same direction the doctor had come from.

Mariama lowered her head. She couldn't meet Hakeem's eyes. For the next few seconds, they stood in awkward silence before he spoke.

"Did I just find out in the middle of the hospital that I have a son?" His voice was brazened. "Did you dare keep my son away from me?"

"Please let me explain," she whispered.

"Explain what? You wanted to hurt me that bad?"

"No...I've been trying to tell you..."

"Apparently you didn't try hard enough. I seem to recall you being able to get everything else off your chest, but you weren't able to tell me I have a son?" he barked.

She jumped. "Hakeem, please let's just go and see..." she lifted her hand to touch him.

He shrugged her off. "Don't you dare touch me. I don't even know who you are. I trusted you. How could you keep a child from me?"

His rejection, although deserved, stung. She felt anger seep from his pores. Words to make this better escaped her. She didn't even know if that was possible. The man she knew and loved had morphed into someone else in a matter of minutes.

"He's in room 534. Let's go see him. We can talk about this later, please."

"I have nothing to say to you." He walked off in the direction her parents went earlier.

Her heart broke when she caught up with him and he was standing at the door with his head bowed. He hadn't entered. Mariama walked up to him and opened the door. Her eyes immediately went to her mother who gave her a disapproving stare. Not having the energy to dwell on that now, she walked up to HR's bed. He was sleeping. She bent to kiss his forehead. Feeling a presence behind her, she turned to see Hakeem staring at his carbon copy. The only difference between father and son was age and the fact that HR was a shade lighter. Every day, looking at her son was like looking at Hakeem. His hair, his nose, jaw line and mannerisms were all a copy of his father.

"Ma, we got it from here. You and daddy please go home and get some rest. We'll keep you updated," Mariama said.

Her parents looked at one another, communicating nonverbally like they'd done since her teenage years. They stood.

Hakeem turned to them. "Thank you, Mr. and Mrs. Niang."

"HR is our grandson. No thanks necessary. We only wish you would have met him under different circumstances," her father said.

Hakeem gave a weary smile. "Me too."

Her parents left the room and dread returned. Mariama pulled up a seat and sat next to the bed and Hakeem occupied the one on the opposite side. In silence, he watched his son. Now in retrospect, the pound of flesh, anger, and things she told herself to justify her actions over the years seemed foolish.

"Hakeem, I—"

"Don't."

Mariama put her head on the edge of the bed and closed her eyes.

AFTER THEIR MOTHER DIED, and Hakeem and his brother were put into the system. No single family member came to their aid. Every time they got their hopes up that they would be adopted, the family suddenly lost interest. They learned to survive on their own and trust no one. Trust no one. It was just the two of them against the world – that was until they met Darius. All through his early adult years, Hakeem never took anyone else at their word. He knew humans were only out to look after *numero uno*. He had girls and women a dime a dozen, but the only one that changed all of that was Mariama. Now he didn't even know if he could trust what his heart was telling him. In fact, he knew he couldn't. That's why, unless it was about this little boy before him, he had nothing more to say to her. Never again would he give her the opportunity to lie to him.

How could she make him believe she loved him and hide his son? She, of all people, knew how he felt about family. Her feelings were hurt so she deliberately set out to rip his apart. Hakeem bowed his head and cradled it in his hands while a thousand thoughts ran a mock.

"Mummy?"

Hakeem raised his head and met Mariama's eyes at the sound their son's voice. They both stood. He wasn't fully awake, but was crying out to her from a dream.

"It's okay, Mummy's here."

Hakeem watched as his son's eyes flew open. His chest tightened when the boy smiled at his mother. He had missed that smile and a whole lot more. Would HR ever give him a smile like that?

"Mummy, you're back," HR squealed.

Hakeem observed their interaction in silence. Regret, pain and disdain were the emotions he felt.

"Yes baby, I'm back. How are you?"

"I'm fine Mummy. See my cast, cool huh?"

"Way cool." She paused. "I'd like you..."

HR turned. "Daddy?" His brows knit together in confusion that quickly changed to realization and, dare he say, recognition.

"Daddy! You're back from business. Mummy, daddy is back." HR stretched out his arms to him.

Hakeem stood still, his body not cooperating with the instructions his mind gave it to move. He knew who he was? She named their son after him and ensured her son knew him. He glanced over to Mariama. She nudged him forward with her head. He walked forward and hugged HR.

"Yes, I'm back, son."

"I missed you. Don't go way for that long anymore."

Hakeem's eyes glistened over, his cheeks heated. "I won't. I promise."

The next several minutes, Hakeem listened to HR give him a recap of his summer so far, ending with how he got the cast. Mariama went to the cafeteria to get coffee, giving them time to talk.

The second she opened the door, HR asked, "Mummy, can daddy stay with us now? Since he says he won't be gone long anymore? Please, please..."

Mariama eyes met his. They shifted in nervousness and he kept his expression blank. He felt no need to give her any relief. However he silently dared her to say the wrong thing.

"Let's get you out of here first. Okay?" She set her coffee down on the counter.

HR started to sniffle. Mariama rushed over to pacify him. Hakeem had seen enough. "We can go to my house buddy. Ever been to New York before?"

"HR rubbed his eyes. "No...no."

Hakeem glanced over at Mariama. The flash in her eyes didn't move him in the least. She had years to give him what he wanted, now it was his turn. Whether she liked it or not, she no longer called the shots.

"We'll go to my house then," he said with a smile, then bent to kiss his son's forehead.

"Yay! Mummy, we're going to daddy's house." A wide grin spread across HR's face.

Mariama gave him a faint smile. She picked up the remote from the tray table, turned the television on, and browsed the channels for a couple of seconds for a cartoon.

"Okay, my big man, watch TV for a little bit. Let Mummy talk to Daddy for a minute," Mariama said.

HR nodded. "Daddy, are you coming back?"

His question pierced Hakeem's heart. He raised his eyes

and shot daggers to the target he once thought was the love of his life. Her eyes were glossy, but he didn't care about that. She would pay for what she did to him. To his son.

"Yes, buddy. I'll be right back."

Mariama left the room and Hakeem was right behind her. She walked a short distance from the door and turned to him.

"Hakeem I'm sorry." Her tone was low and remorseful.

"Sorry you didn't tell me or sorry you got caught?" He ran his hands over his head. "If I hadn't walked in on that meeting two weeks ago and saw you, would I ever have known?"

"Yes..."

"When, because you've been back in the US building your business for three years. So, when?" His voice rose with tension. The rage he felt rolled off him in waves.

Mariama remained silent. A beat passed between them. He paced like a caged animal. He wanted to shout. So many emotions welled up inside of him. He needed to get away from her, but his son was so scared that he wasn't coming back.

"I know you are angry with me..."

"What I feel for you surpasses anger."

"And I deserve it. But you can't uproot us to New York."

"I'm not uprooting you. I am taking my son to where I live. You're welcome to come or not come, but HR is coming with me."

"He needs his mother. I can't go to New York. I have a—"

"And he needs his father. Oh, and let me guess, you have a business to run." He sneered. "Well, let's see if you put your feelings aside this time for the sake of our child."

"That's not fair. How dare you?" Her nose flared.

"My son thinks I went on a six-year business trip. At this point I could care less about what's fair." He growled.

"Hakeem please listen to me, you owe me that much—"

"Owe? Owe? I don't owe you a thing except maybe custody

papers." He put his hand on the nape of his neck, done with this conversation. "You've got two days to put your affairs in order, or that jet will leave without you. The choice is yours."

Hakeem walked off and returned to his son's room. HR's cheeks lifted in a smile. Hakeem took of his shoes and got in the bed with him. HR settled in while his brain reeled.

Mariama had lied and betrayed him in the worst way. He never would have thought she had it in her. How could he love someone who could do what she did? How could she be so malicious? She had nine months to prepare to be a mother. He had no time to prepare at all, but here he was, and he was going to do his best, even if he died trying. First up, home. He meant what he said. Two days was all she had, or they would be leaving without her.

TWENTY-FOUR

It was the wee hours of the morning but the calming sound of raindrops landing against her windowpane did nothing to soothe her slumber. Mariama laid in a fetal position, in the center of her bed while tears rolled down her cheek. The guilt and regret still ate at her and even after eight weeks. The tension between her and Hakeem hadn't gotten any better. In all its opulence, the room she had called hers for the last two months did little to lift her mood. Red and grey were her favorite colors and she was certain he had the room done with that in mind. Now if only she could get him to talk to her. She was at a loss at what else to do. Her eyes shifted to the paper that were strewn across the bed. She had tried to work earlier but couldn't train her thoughts to focus.

The day after HR was released from the hospital; Hakeem flew them to Atlanta for a couple of hours to gather any necessary items. Mariama also stopped over at her office and left instructions. She knew she could've fought a little harder, but she wasn't in a position to do so. All she wanted was to make it right, so she went along with Hakeem's plan. She had no desire to win the battle and lose the war. Several hours later the same day, the three of them boarded his jet again for New York.

Hakeem has spared no expense on the décor in HR's room and his clothes. The day after they landed in New York, his personal shopper came to the house and took all HR's measurements. The woman wanted to take Mariama's, but she declined. She didn't want his money, all she wanted was him. To her surprise, when the woman called Hakeem to tell him, she'd declined, all she heard him say was "fine." He didn't insist, threaten, or try to bully her into doing his bidding. All he said was "fine." The lady left and returned with tons of clothes, sneakers, and toys for her six-year-old

The first week of their arrival, she focused on getting their son adjusted while at the same time, relegating herself to the background to give father and son time to bond. By the second week, she started working again. One night, Hakeem had returned home to see all her things on the kitchen table. They gave each other a silent stare down before he stalked away without saying a word. Two days later, he showed her a home office he had redone for her. It wasn't just a spare room she could use. It was one he had decorated like her office back in Atlanta. Identical colors and the works. As good as that felt, she'd give anything for him to smile at her again.

Days turned into weeks and weeks turned into months, he still hadn't bulged. Any conversation they managed to have, revolved around HR, nothing else. HR however was having a blast. He had taken off the first month to bond with his son. They went everywhere together – ice cream parlor, camping, movies, arcades – anything their son could think of, Hakeem made happen. He also Facetimed with his Uncle Brice and Darius almost every day. He was the happiest little boy Mariama had ever seen and truthfully that made her a little jealous and ashamed. Every time HR called Hakeem daddy or looked up to him with so much love, a piece of her heart chipped away at how she could've ever thought it was a good idea to keep them apart.

Initially, she went on the outings with them on HR's insistence. Hakeem was a pro at putting on a pretentious façade for the sake of their son. But when HR wasn't within earshot and people would mistake them for a family, Hakeem was quick to correct the notion. It was as though he was intentionally out to hurt her. After six weeks of him ignoring her or answering her in clipped short sentences, she gave up. His anger was understandable, so she gave him space. Mariama knew she was wrong, but not having him in her life was punishment enough. She had gone through a lot to get over him the first time. They reconnected, and it was the best week of her life. Losing him again was too much. Granted, this was her consequence, but that didn't make it any less painful. Nowadays, she dedicated her time to solely caring for her son, when she wasn't with him, she threw herself into running her business.

Thankfully, summer would soon be over, and they'll have to head back home. She couldn't take this torture anymore and HR was starting the first grade in a new school. Although they hadn't spoken about it, she hoped Hakeem didn't expect for her to continue to live here with her life in limbo. She was ready to cut her losses. In due time, she was sure that he would hear her out. But for now, they had to reach an agreement concerning HR. She had to get back to living her life and being the best co-parent, she could be. He went out of town two days ago and would be back tonight. She had to have a talk with him.

SEVERAL HOURS LATER, Mariama stood in front of the stove flipping pancakes. The cup of coffee she had did little to perk her up, but HR had begged her to make her smiley face pancakes. Hakeem obviously had a cook, but she asked him to take the weekend off. Hakeem wasn't in town and she could cook for her and HR.

"When are you coming home, Daddy?" HR asked through Facetime, sitting at the island. His cast came off a week ago and he was now a fully functional six-year-old again.

"I'll be home before your bedtime," Hakeem's voice came through the device.

"You promise?"

"Yes, I promise. So, what have you been doing while I've been gone?"

HR began to rattle off the places she'd taken him. They'd been to the park, the library and the museum.

"That's nice. Did you have fun?"

"Yes, it was fun but not as fun as the places you take me."

Mariama flipped the pancake over in the pan and shook her head. Slowly but surely, she was becoming boring old mom and Hakeem was now the fun hype parent. She tuned out as father and son continued to converse for a few more minutes.

"Mummy."

Mariama turned. "Yes, my big man."

"Daddy wants to talk to you."

Mariama took the phone from him. She took in a breath and exhaled. Looking at the screen, she said, "Give me a minute."

"HR, do you want strawberries or bananas with your pancakes?"

"Strawberries, thank you." He glanced up at her and quickly refocused his attention on his computer game.

Mariama picked up the phone and walked to the other side of the kitchen. She brought the phone up to her face and met

Hakeem's scowl. She really could do without his attitude, this morning.

"Yes, 'Keem?"

"Why are you the one cooking?" He growled.

"Because I can. You aren't here so there was no need for the cook to stay."

"That's what he's being paid for and it isn't your place to tell him otherwise." He seethed.

She rolled her eyes. "Okay, I'll remember my place next time. But I'll still cook my food if I want to." He was picking a fight with her for no reason. "Is there anything else I can do for you?"

"I'll be home sometime late evening, but I have to attend a compulsory engagement later. Please keep HR awake so he can see that I came home."

Mariama creased her forehead. "You know you can't keep making those kinds of promises to him. They're unrealistic for a businessman of your standing. You might get caught up somewhere or have to make a detour."

"And whose fault is it that my son thinks that my going to work is potential for me disappearing for another six years?" he scoffed.

"Hakeem, I'm tired of fighting with you. I've tried to talk to you, to explain and apologize, but you've completely shut me out—"

"Because nothing you can say can explain away what you did."

Mariama opened her mouth to speak but was met with the home screen. Hakeem had disconnected the call. Now he was being disrespectful, and she was no longer going to take it. They had to sit down and talk. Something had to give.

THE NEXT COUPLE of days passed with no improvement. She and Hakeem were functioning as complete strangers living in a house to please their son. He didn't want to be around her but pitched a fit when she had the initial conversation about going back to Atlanta. That day, they had the ugliest fight they'd ever had. She needed to go and close the Spartan deal, but he accused her of abandoning her son again because of her needs. He was being completely unreasonable.

That night, she vowed never to shed another tear over Hakeem Richardson. The next time they had a conversation, she wasn't going to let him guilt her into backing down. She'd questioned a lot of things. How could he hate her that much? Did he ever love her? That question was answered when he returned from another business trip some days later with papers to a closed Spartan deal. How he did it, she had no idea. He'd walked in on her having a conversation with her assistant about it but hadn't said anything to her. Him closing the deal showed her he cared for her at least, but would she be able to live with him under the same roof without his love?

TWENTY-FIVE

"You know I love you like a brother—"

Hakeem turned away from the bar in the corner of his man cave and furrowed his brows at Brice. "I am your brother."

Brice waved him off. "You know what I'm trying to say."

Hakeem laughed. Brice arrived at his house earlier in the day and had been at his neck ever since. Hakeem strode over to him and handed him a drink before powering on the television. He wanted to read a book and relax, but he needed the extra noise to drown out the conflicting thoughts in his head and Brice's unwanted lecture.

"I'm being serious, 'Keem. How long do you think you can treat Mari like she doesn't exist, and she takes it?"

"I didn't do this to us. She did." Hakeem seethed. The thought of what they'd become angered him, but he wasn't sure he was ready to forgive her or even if he could. Her betrayal cut deep. It had been a week since they had their last conversation, which, as it had for the past few weeks, ended up in an argument. Like her, he was tired of fighting, but the need to make her hurt the way she hurt him, prevailed.

Hakeem's eye caught something on the side of the couch. He felt Brice's eyes following him and knew that he was still waiting for him to elaborate, but he had nothing more to say. He was tired of Darius and his brother breathing down his neck. None of them had to go through what he had.

He smiled and picked up the toy fire truck. HR and Mari were currently out in the city. She decided to take him to the museum and later to watch a play in the park. Hakeem wasn't oblivious to the look in Mariama's eyes when HR basically abandoned her and wanted to be around him all the time. At first, he didn't care how she felt, but he honestly couldn't stand to see her suffer. So earlier, when HR had insisted, he accompany them, he declined.

"I know you feel me staring at you."

"Yes, I do and I'm choosing to ignore you. Mariama will be fine."

"You sure about that? What happens when she finds out you took Elaine to the gala last week?"

Elaine was his long-time, off and on-again companion. Currently they were off, but that didn't stop him from calling her up when he needed a date to the gala. He really wanted to have Mariama with him, but he didn't have the energy to pretend to be okay with her.

"Last time I checked, I'm a single man. As long as my son is well taken care of, Mariama has no say in anything." He shrugged.

Brice laughed. "I see your anger has you delusional. Remember you said that when she gets tired of trying and leaves you. And that guy..." Brice snapped his fingers trying to remember Roberts' name. "Dude she was seeing in the UK..."

Hakeem's jaw clenched, and his fists balled up.

"Yeah, Roberts. Don't be mad when she leaves you and hooks up with him."

"Over my dead body," Hakeem murmured to himself.

"What's that? I didn't hear you. Oh, so it's good for you to get a kick out of punishing her by ignoring her and taking other women out, but she can't decide she won't take it anymore." Brice's stoic expression told him that he really didn't need him to answer.

It was just as well because Hakeem had no intention to. He picked up the remote and flipped through channels. In silence, he let Brice's words play havoc in his mind. As though he knew he'd given him something to ponder upon, Brice changed the topic and for the next several minutes, they got caught up on his next business venture and, of course, his best friend Imani.

Brice placed his elbows on his knees and leaned forward. "Look man, I get it you're still upset. I am, too. I hate I just got to meet my nephew. But the fact remains that you have to take some responsibility for the reason she didn't tell you. She could've gotten rid of him, but she didn't. She even gave him your name. You have to ask yourself, do you want your family or is this sin so grave that you can't forgive? You do not want a situation whereby you're not on good terms with the mother of your child. Because it will get to a point where Mari will begin to push back." He leaned back into his chair.

Hakeem nodded. He was about to speak when he heard HR running through the house. They were back. Hakeem's heart leaped. The joy he got from seeing this being he and Mari created out of love knew no bounds. God had blessed him with a precious gift. A lifeline. But she kept him a secret. Did she think he was that unworthy?

"Daddy? Daddy? Where are you?"

"Stop running, HR. Walk. He's probably in the den," Mariama cautioned.

Hakeem stood and walked to the doorway. A few seconds

later, HR came barreling into him. Hakeem picked him up and twirled him around. "How was your day, buddy?"

HR began recounting the day he'd just had but stopped when he noticed Brice in the corner. "Uncle Brice!" He wiggled out of Hakeem's arms. Brice walked up and picked him up.

"What's up nephew?" Brice asked.

Hakeem admired their interaction for a few moments, before shifting his gaze to the new presence in the room. Her beauty still took his breath away. Her aura made his heart skip a beat while his stomach did flips – all emotions that didn't go away over the years, or with the hurt, anger and pain. His eyes roamed her attire of ripped jeans and a simple button-down white shirt that was unbuttoned showing her pink tank top underneath. Her hair was held in place by the sunglasses that sat on top of her head. His eyes rested on hers and there was no denying the fire in them. It wasn't that of desire though. If he could still read her correctly, which he probably could, she was controlling her rage.

"Hey, RiRi." Brice smirked.

Hakeem cut his eyes to him. He knew his brother was trying to get under his skin. Mariama walked over to Brice and he kissed her on the cheek. They engaged in small talk while she ignored him. Moments later, she turned to him.

"I need to talk to you. Now," she said through clenched teeth.

Hakeem wasn't the only one that noticed the iciness of her tone.

"Uh oh, come on nephew. Let's go to your room and build this toy set I got for you."

"New toys. Yay!"

Brice chuckled and led HR out of the room. Not before whispering to Mariama, "Go easy on him."

Hakeem folded his arms across his chest and narrowed his eyes at his brother. Brice found the situation hilarious as he walked out of the room. Hakeem's eyes returned to Mariama, who was now standing with her hands on her hips. She stepped back a little so she wouldn't have to stretch her neck to look up at him. Hakeem arched his brow, telling her that he was waiting for her to speak.

Mariama reached into the oversized bag she was carrying, took out something and slammed it on the coffee table. Hakeem looked down at it. His eyes searched for how it concerned him until he saw it.

Shoot! How did this happen?

Mariama started to pace. "I've taken about all the disrespect I'll take from you Hakeem James Richardson. At first, I took it because you were angry, and you had a right to be. I did a terrible thing. So, heck I thought I deserved it and allowed you have your pound of flesh. But you sir, decided to become disrespectful with it. Enough is enough. You took my son to get ice cream with your girlfriend. Are you out of your ever-loving mind?" She stopped and folded her arms across her chest.

"Look, you're blowing this out of proportion. You know the tabloids will write anything." He walked back over to the couch.

"Pictures don't lie, Hakeem!" she yelled. "I'm not even going to argue with you on this. We've been here for almost two and a half months and nothing has changed with us. I don't even care at this point. For the last time; I'm sorry about keeping HR from you, but we're going back to Atlanta."

He could see her eyes water. He wanted to go to her, but her last statement stopped him in his tracks. He could feel the rage mixed with panic creep through him from his toes all the way to his head. He narrowed his eyes at her, trying to gather the words.

"Why are you looking at me like that? Did I speak French?" her tone laced with anger.

"I'm trying to figure out where you get off telling me what's going to happen with my son," he asked.

"*Our* son. In case you forgot...our son." She let out an exaggerated breath. "I'm so sick and tired of you acting like—"

"Spare me the dramatics. You're not the victim here, Mari. You kept my son from me. I missed so many firsts. He missed having his dad. All because you were angry and hurt?"

"Okay, I get it. I've begged, cried, apologized, tried to explain, but you've refused to listen. All this time? It took you barely two weeks to bulldoze your way into my life and force me to listen to you. But I forgot everything is always about you. I'm done, Hakeem. Having that woman with HR then getting photographed while I'm under this roof is the last straw."

"I'm single!" The minute the words left his mouth he regretted them. He heard her gasp and lower her head.

He and HR were in the ice cream store some days ago when Elaine walked in with her niece. They sat together, and nothing happened. He could see how it looked to Mariama, since not even a few days earlier, they'd gone to the gala and were plastered all over the news. To that surprisingly, she hadn't said a thing. But now, his pride wouldn't let him back down. The minute she threatened to take HR back to Atlanta, every sensible bone he had left his body.

She raised her eyes to him. "Yes, you are." She moved closer to the door and stopped. "I'll leave HR with you, but school starts in a week and we have to come to a co-parent agreement by then." She walked out.

Hakeem slumped down in the chair. He wanted to go after her. He should go after her. But his heart was conflicted on his love for her. He was at a loss about what that even was. What he now realized was if he couldn't forgive her, it just might be in their best interest to let her go.

TWENTY-SIX

The moment Mariama landed at Hartsfield-Jackson airport, she let the tears she'd been holding on to flow. She couldn't do another night under the same roof as Hakeem. Her heart tore that she had to leave HR, but it was only for a week. A week she desperately needed to get herself together. She was no good to him in the state she was in. She'd endured and put up a front as Hakeem shattered her heart repeatedly. Even when he started being disrespectful, it was as though he could see she was coming to the end of her rope, and then he would do something nice. He helped her close the deal with Spartan. There was a time she caught a twenty-four-hour stomach bug, and although he didn't say more than a couple of sentences to her, he personally nursed her back to health. It showed her he still cared, so she stuck around.

Never in all of that had he flaunted a woman in her face. When she saw the news of the woman the week prior, she was hurt, but then he came home to her. To them – her and HR. That was the lie she told herself. Imagine her surprise when she was walking down the street with HR and saw the tabloid on the stand. Her son was where she drew the line. She couldn't take it anymore. She really thought he would come after her when she left the den. He didn't. Now it was two days later and here she was back, in Atlanta.

Mariama looked out the window as the Uber driver drove down the Atlanta highway toward her house. She took out her phone and called Priscilla, Hakeem's housekeeper. She had promised she would tell her when she arrived, and she also wanted to get an update on HR.

"Hey Priscilla, I wanted to let you know I've arrived in Atlanta safely," Mariama said, once Priscilla answered the phone. "How is HR?"

"I'm glad you made it safely. HR is down for his nap, but I'll make sure he calls you the minute he gets up." A few beats of awkward silence passed between them. The two of them had gotten close in the last couple of months, so Mariama knew a lecture was coming, but she wasn't up for it right at this moment.

"Okay, I'll—"

"Hold on Mari, are you sure you know what you're doing? Mr. Richardson loves you. I've worked for him for four years now and I've never seen him this happy. Despite his front, I see the way he looks at you when he thinks no one is looking."

Mariama closed her eyes and counted to five. She was tired, angry, and hungry. She was done with all these "are you sure" conversations. She'd had them with Brianna, and her mother the day before. If Hakeem still loved her, he would've come to see about her. Two days, two whole days after their fight and he was nowhere in sight. It wasn't their heart being trampled on, it was hers. So yes, she was sure she couldn't do it anymore. Instead of screaming like she wanted to, Mariama told her she was and then disconnected the call.

As the driver pulled up to her driveway, Mariama exhaled and winced in pain at the same time. She was back home, but missed her baby. The driver placed her luggage at the door and left. She opened the door pulled her bags inside and looked around.

First things first, I need a shower, some food and something for this headache.

WITH HER EYES STILL CLOSED, Mariama felt for the device that was vibrating. Finding it, she brought it to her face and squinted her eyes. The timer told her it was after six in the evening.

"Wow," she murmured to herself. She raised her head and scooted back against her headboard. The memories of the last couple of hours came flooding back. She took a shower, had a light dinner of tacos she'd ordered through Uber Eats, taken some pain reliever and was knocked out within minutes. The phone in her hand stopped buzzing. She remembered she hadn't looked to see who it was the first time. Looking through her notifications, she saw Brianna, her mom, Priscilla and Abby had called. But only one time each. She did, however, have ten missed calls from Hakeem. Mariama really didn't want to talk to him but he was her child's father and they needed to have a cordial relationship. Her phone buzzed again.

"Hey, Hakeem," she said dryly.

"Where are you?" His tone was brash.

"At home."

"That's funny because I'm home and you're not here," he chuckled, but there was no humor behind it.

Mariama scoffed. "Are you feeling okay? That's your home and the one I'm in is mine."

"Mariama, get on a plane and come home. I know you run each time things get difficult. Well, you're not doing that now."

Mariama took the phone from her ear and looked at the screen to make sure she wasn't talking to her father. "Umm, Hakeem, you see that door down the hall? That's your son's room and he's the only person you can tell what to do. Remember you have a week to figure out what to do."

Hakeem laughed. In fact, he laughed so hard that the sound switched from humor to menace. She waited for him to get done because she too wanted to know what he found so hilarious while she was two seconds from blowing a gasket.

"I actually miss this..."

"Huh?"

"I miss this. You thinking you're in charge of anything and me having to show you better than I can tell you that you belong to me. That you somehow think that now that I've found you and HR that I'll be okay with you living under different roofs."

Mariama's mouth hung open. How did she end up with the crazy guy? "'Keem, I don't belong to you. And I didn't run. I removed myself from a toxic, hurtful situation. How long did you expect me to wait for you to come around to listening to me?"

"As long as it takes," he barked. "You don't get to decide when I should get over you keeping my son from me."

"And I'm not saying I should, but I'll wait in my own house. Whenever you're ready to listen, I'll talk, but I'm not coming back to New York."

"Mariama, a flight leaves in two hours. Be on it."

"No. Good night." Mariama hung up the phone. *The nerve of that man. I belong to no one.* He made that perfectly clear with Elongated Elaine. She smiled at the nickname she'd given the tall blondie that Hakeem had been hanging out with. She went to the kitchen, got some ice cream and headed back into her room. She needed to take her mind off of her problems and a *"Waiting to Exhale"* replay would do the trick.

TWENTY-SEVEN

It had been five hours since he had talked to Mariama. Once Hakeem realized she wasn't on the plane, he hopped on his and headed to her. He'd prepared in advance because a part of him knew she wouldn't do as he'd asked. Well, more like demanded her, but he was desperate.

He sat in her driveway in a black Mercedes. So many emotions passed through him. He decided to call her bluff, and this was exactly what he got. He was more than certain she wouldn't leave HR with him and go back alone, but she did. That told him that she had thrown in the towel. Well, he was about to throw it back. As he owned her, she also owned him.

In the days that followed their fight, he made sure he left for work in the morning and didn't return until he knew everyone had gone to bed. Earlier, however, he decided to come back a little early. He wanted to fix things. Darius and Brice had another intervention and this time didn't go easy on him. They reminded him of how long it took him to get over her the first time and asked if the grudge he was holding was worth going through that again. He'd already made up his mind to apologize. But he was going to do it at his own pace. That was until he got home, and she wasn't there. The room she had been staying in was empty, her presence completely wiped away. He ran to HR's room, he was there, playing without a care in the world. An update from Priscilla told him that Mariama had left but she had been in contact with HR.

Now that he sat in front of her house, the breath he had been holding escaped through his lips. He went from full blown rage when he called her, to panic at the nonchalance in her voice. Hakeem stepped out of the car. The darkness was illuminated by the moon. He walked up to the door. He thought to press the doorbell but refrained and called her instead. On the last ring before voicemail, she answered.

"Hello?"

The sexiness in her voice stirred his insides. They hadn't made love since Abidjan. He never stopped longing for her, he however let his anger take center stage. He did know that before anything, they had to talk.

"Open the door."

"Who is this? 'Keem?"

"Do you want me to think there are other men asking you to open the door at this time?" he asked.

She hissed. "'Keem, go away."

"Open the door, Mariama." He disconnected the call.

A few moments later, the lock turned and she let him in. He locked the door. His eyes raked over her. He smiled inwardly because she had on his shirt. He was sure it was from when they were in Abidjan. He looked around her home. Its warmth enveloped him. She stared at him as he walked into her living room. Making himself comfortable on the couch, he glanced over at her next to him. She was still standing.

"Hakeem, it's almost midnight. Are you going to tell me what you're doing here?"

"Talk."

"Huh?"

He glanced up at her. "You wanted to explain, so talk."

Mariama wringed her fingers together and sat on the adjacent seat. She folded her legs under her and let out a deep breath.

"Soon after your decision to slow things down, you left for New York. I cried so much 'til I had no tears left. My heart was broken. I called you and tried to keep our lines of communication open. But between my workload and your new job, things got hectic. But it seemed to be only me trying to reach out to you. Any time you did call, you had to go suddenly, or the conversation seemed strained.

"Then I found out I was pregnant. It was something we didn't plan for, but I knew we could deal with it. I decided to make a surprise trip. The joke was on me because when I got to your apartment, you were throwing a party and had some skanks in your lap. I was furious. How could I be going through so much pain and you were partying?

"I turned around and left. I called up my aunt in Manchester and was out of the country a week later. I could do every other thing I needed to graduate online. And I did.

When HR was born, I called you, but by then you had changed your number and you never were the social media type, none of you were. When he was one, I tried again from a number one of our friends gave me, but some lady picked up the phone claiming to be your woman. That was it, the years went by and I healed. Well kind of because my heart still wanted what it wanted. I couldn't do anything because what it wanted didn't want it back. Then you hit it big, were all over the news. I wasn't going to come to you then but knew HR needed to know you. Especially, to prevent any future scandal. I moved back to the US to grow my business and summon up the courage to look for you. Nothing justifies what I did. It's just my truth. I'm sorry."

Hakeem looked into her eyes that were now filled with tears she'd been holding on to. He saw guilt, hurt, shame and most of all love. She hurt him, but listening to her, he knew he had hurt her too. He'd hurt her deeply and he regretted it. He also wanted to kick his own behind for not listening to her sooner.

"I'm sorry I pushed you away. I'm sorry I made you feel you couldn't depend on me. That party...I think I had just gotten my first hundred thousand-dollar trade. And I only remember changing my number when the old one had been compromised. I'm so, so sorry for how I have treated you these past months and if you let me, I'll spend my life making it up to you."

Mariama nodded but was silent. Hakeem stood and walked over to her. He picked her up and her legs went around his waist. "Please tell me you forgive me."

"As long as you can forgive me," she replied.

"I couldn't breathe when I thought you were done with me. Brice warned that you'd soon push back. I was still too angry to listen, but the emptiness of your room forced me to the realization that I might've pushed too far."

"It hurt too much to stay," she whispered.

"I know, baby, and I'm sorry. Come back with me."

"On one condition." She smiled.

"Tell me."

She whispered in his ear and a grin appeared on his face. "Anything you desire is yours." His lips crashed against hers as he carried her down the hallway to what he hoped was her bedroom.

The END

EPILOGUE

Hakeem rubbed his hand across Mariama's swollen stomach. Her head lay restfully on his broad chest as they looked at the lagoon view from their private bungalow villa in the Gorée Island off the coast of Mariama's home country, Senegal.

Eighteen months ago, they stood before family and friends and vowed to have and to hold each other till death do them part. She hadn't wanted a destination wedding, so they had their ceremony on their New York estate. Two weeks later, she and their son packed up everything they owned and moved in with him. She still had her office in Atlanta, but New York was the new headquarters.

Hakeem smiled as he remembered all they had been through over the years and how love and God's grace had brought them back together. He had his family with him again and couldn't wait to meet his baby girl, Mykaela, who would make her appearance in a little over five months. He felt his wife's head tilt upwards. He brushed his lips over hers and a moan escaped them.

"Did I fulfill your desire?" he asked.

Mariama's condition was that after their wedding, they would travel to Senegal to see her brother. They did. While there, they visited the Gorée Island. The light in her eyes gave him an idea. He bought a piece of land and built their own personal getaway. This was the first time they were on their property which he presented to her as a wedding present.

"More than you'll ever know. I love you Hakeem Richardson."

"I love you too, RiRi, with my heart body and soul. Thank you for giving me a second shot."

PRETEND BAE

Billionaire Pact Book 3

TWENTY-EIGHT

How freaking difficult is it to find a fuchsia hat in New York City?

Imani Sharif parked her car and hopped out. Narrowing her gaze ahead, she made a sprint toward the fifth store she'd been to in the past six hours.

"Hi, where can I find your hats?" she asked, her gaze traveling the expanse of the store.

"Hello, between Women's and Shoes."

"Great, thanks." Imani jogged toward the location she'd been given. Her eyes perused the shoes which, under normal circumstances, would've had her over the moon, her being a shoe addict and all. But her current situation wasn't normal. She was on the prowl for a hat. And it had to be fuchsia. The future of her twenty-year friendship hung in the balance. It was either that or settle for her college roommate/best friend's wrath.

Nicole Johnson, soon to be Mrs. Barnes, and Imani met on the first day of college and had been tight ever since. When Nicole broke the news of her engagement to Desmond, Imani was happy for her friend, but shocked at the same time. Nicole was the girl who was upfront about not being anyone's Mrs. She was Ms. Independent with a side of "I do not need or want a man."

Her words.

Imani, on the other hand, was the half of the duo that had been dreaming of her wedding day since she was a little girl. It was kinda hard not to do when her mother prefaced or ended every sentence since she hit puberty with the words, "in your husband's house."

"Stand up straight, so when you get to your husband's house..."

"Don't buy a house yet, when you get married your husband will have a house..."

"Watch what I'm cooking, so when you get to your husband's house..."

It was kinda written in the African DNA that a female child's aspiration should be marriage. Her Zimbabwean parents weren't an exception. The difference for Imani was, as an immigrant whose family had been living in the United States since she was six, she wanted more for herself. She definitely wanted love and marriage; she just didn't listen to her mother's advice about dimming her own light to get it.

Maybe that's my problem since I can't seem to find a man.

Shaking her head to free it of thoughts that would lead her down the rabbit hole of what ifs, Imani scurried to the other end of the aisle. She released a huge breath when her eyes fell upon exactly what she'd come for. As though sensing her relief, the ring tone assigned to Nicole began to play. Imani picked up the hat with one hand and her phone with the other. She put in her earbuds and answered the call. Imani smiled when she heard Nicole arguing with someone in the background.

"Girl, stop all that fussing." Imani walked to the mirror at the end of the aisle and adjusted the hat on her head.

"I'mma fuss at you in a minute if you don't tell me you've found the hat and you're on your way to Jersey," Nicole chided.

Imani chuckled. "Meanie. I found a hat. As a matter of fact, I'm trying it on right now. And I'll be in Jersey bright and early tomorrow morning."

"You're lucky I love you. First, you run to Harare and stay there for almost two years. Then, you forget the hat you insisted on making for yourself on the plane."

Imani rolled her eyes. "You've already fussed about all of that. Let it rest. Besides, you loved the hat when I sent you a picture of it. Same color and everything. What I look like wearing the same hat as the other bridesmaids? I'm already not the Chief Bridesmaid, and I'm still salty about it."

Nicole and Desmond opted not to have a best man or chief bridesmaid because they didn't want to hurt anyone's feelings. They failed; hers were hurt. The friends talked about the Chief bridesmaid thing so many times during the engagement. Then suddenly, the couple had a change of plans.

Nicole let out a sigh. "Please don't start that again."

"I won't start if you get off my case."

"Deal. I guess I'll settle for seeing you tomorrow."

"Yes. Love ya."

"So, you say." Nicole chuckled.

Imani shook her head. She had too many things to do before morning to go down this path with her friend. It was all love though.

"Okay, I'll see you tomorrow then."

"Is what's-his-face coming?"

"You do know his name, right?"

"I prefer not to say it. Is he coming with you?"

"No, Brice is in Europe on business."

"Is that code for he's rolling around in another random woman's bed?" She sighed. "I don't know why you still bother with him. You should've left him where you met him."

Imani laughed. "Well, that's kinda hard to do since I met him in the tenth grade. But leave Briceson alone."

"Gladly. See you tomorrow, sis."

"Bye."

Deciding to take the hat, Imani made her way to the cash register. Her thoughts returned to B, or as the world knew him, Brice Richardson – the silent second half of Richardson Investments and her best friend. Who was she kidding? They had crossed that bridge a while ago. At least she had.

Despite all her attempts to put the proverbial Jeanie back in the bottle, it never complied. Instead, she'd become good at ignoring the complication that was her relationship with Brice. He, on the other hand, didn't seem upended by the shift in their dynamic. He was out there living it up and that brought on Nicole's disdain. She was the only person Imani told about what happened and how she felt.

A decision she sometimes regretted.

IT WAS late evening four days later when Imani pushed open the door to her Manhattan Brownstone studio and tossed her keys on the side console. Her friend had a spectacular ceremony and was now in Cabo, Mexico for her honeymoon. She'd stayed an extra day on Mrs. Johnson's insistence, but alas she was back in New York, in her cold apartment.

Aesthetically, her home was great, cozy, and comfortable, decked out with art and African sculptures. However, Imani wanted more. Her job as a Human Resources Manager for Plastek LLC afforded her a decent living. It also funded her side hustle, Mani Consults, a branding company she was desperately trying to make her full-time gig.

Plastek LLC was the reason she now lived nine months out of the year in her home country of Zimbabwe – Harare, the country's capital city to be exact. The company, like many multi-nationals, decided to expand to Africa some years ago and made Harare their headquarters. They subsequently started a program in which African immigrants living in America or the United Kingdom could relocate back home to help with integrating the local culture with that of the company. They also did this for their offices in Senegal, Kenya, and Egypt.

Her parents had relocated back home the year after she graduated from college several years ago. She decided to stay in the U.S., with her brother and sister opting to live in Germany and London where they attended college. With early retirement and too much time on their hands, her parents had her little sister who lived in Harare with them.

Imani rolled her carry-on to the corner and trudged to the kitchen. No matter how fulfilled she was in all other areas of her life, her love life was lacking. She thought she was slowly coming to terms with this. However, being a part of her best friend's nuptials, for a shameful moment, she felt jealous.

She didn't want Nicole's life; she wanted her own. With her own man in it. Now, here she was in another wedding, in another role as bridesmaid. Yet, a man still eluded her. She came awfully close to thinking she had hit the jackpot when one of the groomsmen took an interest in her. He was fine with a well-built physique to match.

When he opened his mouth, her eyebrows almost flew off. How could a creature that fine have a mouth that smelled like socks and stale cabbage? After him, no one else gave her the time of day. She was beginning to think something was wrong with her. Or the U.S wasn't the place where she'd find her Prince Charming.

Imani opened the freezer. Surely, there was a tub of Ben & Jerrys she could drown her sorrows in with reruns of *Girlfriends*. Dipping her head in the freezer, she sighed at her miscalculation. She was out of ice cream. In its place, there was a pound of oxtails. Her eyes darted toward the timer on the microwave. It was a little past eight p.m. Her mind was so chaotic that her desire for an early bedtime was a lost cause. Deciding on oxtail stew over rice, she put the meat on to boil and went to unpack and shower.

A few hours later, with a half empty plate and a half glass of wine, Imani sat at her kitchen island, scrolling through her various social media pages. She stared at the image on Facebook where Dineo tagged her and expressed how much he missed her. Dineo Pule was another complication she didn't see coming. When she left America the last time, it was with the resolve that love wasn't for her. She was probably never destined to have it. Just as she settled into that thought, Dineo comes along. He was an engineer from neighboring Botswana who was in Zimbabwe on assignment.

What started off as a group lunch date with other friends, soon became them hanging out together. She wasn't attracted to him and didn't harbor any kind of deep feelings, but he was safe and comfortable, so she enjoyed his company. Her mind drifted back to the last time they spoke, right before she boarded a plane to head back to the U.S for Nicole's wedding.

"I'm serious, Imani. In this short time, I've come to develop deep feelings for you, and I'd like to explore them," Dineo urged.

"You're a decent person, Neo. A good guy, but I'm not the woman for you."

"But we have fun together. I believe if you give us a chance, you'll find out we'll be great together."

"But—"

"Don't give me a definitive answer now. Think about it. We have a lot in common, have a good time together and can talk with ease. I know you can come to love me."

Imani had stared at him. He wasn't entirely wrong. If she had known, *he* was going to develop feelings for her, she would've told him of her emotional unavailability. Stupid because the person who indeed had her heart was doing a poor job of taking care of it.

To fill the awkward space between them, she promised to think about it. Would she learn to love him? The question plagued her mind throughout the day plus journey to JFK International. She still didn't know the answer. Instead, she decided to tell Brice how she felt about him. How she *still* felt about him. She didn't want to live her life with regret. She had done that enough. Before she thought seriously about settling for the one she was with, she was going to see what was up with the one her heart desired.

Imani logged into Instagram and saw that Dineo had commented on all the pictures she posted from the wedding. She responded to some of them and scrolled through her feed until she landed on Brice's page. She always called him a beautiful man and he hated it. That didn't stop her or make the statement any less true. She squinted her eyes when she saw one particular woman whose hand wasn't where it was supposed to be. Her seductive pose with Brice turned Imani's insides. She followed the username to the woman's page.

Daphne.

Brice never put women on his social media pages. How had she missed this? The woman's page was worse; she had him all over it.

Imani's heart thudded in panic. Was he seeing someone? He would have told her. He told her about all the other meaningless dates he had. Or did he not tell her because this woman was special to him?

Imani's eyes darted toward the time. Brice should be getting out of bed by now. Feeling the sudden urge to hear his voice and relish in the comfort it always provided, she dialed.

"Hello?"

"You up?"

"I am now. What's up, Manny? You good?"

Imani scoffed. That question was always irritatingly annoying yet satisfying at the same time. Although she was six months older than him, he always treated her with so much care, and protected her to the point of insanity. Well, until that one time.

"Yeah, I'm fine. Are you still flying back tonight?"

Imani heard movement on the other end of the line. She thought it was Brice until she heard a moan. She rolled her eyes. She should've known there was never anywhere he went that he didn't have someone to warm his bed on standby. Sometimes, why she even wanted him was beyond her.

"You hear me? Manny?"

"Huh? No, I didn't hear you. What did you say?"

"What has you so distracted? I can feel it... and don't lie to me either."

"I'm fine. I have a headache. So, what—"

"Yeah, right. Anyway, I said I'll be here another couple of days. I have to help a friend do some things."

"A friend? Since when do we speak in code?" Irritation laced her voice.

"Chill out. Her name is Daphne. Her uncle is one of our new clients," he responded in the same tone.

"Hmmm."

"Don't start; it's too early. I'm not the one that volunteered for some job on the Continent without even discussing it first."

"It's not some job. It's my career and that place is my home."

"You know what I mean."

"And it's been almost two years. When are you going to get over that?"

"Never. Or when you come back for good."

"I'm here now and you're nowhere to be found."

"Yeah, whatever. I'll be there—"

"Baby, who's..." a woman's voice interrupted his statement.

Imani rolled her eyes. Her chest tightened. "I'll let you go. See you—"

"Manny, don't you dare hang up."

"Bye, B. I'll see you when you get back."

Without waiting for his response, she hung up the phone. She cursed herself under her breath. Once again, she had let Brice get to her. What she wanted was an honest conversation between them. But for a while, they seemed to have their wires crossed.

Yes, she was a runaway.

What else was she supposed to do?

Darius Gray, one of their friends, had a wedding reception in Atlanta for those who couldn't make it to Tunisia for his wedding. The eve of the reception, there was a party at one of his hotels, and she and Brice shared a kiss. Not just any kiss – a soul snatching, "I think I'm losing my mind" kiss. Their chemistry couldn't be denied.

They were interrupted by some drunk party goers and his phone ringing. Darius needed him. He kissed her forehead and left. She went to her hotel room, and plopped down on the bed, full of hope. Hope that this time, they could get it right.

Imagine her surprise when he showed up for the reception

with a date. He had to know they had unfinished business. For the second time in their friendship, he'd cut her deep. For the rest of the weekend, she gave him the cold shoulder, which he couldn't handle. They argued; she refused to reveal her true feelings again. Once they got back to New York, she took the offer from her job and left. In hindsight, she wished she hadn't been so hasty. She wished she had stayed and talked it out. Now it might be too late.

TWENTY-NINE

"Thank you for helping me with the warehouse walk today." Daphne Wilcox's voice broke through his thoughts. "Uncle always likes a Wilcox to be there. Why, I have no idea, considering we pay all these people."

Brice focused on the woman seated before him and gave a faint smile. This was the part of his new status he didn't particularly care for. He'd always been a silent partner in the investment company he and his brother Hakeem owned. He enjoyed traveling the world, playing with the stock market, and modeling. His brother was the more rigid one. He had always been that way. It came with the territory of being the eldest. Brice didn't envy that role but was grateful for it. With an absent father and a mother who had died when they were just little boys, they were sent to live in an orphanage and Hakeem had stepped up in a big way.

"You're welcome, Daphne. No need to keep thanking me. Nolan had other obligations, and I was glad to help out."

Nolan Wilcox had become one of his closest friends in the last few years, and the nephew of the patriarch of the Wilcox empire, Sir Edward Wilcox. There were certain clients Hakeem insisted on handling personally. The Wilcox's were among them.

Brice could never have predicted that his brother getting married would change so many things in *his* life. His brother decided to step back and take six months to be with his new family, which meant Brice had to step up.

Another wedding that messed with his life was Darius's. It was the start of the shift in the dynamic between him and Imani. His life had been off kilter since then, and he had no idea how to fix it. How come his boys were getting tied down, but he was the one bearing the brunt of the shift? A cure to what was broken between him and Imani was one thing his money or status couldn't buy.

"I'd like to think you went out of your way for me and not only as a favor to my brother." Daphne reached across the table and covered his hand with hers.

Brice's eyes traveled to his hand. His lips turned up in a faint smile. He gently removed his hand from under hers and reached for his glass to drink. They were in a restaurant in the heart of West Brompton where she insisted they have lunch so she could "thank him properly."

"Daphne, I thought we discussed what this was. No strings attached."

"Yes, but that was four months ago. Are you telling me nothing has changed?"

Brice studied her. Daphne was an attractive woman who was wealthy and spoiled. The one thing that made him keep her around for so long was he knew she didn't need him for his money. She had her own. He had come to find out, however, she needed him for his status. American billionaire and English Socialite. He'd let her know time without number this was no Prince Harry and Meghan Markle situation. With the current glint in her eyes, it seemed his words weren't sticking. It was time to cut her off.

"Sorry Daph, I promised to always be honest and no, nothing has changed." His phone buzzed and his eyes darted toward the display screen. He could feel Daphne watching him, so he hid his displeasure at the message not being from Imani. She was begging him to jack her up and he was never one to disappoint. After hanging up on him earlier, he called her back, but knew she wouldn't budge. She was so stubborn it made him crazy.

"Is it because of her?"

"Who?"

"Give me some credit, Briceson. Your countenance changed after your phone call this morning. Are you sure she's just your friend?"

"Imani is not up for discussion." His expression was stoic.

"I don't understand it, Briceson. You stop whatever you're doing for her. You take her phone calls even in the middle of important meetings. You two argue like a married couple. You claim there's nothing between you two, yet you wouldn't give us a true chance."

He didn't know what annoyed him more. The fact that she kept calling him Briceson after all this time, or that he had gotten so close for her to know his habits where Imani was concerned. If it were any other person, he would've walked away from the table.

The bigger picture with her family kept him seated. He now regretted not listening to 'Keem when he said it was a bad idea to start anything with her. Even if she claimed to understand the rules of engagement. Not one to back away from a challenge, he forged ahead.

"Drop it, Daphne. Imani is not a topic we'll ever discuss. She is what I said she is. End of discussion."

Daphne sat back in her seat and pouted. She did that when she couldn't get her way. She would have to get over it. Imani wasn't only his best friend; she was his freaking lifeline, his Mother Teresa, and nobody would ever have anything to say about her but him.

He rubbed the back of his neck. He had to get back to New York and see what was up with her. Them. She was in the U.S. for three months and his mission was to make sure she remained there. He understood Harare was her home; he'd visited with her many times before. However, they'd always been home to each other; then she changed that, and he wanted to know the real reason why.

He signaled for the check. His business in London was done; it was time to head home.

SEVERAL HOURS LATER, Brice looked through the documents that landed in his inbox earlier. Leaning back in the leather seat of the Richardson jet – more accurately, the jet Hakeem named after his wife, Mariama. He chuckled to himself as he stared out the window at the clouds they were passing over. Who would have guessed that they would one day have a family jet?

Brice pulled a folder out of his briefcase and went over the requirements his South African contact had sent over. Brice and 'Keem did most things as a unit. Winemaking however was something Brice wanted to do on his own. He'd always loved different kinds of wine, but he had taken a deeper interest in it when he was in South Africa on business some years back. Stellenbosch to be exact. He got to tour some vineyards and his interest grew.

He wasn't interested in starting from scratch; instead, he

wanted to buy a vineyard that came with a winery. One that he could fix up, rebrand, and take to the next level. The search started three years ago, and the dream was almost becoming a reality. He longed for it with a passion that wouldn't let him go.

Browsing the document again, one thing had him stuck. He didn't understand what his family status had to do with anything. He had a couple more hours in the air, so decided to find out. When he touched down, he wanted to spend some uninterrupted days with Imani, so he needed to wrap up any business matters before he landed.

"Hello, Mr. Richardson?"

"Hello, Lethabo, I got the documents you sent and have gone over them. Are you free to chat now?"

"Yes, of course."

"I read the part about family values. Explain what that means exactly," Brice said.

"It is a requirement the sellers has for any potential buyer. That vineyard you're interested in is very lucrative—"

"That I know, which is why I want it."

"Ah yes, but before the owner died, his will stipulated that any potential buyer had to have a family. As you know, if a buyer can't be found in four years, the vineyard will go to the government."

"Why didn't you tell me this before? Before we put all the time into researching the property." His irritation couldn't be curbed. All the years he had spent searching and negotiating and still, he needed to be a family man? It didn't make any sense.

"I went to submit all the paperwork to the new lawyer, and I was told of that tidbit the former lawyer forgot to mention," Lethabo explained. "You don't have to be married. There's nothing that says that. I think they want to make sure a bachelor wouldn't turn the place into a party zone." A beat passed between them before Lethabo continued. Brice could detect the hesitation in his voice. "The trustees researched you, Sir."

"That can't be good." Brice rubbed a hand over his head. The internet wins again. Half the stories they had of him were either not true, or an exaggeration of the truth.

"No sir, but maybe we can get your brother to be the front person?"

"No." Brice was determined to do this on his own. The vineyard had been up for sale long before he expressed an interest in it. By his calculations, the four-year waiting period before it became the government's property was around the corner. Something like six months. There was no guarantee he would be in a committed relationship in that time. Or that someone else that met all the requirements to buy the property wouldn't come along.

"What about if I doubled, or tripled my offer?"

"It's not about the money with this particular vineyard. I've bought property for you in South Africa before, so I know what your counter would be, and already offered," Lethabo said. "The late owner was a widower whose family died in an unfortunate crash. His last wish is of sentimental value that has no price tag. I'm sorry."

Brice knew he would've done all he could before coming to him. He was the same person that had negotiated and purchased the land where he had built his home. Brice took in a deep breath and exhaled. He toyed with the idea of starting his search over but cleared the thought from his mind.

He, 'Keem and Darius had a pact that they'd become billionaires by thirty-five. Thanks mostly to his brother's hard work, they'd achieved that goal, and he was only thirty-two. This was his chance to build and transform something he was passionate about, and now he was being denied because of his personal life, which was no one's business but his own.

"One day you'll want someone so bad who neither your charm, nor your money can get you."

Imani's warning intruded his thoughts. Any time she said that, it was always when chiding him about another no strings attached relationship. He always laughed at her. Her words now were coming back to jinx him. It wasn't someone, but something.

Since she used her mouth to mess his deal up, she was going to use her brain to fix it.

"Okay, let me think. Can I get back to you within the next few days?"

"Yes, sir. I'll hold them off until I hear back from you."

After disconnecting the call, Brice leaned back into his chair with his fingers steepled under his chin. He pondered who, if anyone, he could get to play the role of devoted partner. At least till he signed on the dotted line. He scrolled through his phone. No one on his roster hadn't hit him with the "so nothing has changed?" talk. With what he was trying to do, that would only spell disaster.

I need some new options.

Imani.

He thought about her recent attitude and developed an instant headache. He checked the email confirming their reservation for Le Bernardin. She hated surprises and would be mad at him, but it was a risk he was willing to take. He missed his friend and strong arming her was no longer working. He needed her to talk to him. Really talk to him so they could get whatever was between them cleared away.

He went over to IG and scrolled through her feed. She hadn't posted a picture of herself in a while, so he was surprised when he saw photos from the wedding. He was glad Nicole was now married. Maybe she could finally get some business of her own to mind.

He was about to close the app when the multiple comments by someone named Dineo caught his attention. Brice was used to Imani getting the attention of men. He also wasn't shy about discreetly letting them know she was off limits. A few needed further clarification, something he was always willing to supply.

Those were the good old days. Now she was far away in Zimbabwe and he wasn't sure what she was up to. There was something about this man that rubbed him the wrong way. How did this guy know she'd cut her hair before he did? They shared everything. Apparently not anymore. And that made his stomach churn.

THIRTY

The burning wood in the fireplace crackled as Imani strolled through the small foyer of her home to the front door. She raised the mug of hot cocoa to her lips and sipped when she heard the door lock turning. Then the doorbell rang, again. Rolling her eyes, she turned around and retraced her steps to the living room. If he was going to use his key, she wondered why he bothered ringing the bell.

Imani sat with her legs tucked underneath her and drew the blanket across her lap. The longer she stayed away from New York, the more she appreciated the cold weather, which was a huge contrast to the dry, hot climate of Harare.

"That key is for emergencies only, B," Imani scolded as the heavy footsteps got closer.

"Well, hello to you too, Manny. Your funky attitude is about to drive me insane."

"You're one to talk," Imani murmured.

She wasn't really mad at him. More at herself for not being able to express what she felt for her best friend. Or to get rid of the emotions all together. "My bad."

"Your actions don't match your words. Do I get a hug, or you're stingy with those too?"

Imani smiled and stood. At a little over six feet, Brice stood before her in all his chocolate glory. He loved keeping his hair cut low and face clean shaven. She walked into his outstretched arms and rested her head against his firm chest. His strong toned arms encased her against his body, while his cologne invaded her nostrils, sending her dopamine levels into a frenzy.

She missed him even though she didn't want to. This was the main reason she decided to live so far away, but any time she saw him, her heart reminded her that her strategy was failing miserably. After having his hand rub up and down her back a moment too long, she pulled away and lowered her gaze. Brice lifted her head with his finger.

"You all right?"

Imani walked back to her place on the couch. "Yeah, I'm fine. How was London? And why are you out in this weather?"

Brice shrugged out of his coat and tossed it on another chair in the room. "I missed you. London was fine. I got back a few hours ago. And I've been in New York for a while now. The weather is what it is."

He was dressed down in navy blue sweats and a hoodie. Apart from the numerous women who rotated in and out of his life, nothing had changed about him since they were teenagers. That was one thing she loved. The money never changed him.

"What's with the haircut?" he asked, plopping down next to her. He tousled her hair with his fingers.

Imani raised her hand to rub down the back of her head and creased her brows. "What? You don't like it?" His opinion was important to her. It no longer reached the middle of her back but stopped at her neck.

"I love it. But you haven't cut your hair since Soul Brother Steve."

Imani cackled and flung a pillow in his direction. "Shut up. I can't stand you."

Brice laughed with her and stood, walking toward her kitchen. "You know I'm speaking facts. You were so in love with dude in the eleventh grade that he convinced you that to be his girl, you had to embrace your natural roots."

Imani followed him. "And my dumb behind pleaded with my mama to cut off my good perm." She no longer wore a perm, but back in the day, she loved hers.

Brice opened the refrigerator. "Yeah that was dumb, but we weren't that tight yet for me to put you on game." Brice brought out some of her leftovers.

"Oh, help yourself why don't you."

"I always do, don't I?"

"Annoyingly so. "Imani bumped him with her hips. "Move, I got it. You never clean up after yourself no way."

Brice raised his hands in surrender and walked around the small island to take a seat. Over the next couple of minutes, while she prepared his plate, Brice caught her up on the latest with his nephew and niece. Seeing Brice in his uncle element was still a new thing for her. He would be a great father.

Most of the time when they had deep conversations about the future, he always told her that he wasn't sure how to be a dad, but he knew what a dad shouldn't do. He vowed to give his family the best when he did have one. The thought brought her back to what she promised herself she would discuss with him.

Her feelings.

"Sometimes, I still find it hard to believe that Hakeem and Mariama could get back together." She slid the warm plate in front of him.

Brice bowed and said grace. "Married with children. After all this time." He blew on a piece of oxtail and lifted it to his mouth. "That love thing does work for some people. Their story gives hope."

Her eyes bugged. "Hope? Are you telling me you've sown enough wild oats?"

Brice shrugged. "I won't say all that. I'm just saying it gives others hope."

Imani folded her arms across her chest and leaned against the counter opposite him. She studied him. Was it this Daphne woman who had him singing a different tune? This was new even for him.

"So, tell me about Daphne?" Imani asked.

"Who?"

"Don't give me that...you heard me."

Brice shrugged. "There's nothing to tell really. She's the niece of this client we have. You know when 'Keem took time off, I had to step up."

"Hmmm."

Brice placed his fork on his plate and leaned back. His brown eyes pierced her. Imani shifted her weight from one foot to the other. He always stared at her like he could read her, and most times he could. This time, however, she couldn't reveal her true thoughts until she knew his. This wasn't high school or anything, but she was still weary of putting herself out there. Especially after what happened during their freshman year and Darius's wedding.

Suddenly, the bravado she seemed to have days ago disappeared. Besides, she wouldn't want to be the one that messed up anything he did have going on. Especially if it was leading to somewhere.

"Out with it."

"Out with what? I just asked you a question." She turned to put on the kettle.

"What? No judgements?"

"Should I be judging you. Why are you so testy?"

"Because you've been acting strange ever since—"

"Ever since what?" Her heart throbbed, thinking he knew her issue and the fact jealousy was overrunning her.

"Look. I've missed you. I don't like this strain between us. Daphne is nobody," he pleaded.

Imani sighed, not wanting to argue with him either. She opened the cupboard and removed two mugs. "Tea or hot chocolate?"

"Tea." He continued to eat.

Imani walked over to the sink to rinse the mugs out. "Does she know she's nobody? You're all over her Instagram feed."

"That has nothing to do with me. She can do what she wants as long as she understands what I communicated." Brice stood and walked over to her. "Manny, what's wrong, babe? I know you can't still be mad at what happened at Darius's wedding three years ago."

"And why can't I be?"

"Because I asked you if we were good after we talked, and you said yes. I didn't invite her. How was I to know she was still a sensitive area and so to avoid walking in with her?"

Yeah, that was the part that hurt so much. Not only did he have a date the following day to the reception, but it was with Maxine Bedford.

Imani scoffed. "Look, let's forget it."

"Let's not. Because apparently you haven't. I didn't know it was a big deal."

"But you knew the history."

"But I didn't think..."

"Yeah that's it, B, you don't think..." Imani turned from him to pick up the whistling kettle. She picked it up to pour when Brice placed his hand over hers.

"I got it."

Imani glanced at him then resumed her position near the counter.

"When I left you, I was drunk. I met her at the club when I went to meet 'Keem and Darius. It wasn't planned. It just happened. She knows all of us." He paused and glanced at her. "Why are you still so angry anyway?"

Imani sucked her teeth. "I'm not angry. I'm only stating the facts."

"Okay, what do you want me to do? I want my friend back."

Imani sighed. She was being dramatic and unfair. He wasn't a mind reader; this she knew. She couldn't provide him with an answer really because she didn't have one. Except for him to see her. Really see her. The memory of what happened the first time she spilled her guts to him stopped her from shouting her need from the rooftop. He finished making their tea in palatable silence.

"You gonna answer me, or are we good?" Brice asked after a beat of silence.

"Yeah, we're good." She missed him terribly and she had three months to muster up the courage to tell him how she felt. She desperately wanted to enjoy her friend and for them to go back to the way things were. If they stood any kind of chance, she needed to let that hurt go. She promised herself to have the talk and she would, but she could hold off for now. Daphne was a nobody and that was good enough.

"Yo, I don't wanna hear about it no more, Manny. I'm serious."

"I hear you."

"But do you understand me tho?"

"B leave me alone. You said you had some news to share. What's up?" She blew on the hot liquid and took a sip.

Brice stared at her for a few seconds before he picked up

his mug and walked back to where his empty plate was. "Yeah. Remember the winery I told you about?"

"The one in South Africa? Yeah, I remember. Have they agreed to your offer? That's so exciting, B. I remember when you were going on and on about it—"

Brice laughed. "Slow down so I can tell you the story..."

"Okay, I'm calm. What's up?"

"The money part is settled. I got all the papers and permits, but your behind jinxed me."

Her brows came together. "Me? What did I do?"

"Remember that time you called yourself checking me?"

"I've checked you many times. You gotta be more specific."

"The time you told me that I'd come across someone or something I want that I can't get with my money or charm."

"Well, it's true, but what does that have to do with the vineyard?"

"The sellers claim the late owner had something in his will about the vineyard being sold to a family man."

Imani stared at him, thinking he was going to laugh any minute now. When his deep baritone chuckle wasn't forthcoming, she let hers rip. She threw her head back and clapped her hands as humor ripped from her belly. Once she saw Brice's stare get deadlier, she tried to stifle her laugh. He looked like he wanted to strangle her.

"Are you done? I don't see anything funny about it."

"I'm sorry...when I said that, I didn't mean your business. I meant your heart."

"My business is part of my heart. But I'm glad you think it's funny, so this next part won't be hard."

Imani placed her hand over her mouth. "What...next part?" She cleared her throat.

"The part where you, my best friend, gets me out of this." He smirked.

Her eyes widened because the mischief in his was one she recognized. "Me? How?"

Brice stood and took both mugs and his plate to the sink. "But what do they need with my personal life? My money is green—"

"The South African Rand is actually orange, blue, and red. Well, the large bills..."

"Thank you, smartie."

She shrugged. "Glad I could help. But we're talking about Africans. It's our business to know other people's business, especially the personal stuff."

Brice raised his brows.

"Of course, I'm exaggerating a little, but most times there are no boundaries. Besides, family is more important to a lot of family-owned businesses than the color of your money."

"Well luckily, I don't have to be married—"

"Oh, thank God. Marriage is so, so terrible..." Imani rolled her eyes at him.

He started the water for the dishes. "I'm not marrying because of business. It might have worked out for Darius, but that's not me."

"Okay, so what do you have to do? And how can I help? You know I don't have a family to lend you. Or is it because I'm African?"

"Huh? 'Cause you're African? Really?"

Imani swatted his shoulder. "My bad. Okay, so spit it out..."

Brice lifted her left hand. Imani lowered her eyes to where their hands connected. Then she lifted her eyes to his face and was met with a smirk.

"What's going on, Brice?"

"Trying to figure out what size ring to get for my pretend bae."

"What? Are you out of your mind?" She snatched away from him, reaching for a towel to dry her hand.

"Do you remember the vow we made in high school?"

Imani hesitated. How could she forget that corny vow?

"Come on, say it. You remember. I'll even say it with you." Brice lifted her hand again.

"From the highest mountain to the lowest valley, when it comes to each other, we'll always be down for the other." They said in unison.

Imani removed her hand from his. "I can't be down this time."

"Why? We've always been there for each other."

"That was a high school vow..."

"And? We've abided by it through high school, college and grad school, so what's the problem now?" He furrowed his brows.

"I know but I can't be your pretend...what now?"

"Bae." He wiggled his brow.

Imani waved him off. "I hate when you do that. But yeah whatever, I can't be that."

"And again, I want to know why? The only time we agreed to reevaluate was if we were married or in a committed relationship."

Imani rubbed the back of her neck. "Yeah, about that..."

"What?" His tone held an aggression she wasn't expecting.

"I'm kinda talking to—"

"Talking? Then you're not in a committed relationship, so he's a non-factor." Brice kissed her cheek and walked into the living room. He picked up his coat and put it on.

"Brice, we're not done talking."

"Then we can continue at the birthday party tomorrow. But I know you won't let me lose my heart's desire because of someone you're *talking* to."

Imani shook her head and walked behind him as he headed down her short foyer. "Brice—"

"Goodnight, Manny. Love you. Make sure you lock up." He opened her front door and stepped out into the frigid evening.

Brice always did this when he wanted to get her to buy into his idea. This time, however, the cost was too much to bear. Could her heart take the charade? It could work out in her favor. But what if it didn't? That's the question that kept her tossing and turning into the wee hours of the morning.

THIRTY-ONE

"I can't believe she fell for that."

Brice looked over at his brother who was at the indoor grill. "She didn't exactly agree. But she will."

"Why? Because of some high school vow?" Hakeem asked.

"That's part of it, but I intend to have a counter for any objection she raises. I don't know this dude she's talking to, but I don't trust him."

Hakeem chuckled. "You don't even know him. But you don't trust any dude she talks to."

"But this one in particular."

"Why? Because he's African? Or you scared he'll take her from you, being so close to her?"

"What are you yapping about, bro?"

"You know what I'm sayin,' but let's keep pretending you don't." Hakeem shook his head.

"Whatever, man." Brice waved him off. His thoughts went to the real reason he was rattled by this Dineo guy. He didn't let Imani talk about him, but he knew that was who she was referring to. The comments on her IG post now made sense.

"Don't tell me you'll have him investigated too. I don't want to be there the day Manny finds out about all these investigations and the warning men off you've been doing for years."

Truth be told, Brice didn't want to be there either, but he wasn't going to admit that. "It's for her own good. Besides, she won't find out—"

"Find out what?"

Brice narrowed his eyes at his brother when Mariama, his sister-in-law, entered the kitchen. He turned to face her. "Find out how much I love my sis-in-love."

Mariama walked into his open arms. "Tell me anything."

"Aye, you've had your arms around my wife for too long."

"Chill out." Brice placed a kiss on her cheek, a move he knew would irritate his brother. The man wasn't normal on an ordinary day, but when it came to his family, he was another kind of beast. When Mariama was sick up until and after the birth of their daughter, Hakeem was a shadow of himself. It was great to see him back to his old self.

"Please don't get him started." Mariama walked over to her husband, tugged on his beard bringing his lips down to hers.

Based on the way she tried to wiggle out of his arms, Brice could tell the kiss was deeper than she wanted it to be. In front of him at least.

"Where's Manny?" Mariama asked when she finally broke away.

Although they all went to the same college, Imani and Brice were two years behind Hakeem, Mariama and Darius. The ladies knew one another but weren't super close. Brice wished they were. Anybody except the hater Nicole.

"She's on her way. One of Nicole's cousins dropped by her house last minute for something."

"The same Nicole? I don't envy you, bro." Hakeem laughed.

Mariama giggled. "Well, whatever she's saying hasn't driven Imani away from you *yet*, so..." She shrugged her shoulders and walked back over to him. She placed her hand on his shoulder. "If anyone's going to do that, it will be you, little brother."

Brice was about to ask her to expound on that statement when the doorbell rang. Mariama hurried out of the kitchen. Brice looked at his brother.

"What's your wife on about now?"

"I learned a long time ago not to get between what you and Imani got going on. All I'm gonna say is, the worst kind of deceit is self-deceit. You do too much to just be her friend; she does too. But after a while, she'll move on, case in point, this other dude. I want you to think carefully about this South Africa thing. You'll come out smelling like a rose, or it will go terribly wrong..."

Hakeem allowed his words to trail off when the laughter between two women became louder on approach. Brice swiveled his stool around, the words Hakeem uttered running on repeat in his head. He took in Imani with fresh eyes. He could never deny her beauty – blemish free dark skin, onyx-colored eyes and high cheekbones that shaped her oval face.

Her outer beauty was something he didn't allow himself to enjoy. The blinders he wore became a necessity when his feelings for her shifted. Especially after the damage their friendship suffered in freshman year. Ever since then, he settled for what she was willing to give him as long as she was speaking to him again. Although he never set out to hurt her, she was hurt, and he didn't like it. Currently however, he allowed himself, even for a moment, to take the blinders off.

"Hey 'Keem!" Imani walked up to his brother.

The same way Hakeem looked out for him was the same

way he looked out for Imani. She was like his little sister. After their falling out, Hakeem was their mediator and helped fix things between them. It was then he advised them to set boundaries, so they didn't unintentionally hurt one another again. They never did set those boundaries, and Hakeem washed his hands of what he called their "situation."

"Hey, sis. What's it been? A year?" Hakeem drew her in for a quick hug.

Imani put some chips in a plate and chuckled. "I think it has been. But you're in good hands now, so I don't have to worry."

"I am in the best hands." Hakeem winked at Mariama, who put the presents Imani brought on the table in the corner.

"Where's the birthday boy?"

"Upstairs with his friends. They'll soon come rushing down to eat," Mariama responded.

"So, what am I? Chopped liver?" Brice asked.

"No, more like minced beef. But I'm coming..." Everyone laughed as Imani walked over to him and tweaked the tip of his nose.

"Aye, stop that. You know I hate it."

"Main reason I keep doing it."

Brice gave her a pointed look. She grinned at him and lifted a chip to his mouth. He opened his mouth to take it and heard Hakeem grunt. Brice understood the hidden meaning behind the sound but ignored it. Instead, he stood, grabbed Imani's hand and her bowl of chips.

"Hey, where are we going?"

Her question garnered laughter from their hosts, but he ignored them. Glancing at her, he mumbled. "We have unfinished business."

"Err, give me my chips B, and no we don't."

Brice ushered her into Hakeem's den and placed the bowl on the coffee table. She gave him a stern look and moved to the couch.

"If this is about your South African thing, the answer is still no."

"Come on, Manny. I don't understand why you won't help me out. Six to eight weeks tops, and it's over."

"Are you kidding me?" she glared at him. "Has it occurred to you that I want to get married? Have a family? Not that I'm under any pressure, but I eventually want that...for me."

A wave of heat enveloped his body. He didn't understand the feeling. The thought of her marrying someone else and procreating vexed him. He knew she wouldn't be single forever, but how did she go from talking to someone to thinking about marriage?

"Are you telling me you're getting married?"

"No, I'm not, but being photographed as your fiancée in South Africa, then being dumped two months later doesn't look good." She stood and walked over to the small fridge in the corner. "Girls might be running the world, but it's still a man's. I have the most to lose in this plan of yours."

Imani opened the fridge and Brice ran his hand down his face. He heard everything she said, his mind just couldn't comprehend it. Fear creeped up his spine. The realization that he had always counted on her being by his side hit him. She was his one sure thing. The only woman to ever be there and love him the way his late mother did. But her talk about marrying someone set everything within him on high alert. Hakeem's words came back to him, and he jolted to his feet. He needed to think of something quick.

"Well, if that's the case, breaking up with me will have other men curious about you."

Imani whipped her head toward him at a speed he feared would have it rolling on the floor. "You're joking right? You must think this is the British Regency."

"You're the one that made me watch it." Brice shook his head at her. She had this new series on Netflix she couldn't stop talking about, so they binge watched it together over Facetime. He knew it was a stretch though. "Okay, how about this – we keep the engagement on a need-to-know basis. Right now, the only people that need to know are my lawyers and the sellers."

Her eyes softened and he knew he had an opening, so he went for the kill. "Also, you can work with my marketing team to rebrand the vineyard and winery when the sale is done."

Her eyes widened. "You can hire any branding company in the world."

"Yes, I can, and I want to hire you."

"Brice, that's a big responsibility."

"I'm not saying you'll do it alone, but what do you always tell me?"

"If your dream doesn't scare you, it's not big enough."

"So, what do you say?"

"Are you throwing me a bone, or do you really believe in me?"

"You of all people know I don't play about business. You'll see the vineyard, write up a proposal, present it, the whole nine," he assured her.

She placed her hand on her hip. "What if you don't like what I come up with?"

"Then you'll rework it. I'll pay your fees and add a bonus if I do like it."

"You know I could've just asked you for money to start my business."

"I know. I've been trying to give it to you for years. But you ain't that kind of person. You already give me grief for the things I do manage to get you."

Imani squinted her eyes at him. He could tell she was deep in thought, but he allowed her to marinate on the seed he'd planted. He didn't, however, anticipate her next question.

"What about Daphne?"

The question annoyed him. "Really? She already thinks that we are what we're not."

"Wow, what a shame to have all these women at your beck and call, and you can't call on any of them to do you this favor."

He wanted to ignore her comment so as not to give it life. But then decided to use it to his advantage. "No other woman on this earth knows me as well as you do. We won't have to rehearse a thing."

"I'm beginning to wonder if that's a good thing."

Brice saw she was having way too much fun goading him. He also knew that in the moment, he was the one that needed a favor. It was true that she had the most to lose. However, he wasn't planning on either of them losing. But, telling her that now would spook her.

One thing his Manny was good at was jumping to conclusions. If he showed her that he was even entertaining the idea of them giving a relationship a shot, she wouldn't believe him. Especially because of the timing. Her protection and safety – emotionally and mentally – were his utmost priority, but her agreeing to this wouldn't only get him his winery, but it would also give him time to convince her of his true intentions.

In silence, Imani strolled over to where he sat. He knew she was playing all possible, hardly possible, and farfetched scenarios over in her head. She picked up her now empty bowl of chips.

"Will you let me think about it at least? You can't just

spring this on me, B, and expect an immediate answer." She shook her head. "We're not kids anymore."

With a grin on his face, he walked over to her and pulled her in his embrace. Her thinking about it meant she was five percent away from giving in. "Fine. We don't have much time though."

She stepped away from him with her eyebrows furrowed and asked, "What do you mean?"

"I mean we have to be in South Africa in two weeks."

"Why the rush?"

"Lethabo told me about the clause a few days ago. The timeline for the winery going to the government is approaching. In order to still be in the running, I need to really convince the sellers that I'm not a reckless playboy."

Imani grunted. "Reckless? How did they come to that conclusion?"

Brice shrugged. "Someone's Google search included my pre-reform years."

Imani cut her eyes towards him. "Reformed? I wouldn't go that far." She laughed.

Brice draped his arm around her neck. "I'm glad you think it's funny. That means you'll have no problem remedying that impression."

"I haven't agreed yet," she reiterated.

"Yeah, I got it..."

"Somehow I don't think you do." She paused and thought for a second. "Why is this so important to you? So much so that you're willing to risk our ENTIRE friendship for it? I've never seen you like this about anything before. It must mean a lot to you, or I mean less to you than I thought."

Brice frowned. "You know that's not true. You know you're my ride or die. Since forever."

"Then what is it about this deal?"

Brice took a deep breath and rubbed his head. It made sense for her to want to know his why, considering the risk she was taking. He had always been honest with her about everything. Almost everything. If he was going to expect her to agree, he at least owed her a real explanation. "You know our whole history. If I were to be honest, I'd had to admit that it was Hakeem that made us rich. Everything we've amassed is mainly because of his entrepreneurial skills and hard work. And I'm so grateful. But I've always felt like I've been riding his coattail." Brice turned from her. Even to his best friend, his truth was too painful to be observed.

"This is my chance. This deal is perfect. There's almost no chance I can fail at this one. It's a perfect chance for me to prove myself. I can come out of the shadows and make a significant contribution to the family's wealth. We'll always work together, but I want to get this one on my own..."

He looked up at her, wanting to gauge her reaction. He was glad he didn't see judgment.

"Brice, I never knew you felt that way...I..." Her voice trailed off like she was trying to figure out what to say.

He felt uncomfortable that he had been so vulnerable and wanted the moment to be over. "Anyway, you said you'd think about it. We have a birthday party to get to."

Brice escorted her back into the kitchen. The party was now in full swing. They could hear the music coming from the ground level. Hakeem Jr. or H. R., as the family called him, was with his friends in a room he and Mariama decorated with a Marvel theme. That was his job while Hakeem manned the grill. Imani went to assist Mariama while Brice's eighteen-month-old niece, who was clinging to her dad, spotted him. Brice met her halfway and picked her up. Her arms went around his neck and he twirled her around. She had given all of them a scare for a minute and there wasn't a day that went by that he didn't remember how blessed they were.

THIRTY-TWO

"Let me get this straight—"

"You promised no judgements," Imani warned. She moaned as the masseuse kneaded her shoulders.

"And I'm not judging. Not yet at least. I want to restate the facts," Nicole stressed.

Her friend had returned from her honeymoon some days ago, and they planned a day of pampering in the Peninsula Spa. Imani had mulled over the pros and cons of Brice's proposal. A couple of years ago, it would've been a no brainer. She would have agreed without him having to explain further. But now things were complicated, muddled by feelings she didn't think he shared.

"I know how you feel about Brice, but you're my friend and I need help." Imani sighed.

"Being your friend entails me telling you the truth. If you want me to agree with you, then you know I'm not the one."

A beat passed between them. Imani opened her mouth to speak, but Nicole beat her to it.

"You already know how I feel about Brice. He's cool and all, but there is no way he can be so out of touch that he doesn't realize the feelings you still have for him. He ghosted you in college, only for you to find out he was with Maxine. Then years later, he's at the reception with her after making out with you the night before. Yes, I heard his explanation. He didn't invite her; it was Darius and his crew, but still. But okay, I'm gonna stop. I know how you feel about him. Your romantic feelings aside, you two have an authentic friendship that to me, borders on dependency—"

Imani chuckled. "We're not that bad..."

Nicole rolled her eyes. "Hmmm. That's because you two don't see what others see. The day y'all spent the night in jail because neither one of you wanted to tell the officer whose open drink was in the car was the night, I knew both of you were gone."

The friends shared a laugh, then a beat passed before Nicole continued, "You love this man. Being in close proximity with him for eight weeks can go two ways. It might backfire if at the end of the time, nothing changes for him. You guys end the engagement, and he goes back to doing him. Can your heart take it? On the other hand, God might hit him over the head and he finally realizes what he has right in front of him, and both of you live happily ever after."

Imani turned her head to her friend. "Nic, I know all that. I've mulled over it for two days now. I'm asking what you think I should do."

"Heck. I don't know. This happily ever after stuff has been your forte. You know I just stumbled into the stuff. What would the Hallmark folks do?"

"This is real life..."

"And I know that. Which is why I don't know why you're

acting like you don't already know what your heart is telling you to do. You just want me to cosign your decision to be his pretend bae 'cause I know you've already made up your mind."

Imani groaned. "I had a plan. Come to New York, have a conversation with Brice about my feelings. If he doesn't feel the same, I go back and work on building something with Dineo."

"What kind of cowardice plan is that? If Brice doesn't feel the same, you wait. There's someone out there for you. You sound like you'll settle for Dineo just to be married."

"Soon... yeah."

"Sis, trust me, marriage is hard enough. You have to at least love the person you're with and not settle."

Imani laughed. "Says the woman who's been married for a month."

"And I'm telling you, in that month, I've thought of ways to suffocate Desmond without being caught."

Imani's eyes bugged.

"What? I didn't do it, but when he makes me mad, I think about it."

"You have issues."

"Yeah, and he knew that. But let's not get off topic. If you're going to do this, protect your heart. I know it's hard but try and remember that you're doing your friend a favor. Don't assume anything unless he says it."

Imani sighed. "Okay, I hear you."

Their massages were over, and the attendants left the room. Imani and Nicole stood and reached for the terry cloth robes to cover their bodies.

"I hope so. While you're hearing, I also need you to hear this. If nothing comes out of this after two months, you have to cut Brice off."

Imani's eyes met her friend's. Her heart ached like a shard

had pierced it. Despite her tough talk, could she cut Brice out of her life cold turkey? "Completely?"

Nicole shrugged. "If that's what it takes for you to get over him, then yes."

Imani remained silent.

"Imani, promise me. If you genuinely want to be married and give yourself a fair shot, you must let go of Brice. You can't attract new while holding on to the old. If he's a true friend, he'll understand the need for both of you to cut each other loose for a bit."

Imani whispered her promise as they left the room and headed to their facial appointment next. Nicole was giving the attendant instructions while Imani contemplated the reality of what she must do. She wouldn't be able to live with herself if she didn't help Brice attain his dream. But on the other hand, she wouldn't forgive herself if she held on to a dream and her own reality slipped by.

LATER THAT EVENING, Imani rode the private elevator up to Brice's penthouse on Park Avenue. She was with him the day he bought it and still marveled at how big it was. The six-bedroom, seven-bathroom space had its own library, wine cellar, movie theater, and swimming pool. She never understood why he needed so much space. The building had a staggered roof, affording Hakeem his own penthouse at the other end of the building. However, with a new family, he now lived mainly in the suburbs.

Moments later, the door opened into the spacious, open floor plan. The smell of lemon chicken hit her nostrils and her stomach growled. Any time Brice cooked she was in for a treat.

"Be right there," Brice yelled from the direction of his room.

"Take your time." Imani took off her shoes, tossed her purse on the couch, and picked up the remote. She turned the television to ESPN for the highlights and walked toward the kitchen. They both shared the love of sports, but almost never liked the same teams. Their friends hated being around them if their teams were playing against each other.

After washing her hands, she moved over to the stove. Lifting one lid after the other, she smiled in anticipation. Brice loved to cook, and she had a healthy appetite; it was another reason their relationship worked so well. Imani turned when she sensed his presence. His tall, well-built body moved toward her with a smile that eroded the level head she was trying to maintain.

"How did I know you wouldn't keep your hands to yourself?" His voiced washed over her, leaving slight tremors in its wake. "I was trying to take a shower and be out by the time you got here."

"Ne...next time try harder. I'm starving." She had to pull it together if she had any chance of surviving the next eight weeks.

"Cheap Nicole didn't take you out to eat?"

"Nah buddy, we're not doing that." Imani opened the cupboards and took out the plates so he could dish the food. "Just like I won't let her badmouth you, I won't let you badmouth her either."

"Yeah, whatever. You turned on the game?"

"Yeah, it's about to start, so hurry it up."

"Get out of my kitchen woman. Let me do what I do."

Imani raised her hands in surrender and backed out of the kitchen. She sat on the couch with her legs folded under her and scrolled through her phone. Moments later, Brice walked into the living room with two plates. She hopped up to get them something to drink and soon after, they were eating and watching a game of football. The roasted chicken with lemon, sage and parsley stuffing almost solicited a tear, it was so good.

During the commercial breaks, they discussed the vineyard and his expectations for the place once it was a done deal. He still hadn't settled on a name for the wine he'd be producing, so they went over a few ideas.

She updated him on her job and her family. Let her parents tell it, Brice was their adopted son. He had been a constant part of their household growing up. Till date, he was still close to her family, although naturally closer to her mother. He popped in on her at least twice a year and called almost every month, not missing a beat, especially since her father had passed. When he was alive, her dad liked Brice, but didn't like their closeness. He couldn't understand how she could have a boy for a best friend.

"So, in addition to a vineyard and winery, you want to open a restaurant?" Imani asked.

"Not like a standalone structure. A small, intimate and exclusive place where people that visit not only taste the wine but have a classy meal with it." His eyes lit up as he explained his idea to her.

Imani couldn't take this away from him. She'd never seen him so excited about anything. Everything else she had seen him do was out of obligation, necessity or to prove a point. The gleam in his eyes had nothing to do with any of that; it was pure joy. She would just have to do a darn good job at guarding her heart.

"I thought about it, B, and yes, of course I'll help you—"

"Thank you. Thank you..." He pulled her to him and peppered her face with kisses. It was a gesture he had done a million times before, but this time, it felt different. She cleared her throat and eased herself off his lap. The silence between them became uncomfortable. Hating the awkwardness of the moment, she chuckled.

She stood to take their plates toward the kitchen, sashaying to the theme song of a commercial that came on. She glanced back at him, and grinned as he laughed at her while he typed away on his phone.

"You do know Lethabo's on a different time zone and probably sleeping."

"Yeah, just sent him a text so when he wakes up, he can get the ball rolling again. Thank you, Manny."

"Hmmm, yeah, yeah, yeah. You owe me and I'm warning you Brice...if I'm associated with any kind of drama, I'm never talking to you again."

"I promise. Our engagement will be on a need-to-know basis."

Her phone buzzed. "Our pretend engagement you mean?" Nicole's words about not assuming anything rang in her head.

"Yeah, that," he responded, almost disinterested in her need for clarification.

Her phone buzzed again, and she called on him to get it. Imani didn't hear a response, so she turned around. He was frowning hard at her screen.

"What's wrong with you?"

"I thought you said you and dude where only talking?"

"Who is dude?"

"That Dineo guy..."

"Yeah, we are. Why?"

"You might want to make sure he's on the same page. 'Cause he's talking about marriage in this text."

Imani's eyes stretched in surprise as she wiped her wet hands off and made hurried strides toward Brice. He handed her the phone and walked away without even looking at her.

She didn't know if he had to leave the room for something,

or he wanted to be out of her presence. Which was what he did when he was upset. She looked at her phone and read Dineo's message. She had no idea what he was talking about. But asking him about it could wait. Right now, she questioned the look Brice gave her. Was he jealous? If so, why?

THIRTY-THREE

Brice twirled the pen between his fingers and tapped his foot lightly as he struggled to pay attention to the people in the room. They were in one of the conference rooms at Richardson Investments, and Hakeem sat to his left at the head of the table. On the other side were this quarter's participants in their *Pass the Know* program. They were the owners of a family-owned hair care product from Jamaica. The program was geared toward assisting a worthy local business in expanding their portfolio through other related lucrative investments. Despite their schedules, he and Hakeem personally worked on and handled the initiative. It was their way of giving back.

Brice's mind drifted back to two days ago, to the awkward and disastrous end to what should've been the perfect evening. The anger that rose through his spine when he read that text about marriage didn't dissipate until Imani left. Even though she assured him she didn't know what the guy was talking about, he couldn't shake the emotion.

Apparently, Dineo was out and saw a house that would be perfect for them, but before he "got ahead of himself" he wanted to know where she wanted to live. Manny had told him over the years how some African men could be forward, but this was way out there. Especially since she maintained she didn't know how he came to that conclusion.

Brice trusted her, so he wanted to believe her. But the fact that Imani was talking about settling down, this joker was in Harare with her, and he seemed too comfortable, raised all kinds of red flags for him. Flags that had deprived him of any rest or concentration in the last forty-eight hours.

"I thought my heart would be safe with you. The person I trusted the most. The joke's on me."

Those words had seared a hole in him, and he hadn't forgotten the look in Imani's eyes when she uttered them. It was toward the end of freshman year in college and the memory still haunted him like it was yesterday. It was Valentine Day weekend. They had partied hard and during the kissing booth contest at some festival, Imani confessed to loving him. He wasn't sure of his feelings but didn't want to leave her hanging so repeated the sentiment. They had sex – something they'd agreed on – but he regretted it, because by the time he sobered up, he panicked. Which led to him ghosting her for three weeks. He avoided her and their friends and hung out with a whole different set of people – one of them being Maxine Bedford.

Maxine was Imani's high school nemesis and had transferred in the beginning of the second semester. If he'd been around Imani, he would have known that the ladies had met a week earlier, and Maxine resumed her taunting of Imani. Something she'd conveniently left out when they hung out. Absolutely nothing happened between them, but that wasn't the way Imani saw it when she saw them together at a house party.

In hindsight, he should've talked to her about his feelings.

He had love for her, but wasn't in love with her, at least not then. It was the beginning of college and they had a lot of life ahead of them. He should have talked and not avoided her altogether, because Imani never gave him a chance to say anything else to her. She said those words to him and cut him off for almost eighteen months.

He had done the exact thing his absentee father had done to his mother – something he swore he would never do. Hurt the woman he loved. It wasn't until after Imani was no longer in his life, that he realized he did love her. The damage was already done. It took Hakeem to get them back on track.

Over the years, she'd dated, but he was always in the background and none of her relationships were serious. Neither were any of his situations with other women. Imani had his heart and soul. So, Brice settled for whatever she was willing to give. The thought of hurting her again terrified him. Until now that she was trying to give her heart to another. That wasn't gonna fly.

"Gentlemen..."

Hakeem's voice brought Brice back from his painful trip down memory lane. He blinked and shook his head to refocus on the room.

"We do the recommendations, tell you how it will pay off, but at the end of the day, it's your call to make." Hakeem dropped the clicker that was in his hand and leaned back in his chair. After a few moments of silence, the father and son duo in front of them asked a few more questions.

Brice answered some of them as he was familiar with the details of the project and presentation. After a while, the men were out of questions and seemed satisfied with what they had heard. However, they still wanted to give it some thought.

"I'm glad you could join us there at the end," Hakeem said after the men left.

Brice waved him off. "This is your thing, remember? You got it."

Hakeem took out his phone and smiled as he returned a text. Brice knew it had to be to Mariama.

"Let me ask you something."

Hakeem looked up from his phone. "What's up?"

Brice ran his hand down his face and took a breath. "How did you convince Mari to give you another chance?"

Hakeem studied him for a few seconds and tugged his beard. "Well, I tried bullying her, but that didn't work. Then I threw a tantrum, and that didn't work either, so I groveled. That worked, but I think the fact that she kept our son from me had something to do with her not being angry for too long. Neither of us were squeaky clean."

"Maybe I should've put a baby in her at some point," Brice thought absently.

"Put a baby in who?" Hakeem barked out his surprise.

Brice smiled. "Nah, I'm just kidding."

"Okay, but there's an element of truth in there. Who are we talking about?"

"Manny, man..."

Hakeem stared at him for a few moments and laughed. For some reason, his cackle got louder and began to irritate Brice. His brother's laughter died down when he noticed Brice hadn't joined in on the humor.

"Oh, you serious? But what happened? I thought she agreed to the fake fiancée thing?"

"She did. But then..." Brice stood and walked over to the large windows in the conference room. He stared out at the busy streets for a moment, then turned to face his brother. He explained the dinner and what happened later, but at the end of the story, Hakeem was silent.

"Are you gonna say something?"

"How long y'all gonna be in South Africa?

Brice's eyebrows furrowed. "About six to eight weeks."

Hakeem stood. "Then that's the amount of time you got to convince her you want her. That's if you do. Or maybe you just don't want to see her happy with someone else."

Brice scoffed and walked back to the table. "Man, shut up."

"I'm just saying, because I have no idea why you haven't made a move all this time. Instead y'all playing this best friend game."

"You know why."

"That was something that happened in college," Hakeem insisted. "And don't even mention D's wedding because you ain't the one that invited that chick."

"Yeah, I know." Brice rubbed his neck. "I don't think it's really about what happened, but more so about who it happened with."

"You got the worst luck, man. How you let the same woman trip you up twice? You know, no matter what you and Manny call yourselves, that image won't leave her head."

"I know. I know, but that don't mean I'mma sit back and let her marry someone else." He felt a now familiar discomfort in his chest.

"Then you got eight weeks to do whatever it takes for her to understand you're serious about y'all." Hakeem picked up his jacket and put it on. "Or get ready to have a front row seat while somebody else does."

Hakeem walked out of the room, and his parting words churned Brice's insides. He needed to make sure it was never a possibility.

"BRICE, WHAT ARE YOU DOING?"

He tried to stifle his laughter as he guided Imani out of the car. She had on a blindfold he had to beg her to wear.

"Do you trust me?"

"You know I do, but where are you taking me?"

Ignoring her question, he led her across the private airstrip where the jet was waiting. He took off her blindfold and watched as she blinked her eyes and adjusted her sight to regain her bearings.

"Briceson Richardson, where are we going? It's barely noon and I'm dressed in jeans." She placed her hands on her hips and he shook his head.

"Can you just trust me? I know you have this insatiable need to know the now and the next, but can you get on the plane? We're going to be late."

Their eyes locked in a battle of wills before she rolled her eyes at him and stomped up the stairs. After talking to Hakeem the previous day, Brice was determined to start immediately sowing seeds of his love for her. It was too late to come clean now, because she'd think it was because of his deal. His plan was to sow seeds now. Because at the end of their eight weeks together, when he told her his true intentions, she would definitely question him to death. He wanted to be able to point out these things he was doing now.

A few minutes later, they were settled in and ready for takeoff. He walked to the back of the plane and looked inside the bedroom. The dresses he asked his stylist to get together were laid out on the bed. With Imani, he always had to tread a very delicate line any time he spent money on her. Everything had to be perfect. She would think his words were all in line with the charade, but he would mean every word uttered.

THIRTY-FOUR

A couple of hours passed by, and Imani stirred from her nap. Slight snores coming from her left caused her to turn her head. Brice was asleep with his head leaned against the leather headrest with his iPad face down on his chest.

Imani stretched her body and shook her head. He never listened to her. The number of screens he'd cracked doing exactly what he was doing now were way too many to count at this point. He was so stubborn and always wanted his way.

In those romance novels, billionaires had a reputation of being pushy and bossy. Brice had been that way even when he didn't have a dime to his name. He also could hold a mean grudge, except when he was on the receiving end. Which was why she was shocked when he showed up at her place and demanded that she go with him. After initially giving him a hard time, she agreed. If she had known they would be flying out of the US, she would've questioned him more.

He'd practically ignored her since that night at dinner. While she had absolutely no idea what Dineo was talking about, the gesture was sweet. She responded as such but reminded him that the thought was way off. They weren't in a relationship. His response: Not yet.

She asked Brice if he was jealous, and he called the thought ridiculous. So, her plan was back on. Help him out but guard her heart. Nicole was right, she'd been in love with him for too long. At the end of this, real distance between them would be exactly what she needed to rid him from her system. At least to some degree. She'd wasted enough time and life was short.

She stood and walked over to him. She reached to pick up the iPad when Brice's eyes peered open. He caught her wrist with his hand. The bolt of electricity that passed through her on contact wasn't like she'd experienced before.

"Calm down. I wanted to put your iPad away." She moved back a bit.

"'Preciate it. Since you decided to leave me here with no one to talk to, I decided to do some work."

Imani walked toward the back of the plane. "I'm awake now. Bring out the Uno. It's time for your monthly whooping."

"Where are you going?"

Imani turned back to him and furrowed her brows. "Do I have your permission to go to the bathroom?"

He snorted and signaled for the airhostess' attention. Imani laughed at him and continued her mission to empty her bladder and freshen up.

By the time she got back, she was met with a plate of fruit, baked snacks, and a bottle of wine chilling between them. She settled down beside him, eating and playing cards as he filled her in on the auction they were attending in St. Maarten. He was taking her to one of the most beautiful places on earth, so she had no complaints.

She'd visited the island with Brice years ago and had a ball. In her opinion, he was going overboard with the charade. They didn't need to appear together in these functions. All they had to do was show up in South Africa engaged, and no one would be the wiser. He explained this deal was particularly important to him, and if they were going to do this, it had to be done the right way. So, she decided to cut him some slack and allow him to do his thing.

THE FOLLOWING DAY, Imani stepped out into the private pool area. She set her bowl of fruit down and stretched out on the lounge chair. Her thoughts went back to the previous day when they'd arrived. Brice had rented a two-story, four-bedroom, beachfront villa, which they settled into. The place was so big that they had separate suites on each floor. After resting, they had a late lunch before going shopping for some clothes and necessities for their three-day stay. Later that evening, they attended the auction together where Brice introduced her to some of his super wealthy acquaintances and business associates. The dresses he had her choose from were exquisite, and she could truly get lost in this life of make believe. She knew Brice was real, but all the other stuff, she tried not to get wrapped in it.

After the event, they retired to their separate suites, but chose a movie to watch. While on the phone, they analyzed the actors, the plot and tried to predict what they would do. It was something they always did when they watched movies. They laughed so much, and the memories took her back to when everything was so simple.

It wasn't until she woke up in the middle of the night to use the restroom, that she noticed neither of them had hung up the phone. After listening to Brice's snores for a little bit, Imani disconnected the call. Turning off the television, she eased herself back between the sheets and resettled into a peaceful slumber.

Imani picked up a piece of fruit when her phone buzzed.

Hey you good?

She smiled. She hadn't seen Brice since they had breakfast before he had to attend some meeting.

I'm good. Sitting by the pool. Love this villa.

You want one?

Imani read his text and furrowed her brows. She sent him a couple of laughing emojis and responded.

You gonna buy me a villa?

If you want one?

How is it going?

About to wrap up. Be ready in two hours.

K

Imani closed her eyes as her heart lurched in anticipation of what he had planned for them for the evening.

"Please remember that this is all pretend. You're doing your best friend a favor. Don't get caught up," she cautioned herself.

Two hours later, her lips turned up in a smile, reading her mother's message.

I see both of you are still pretending not to love each other.

Imani responded that she didn't know what her mother was talking about before shifting the conversation. She had debated with herself on whether to tell her mother about her and Brice's arrangement. As the oldest child, she and her mother were extremely close, but she also knew she wanted her to end up with Brice. Her mother loved Brice and thought he could do no wrong. That was an image of him she was going to make sure she protected, always. Which is why she never told her about what happened during their estranged years. After thinking about it, Imani decided to keep the arrangement to herself. There was no need to give the woman false hope.

Imani chucked her phone into her tiny, black purse just as the knock she was expecting came from her suite door. She looked at herself one last time before walking toward the door. As expected, on the other side was Brice in all his glory. She tried her best not to let her gaze linger too long. In one quick sweep, she took in his notched lapel, plaid leisure suit. In typical Brice fashion, he had the top button of his white shirt he had underneath unbuttoned, displaying the gold cross chain she had given him for his twenty-fifth birthday. He never took it off.

"Ready?"

"Yep." She stepped out of her suite and he grabbed her hand and headed toward the elevator.

Sometime later, they were aboard a rented yacht, sailing the open seas and taking in the sunset. They'd gone to the theater first before setting sail. Imani was stuffed from the lovely meal the chef had prepared.

"What are you thinking about?" Brice took off his jacket and draped it around her shoulders.

She shrugged. "Nothing."

"It can't be nothing. I've been talking to you for almost two minutes without a response, so tell me what's on your mind."

"Nothing. I'm admiring the view." She closed her eyes and took in a deep breath. "Thank you for renting this yacht. I kinda feel sad you had to do that considering you have one docked in New York."

"There you go thinking about money again. This was a quick trip. We couldn't have used mine."

"Well. Thank you still. I've always wanted to sail the open seas."

Brice chuckled. "I know. I remember you watching those corny chick flicks, then talking my ear off about sailing."

Imani hit him across his shoulder. "Don't clown on my movies."

Brice laughed.

"But you're right about one thing though."

"What?" he asked.

"Love isn't that easy, neither does it come in a pretty little bow. I've since been delivered." She sighed.

"Hmm, and what caused this deliverance?"

She shrugged. "I guess you can say the years. Love is action. Action you must do whether you feel the mushiness of it all or not. People love differently and you have to be willing to meet them there or love yourself enough to realize they're not for you."

"Is that what you are doing with Dineo?"

Her forehead creased. "As of now, I'm not doing anything with Dineo. Didn't we already discuss this?"

"I guess." He shrugged and sipped his wine.

"Brice whatever, I don't want to argue with you. You either believe me or you don't." She sucked her teeth. "I can't believe you're still on that when it's you I'm pretending to be getting married to. If there was anything serious between Dineo and I, you know me. Am I the kind of person that would do this with you? Friends or not."

A beat of silence passed between them before Brice spoke. "My bad. Speaking of pretending to marry me..." He walked over to her. "Follow me."

"Oh Lord. B, what are you doing now?"

"Will you trust me and come on?" He took her hand and led her to another part of the yacht.

"Hope you've enjoyed yourself?" he asked.

"Yes. Amazing."

"Good. It's been a while since you and I just chilled. I've missed you. Now, I have one more thing to cap off the trip."

"You and these grand gestures. Easy now, I might get used to them and your real wife will definitely not like that." The joke was really intended to remind her that all this wasn't real. But the dry humor tasted bitter even to her.

He glanced down at her and smiled. "Somehow I doubt that."

A few minutes later, they arrived at another section of the yacht decorated with rose petals of varying colors, and huge floral placements lined against the walls. The lit candles were of varying sizes and gave an ambiance to the room that threatened to sweep her off her feet. She could still see the ocean through the glass partition, but it wasn't windy. Soft jazz played in the background. She turned and faced Brice. Her tongue was held captive by surprise.

"B...Brice what's all this?"

"A token of my appreciation for being my friend, putting up with everything I bring and doing me this favor."

She stared up at him, contemplating whether to go for his explanation or to probe deeper. She reminded herself that the onus was on him. She had put herself out there enough. If he wanted anything, he was going to have to say it. Until then, she would go with the flow with a huge clamp of reality around her heart.

Brice guided her to the mountain of cushions at the center of the room and helped her down. Soon after, he was seated beside her when a chef appeared out of nowhere and served them a decadent treat of white chocolate, raspberry cheesecake. She felt Brice's eyes on her as she danced in place. She took a spoonful of the confection and closed her eyes as the flavors exploded on her tongue. In the second it took to open her eyes she saw Brice on bended knee. Her eyes darted to what seemed to be a three-carat, radiant cut diamond in his hand.

"Don't say anything. Let me get this out. The day I walked into Ms. Barbara's tenth grade homeroom; my life changed. Seated in the front row, all prim and proper, was this girl who I knew I had no business looking at. I was already going down the path society expected of me. A prodigal product of the system now in the third school I was sent to. I wanted to pass time and get back to the streets. You and Hakeem saved me.

"No matter how many times I clowned or dismissed you, you made it your mission to bring me over from the dark side. That I graduated high school is because of you. And you've kept pushing all the way through grad school. You get on my last nerves sometimes, but you are my center. My moral compass. Once again, you're stepping out of your bubble to make sure I get what my heart desires. Imani Sharif, will you do me the honor of becoming my wife?"

Imani's eyes roamed the small space. "Brice, what are you doing?"

"You can't be my pretend fiancée without a ring and a proposal."

"But you could've just bought me a ring. This isn't necessary."

"You know I never half step."

Her heart thudded against her chest. This was too close to the real thing. She needed to separate the two in order to remain focused on the role at hand. He had taken her to the island she loved. She looked around and noticed that this was the exact set up she'd described to him so many years ago now that she thought about it. Everything, down to the meal, was exactly the way she'd told it to him several years ago.

One thing was missing.

The thing that kept her from leaping into his arms and grounded.

He hadn't said the words.

He spoke of her love for him but said nothing of his love for her.

"Manny, I'm too old to be kneeling this long."

Imani shook her head and chuckled. "You're thirty-two, but yes and get up."

Brice slipped the ring onto her finger and sat back down. A flash went off and she saw someone had taken a picture. She leaned in toward Brice.

"This is too elaborate, B..."

"I know no other way to be. Besides, we can't just show up engaged and be believable."

"I guess considering your status, we can't." She examined the rock on her finger. He went all out.

She reminded herself again. This is all pretend.

THIRTY-FIVE

Less than two weeks later, Brice ushered Imani into his seven-acre, fenced-in farmhouse in the Stellenbosch province of South Africa. He had built the house a couple of years ago, but Imani hadn't had a chance to see it yet. The property, which was surrounded by olive groves, a small vineyard, and breathtaking views of the Boland mountains, captured his heart the minute he saw it.

"B, did we actually land in your backyard? A landing strip in your backyard?" Imani squealed.

Brice lifted his brows, smiled, and kept on toward the control pad on the wall. He'd spent countless days telling her about his dreams and was proud that she was here to finally see one of them. The lights came on, illuminating the grand room.

"Girl, stop tripping come on let me show you the whole house."

"Are you sure the tour of this place can be accomplished in a day?"

"Very funny."

In the next several minutes, Brice took her around the

expanse of the house. There were seven bedrooms arranged over two floors. Each had an en suite bathroom. Three living rooms were all decorated with a different theme, and there was a library, inside and outdoor pools, an expansive patio, a game room, a gym, a media room, and a state-of-the-art kitchen. Then he walked her to the master suites which were in a different part of the house from the guest rooms.

"I know you don't expect me to share a bed with you?" Imani raised her brow at him when he walked her into one of the two master bedrooms.

"If I say what's really on my mind, you might drop kick me, so no. This is your room. It's next to mine because...appearances."

Brice leaned his shoulder on the door frame as Imani walked through the room. The day she agreed to his plan, he'd called his assistant to get in contact with the original interior designer for the home. He wanted to redesign this room to suit her taste. The decor was pink and gray – her favorite colors.

As he watched her move and admire what she saw, his mind traveled back to St. Maarten and the proposal. He hoped she paid attention to the fact that he made sure the proposal was what she had always envisioned. He couldn't remember the name of the movie they had watched that made her talk about the proposal, but what he did remember were the details.

"Is this what I think it is?"

His eyes connected with hers as she picked up one of the pieces of the set of three Khada Totem, hand-carved sculptures.

"I hope it is, or I've been duped, and heads will roll."

For her thirtieth birthday, he had taken her to Paris where the set was being sold at an auction. It was of African origin, from Zimbabwe to be exact, so he got it for her. That one was in her home in New York. When he was redesigning her room, he had someone locate the same set so she could have one here.

She chuckled and turned the piece over in her hand, examining it. "You want to make a softie out of me."

Brice strolled over to her and tweaked her nose. "You've always been a softie. You just pretend to be a thug."

"Hey, easy with the nose. That's my thing." She swatted his hand.

He kissed her on her forehead and walked to her door. "Now you know how it feels." Before he left the room, he turned back to face her. "We're solo for the next couple of days. I figured you'd want to get settled in without the staff around."

She nodded. "Good idea. We can take care of ourselves."

He smirked and attempted to walk out when Imani called out to him, "Is there any special trick I need to perform for the water to run?"

"You've got jokes."

"I'm just saying. I'm the one from Africa and never in a million years did I think luxury like this existed. It took my American pretend bae to show me."

Brice shook his head at her, laughed and left. There was a lot more he wanted to show her, but all in due time. Now he needed a good night's sleep. The second phase of his redemption plan was about to begin.

THE NEXT MORNING, seated behind his mahogany desk in his home office, Brice stared at his computer screen. The Zoom call between him, Lethabo, his attorney and his accountant had exceeded the time he'd allocated for it. This wasn't how he envisioned starting the day. His ideal start would've entailed preparing breakfast for Imani before she got out of bed. However, with the time difference between the States and South Africa, this was the only time he could get his team together after the email he received from his accountant late last night.

Twirling his pen between his fingers, he listened to his accountant make a case for trying to go back to the negotiation table with a lower offer to buy. He referenced some new numbers about the value of the property. Lethabo, on the other hand, stated that if the vineyard and winery were something Brice was really interested in, going back to the beginning would be a risky move. Especially with them being so close to the expiration of sale date. Brice listened to both men and was about to make his decision when there was a light tap on the door. He looked up and saw Imani walking in with two mugs in her hand.

He waved her in while his eyes darted toward his phone display to check the time. He had to get off this call so they could begin the day. As she approached, her signature cocoa butter scent preceded her, wreaking havoc on his senses. So did the sight of her well-toned legs, visible through the shorts she had on with a Ziedu designer t-shirt. Imani had always dressed like this around him. But now his feral need to claim her as his had him looking at her from a different lens. He needed to get a hold on it if he didn't want to scare her away.

He lifted his index finger to her to wait while he turned his attention to the gentlemen on his screen. "Okay gentlemen, I understand where both of you are coming from, but I tend to agree with Lethabo. It's too late to go back to the drawing board. The concern about the value of the property I'm sure will be addressed by the plans we have to turn the place around. I need to own it first. Any other time, I would always want to spend less, but this isn't the States, and I don't want to upset the status quo. I'll go with Lethabo on this one."

Brice gave out a few more instructions to the trio, then ended the call. He stood, picked up his mug and sat at the end of his desk. "Good morning, Manny." He lifted the cup to her. "Thanks. You sleep good?"

"Morning. Yes, are you kidding me? Those sheets...wow. You better hope I don't ask to move in permanently."

Brice laughed. "What's mine is yours; you know that. But I know you and lounging around will get old quick. Grinding is in your DNA."

"I can work from anywhere, but I get you." She took a sip from her mug. "I'm trying something new, though."

"Really? What?"

"Not letting the grind be the bane of my existence. I'm trying to lean on the grace and favor of God. Doing my part and letting Him blow his breath on the rest."

Brice furrowed his brows at her. Ever since he had known her, she had been a natural born workaholic. She was involved in a little of everything, which was one of the reasons she became a brand consultant. Her full-time job was routine, but her business allowed her to go into different worlds and apply her magic. That way she was never bored.

"Serious?"

"Yeah, which is why I spend the first part of my day in meditation and prayer. I found a nice spot by the pool. I was coming to get you before I heard you on a call."

"Is it too late?"

"The sun is already out, but as big as this house is, we can find somewhere. Come on."

Brice followed as Imani led him to the gym in the house. It was a fully equipped space with press up benches, treadmills, weights, peloton bikes, a water area, a space with fresh towels and a mounted television. Imani walked over to the corner and retrieved two mats.

"Good. You made yourself at home," he said, observing the ease with which she moved around.

"Yeah, when you're jet lagged and wake up at a crazy hour, you tend to roam the gigantic house you've found yourself in. The movie room and library are my favs." She spread both mats. "Why so big though?"

She sat on her mat and folded her legs, urging him to mimic the position.

"The space is for the future. Friends and family vacation."

"As long as my husband and kids can visit too, then we're good."

"They'll do more than visit."

"Okay, good."

Brice was sure they didn't have the same idea of husband and children, but at the end of their stay, he was certain they'd be on the same page.

She gave a quick rundown on how to meditate. He said his prayers every morning, but never engaged in meditation, but what Imani wanted she got, including having him on this mat with his legs crossed as though he was in preschool. After acknowledging that he understood what to do, they were about to start when she stopped.

"Your land is beautiful. I saw some of it this morning. But how do you enjoy it with the mosquitos?"

"I'm only here about two months out of the year tops. But mehn, after those suckers bit me the first time, I had the best people looking for how to treat the exterior. How? I don't know. All I know is I don't have trouble with those blood suckers while I'm here."

Imani giggled and shook her head. They began meditating – something that would become part of their routine going forward.

THIRTY-SIX

For the first week, their days were spent the same. Meditation by the pool before dawn, followed by cooking breakfast together. After they'd eaten, the pair went their separate ways for a few hours. Brice went to his office to check on anything that needed his immediate attention and Imani to her room. She used the time to check on her mom and siblings. Then she'd attend to some business before walking the grounds.

Once she got back, she and Brice would converge in the family room or media room. They watched movies, talked about their visions for her business and his for the vineyard and winery. In the initial stages after opening, the plan was for him to spend a lot of time in South Africa.

He broached the topic of future relationships, but from an angle he never had before. He asked about the number of children she wanted, and whether she'd want to live in the US, or eventually move back home. He wanted to know what kind of parent she saw herself as, in addition to her thoughts on the issue of spirituality when it came to the kids. He told her of his preferences also. They agreed on some things, but it wouldn't be them if they didn't vehemently disagree on others.

Imani absently kicked the gravel along the well-manicured path as she remembered his adamant refusal to understand why she was leaning toward hyphenating her last name when she got married. It wasn't really an African thing, but it was something she wanted to do. The way he argued his case, she almost thought it was his last name she'd be hyphenating.

She smiled at the thought. She was allowing that thought to roam free as the days went by. To the ordinary eye, they were a real couple. He didn't have to say anything when the staff got back; they knew immediately. His touches, light kisses, and whispers felt so real, she was having a harder time remembering it was an act.

"You good?"

Imani's thoughts were interrupted by the voice that always made her heart skip a beat in a whole new way.

"Yea, I'm fine. Just thinking." She let her fingers brush against the bush of Barberton daisies. Brice kept his eyes on her as he approached. A motorcycle accident he had in their final year of high school made him walk with a slight limp. He had turned it into his sexy, signature Brice swag.

"There you go. Whatchu thinking about?"

"About how proud I am of you. I know I say it all the time..." He entered her personal space, and she cupped his face with her hands. She didn't want him to brush her off as he had the tendency to do. "But hear me – I am very proud of you."

He covered her hands with his. "A rise from that rebellious fifteen-year-old that walked into Ms. Barbara's class, huh?"

She laughed. "A huge rise. You've done well, bestie." She nudged him with her shoulder.

"Don't call me that like I'm one of your girlfriends." His irritation was adorable.

She chuckled, but he didn't join in.

"I came to get you because breakfast is ready. But also, to see if you're up for heading outside the villa today."

"Sure thing. I'm so ready for my favorite American to give me a tour of South Africa."

"We'll both get lost if that happens. However, I know people, so we'll have a private tour guide. We going to Cape Agulhas."

As they walked inside the house, Imani pulled out her phone and Googled Cape Agulhas. It would take them about two hours to get there. She was weary thinking about the long drive, but when she saw all the things they had out there, she was more than excited. The Cape was the southernmost tip of the continent. She had no idea what that meant, but quickly found out.

"Do you know that Cape Agulhas is the end of the continent? Like when you look at the map, that point right at the end is where we're going?"

Brice glanced back at her. "Yes, I thought you'd like it."

They entered the foyer headed to the kitchen. She had enjoyed having the kitchen to herself over the first few days. Chef Luan was back and wouldn't let her lift a finger.

"I'm sure I'll love it. It's where the Indian ocean and Atlantic Ocean meet. But if I fall into the ocean, I'm holding you responsible." She giggled, but her statement caused him to halt his steps. She wasn't sure why, but he had a strange look on his face. Almost as though he was irritated or annoyed.

"That's not funny."

"Okay...why so serious?" she asked.

"Nothing. Don't say stuff like that. Don't you trust me?"

"I...I do."

"Then trust that nothing will ever happen to you on my

watch. Even when I'm not there, I got you covered. Always. Now let's go eat."

His voice was stern, and without giving her a chance to respond, he continued walking. Stuck in place for a minute, Imani watched him before she resumed her stroll down the massive hallway. She knew Brice had security watching over her. Even while she was in Zimbabwe. No matter how much she protested, he never wavered in making sure someone was always with her. The only way she finally agreed was if they blended in. That they did, so she never saw them, but she knew they were there.

Imani entered the kitchen, and the aroma of grilled vegetables hit her nostrils. Brice was already seated on a barstool at the huge, oakwood island, waiting on her. The one thing she loved about his kitchen was the fact that although the appliances were state of the art, the décor wasn't cold. It had a mix of modern minimalistic and country living.

"Good morning, Chef," she greeted.

"Good morning, Ms."

"I told you Imani is fine." She glanced over at Brice who had his head down, eyes on his phone. She could tell he was in a mood, but she was too hungry to pry whatever was the matter out of him. Also, she knew him well enough not to poke him when he got like that.

She listened to Chef Luan describe what he had made for breakfast while he poured them glasses of orange juice. There was a choice between poached, scrambled, or fried eggs, some muffins or slices of toast, a grilled tomato and onion mix, sauteed mushrooms and boerewors which she found out were special, South African sausages. Everything looked so good, and she was ready to dive in. When Brice looked up, she took his hand and said grace, then they pounced on the feast before them.

SEVERAL HOURS LATER, the pair had driven through Sir Lowry's pass, a scenic drive along the base of the Hottentot Holland Mountains. They then visited a farm stall where they tasted different local delicacies. Next, they were off to the Cape itself. There were no words to describe how beautiful and breathtaking it was to stand there and take in nature. The strong winds had Brice holding on to her extra tight. The fact that he always kept her by his side and their playfulness, not to mention the rock she wore on her finger, garnered them a lot of congratulatory comments.

At first, she felt uncomfortable, but remembered she was in South Africa to pretend to be his. Pretend being the key word. That didn't stop her from turning on the PDA herself. There was no telling who was watching. It was all part of the act, she kept reminding herself, but no part of the erratic beat of her heart was make-believe. The goal was to leave without her heart being completely shattered though.

Next, they ventured to Hermanus Cliff path where they got to see the whales, a penguin colony and finally, Gordon's Bay Beach where they currently were enjoying a nice meal in a tented space.

"Thanks B, I had so much fun today." Imani thumbed through her phone, once again admiring the pictures they'd taken. "I saw so many different cultures on this tour. No wonder when you mention Africa, the only place the rest of the world thinks exists is South Africa."

"That's not true," he countered.

"Are you kidding me? Which accent does Hollywood go to first when they want to portray an African?"

"The Mandela accent." He laughed. "Point noted."

"All Africans don't speak like South Africans. The only

movie I've ever seen try to make the distinction is *Black Panther*. You heard various accents from the continent. But I get it though. This place is beautiful and advanced."

"True. But don't sleep on Nigeria," Brice said.

Imani rolled her eyes. "Hmm, that's 'cause Afrobeats is now a thing in America."

Brice laughed. "Don't hate. They're not only known for Afrobeats."

Imani scoffed at him and forked lettuce and tomatoes from her salad, then placed it in her mouth.

He reached out to her and pulled her closer to him in the booth. "Don't be jelly. I'm not the one that told you not to have a Nigerian friend."

"You had that one friend in college. Stop acting like you have a lifelong brother."

He laughed again. "Now you just wilding out. If it makes you feel better tho, my most prized possession comes from Harare." He winked at her and took a bite of his food.

Imani willed her heart to not react to his comment, but it was a futile effort. They switched to safer topics for the rest of the evening. The main one being the reason why they were here in the first place. Over the next couple of weeks, they had to meet with the sellers, who Lethabo said were so excited to learn Brice came with his fiancée.

They'd subsequently been invited to various dinner parties, golf games and charity events given by the rich and wealthy of South Africa. She was surprised Brice was part of that group. He always amazed her with his ability to enter, adapt and almost take over. He was a born leader and charmer. His style was more subtle than his brother, but that didn't mean it didn't pack a punch.

In the last two years, she'd deliberately distanced herself

from his everyday life. Although they still communicated, listening to him in the last couple of weeks, she felt completely out of the loop. And she didn't like it. How was she going to cope if their distance ever became permanent?

LATER THAT EVENING, Imani stepped out of the shower and walked to the vanity. There were more places Brice wanted to show her, so he decided to get them accommodations in town. It would save the commute back. The Inn he'd chosen couldn't be compared to his villa, but it was luxurious all the same. They had adjoining suites and agreed to meet at the same time for their morning routine.

Imani hadn't seen Brice this carefree in a while and she loved it. When he was focused on attaining his current status, he acted like if he didn't work, he'd wake up one morning and his wealth would be gone. She understood the pact he, Darius, and his brother had made, but she still worried about his health. There were so many times they'd argue because he was at work until nine p.m. Although he didn't work directly with his brother full time, Brice had other smaller ventures that kept him occupied, in good and bad ways.

Imani slipped into the bed and decided to relive the day again through the pictures in her phone. She posted a few solo pictures on IG, careful as not to let her ring show. To her surprise, Brice had posted one too. He almost never used his page. In fact, she was the one that opened the account for him.

He had a picture of them from earlier at the Cape. Her hair was in his face and his hand around her stomach. Her statement about falling must've still been on his mind because he wouldn't let her go. His caption read, *My day one. First and last.*

Imani really wanted to spend some time dissecting the statement, but her eyelids had other plans, closing soon after. She fell into a deep, blissful sleep.

THIRTY-SEVEN

"All the hard work that's been put in over the years has finally brought us to this moment."

Brice gestured to Imani to stand by him. He lifted his glass in the air and outstretched his other hand for her to take. He couldn't believe that eight weeks had breezed by and he finally got his own vineyard and winery in South Africa. They were in a private VIP room of a restaurant in downtown Stellenbosch for the celebratory lunch. His lawyer, assistant and accountant all flew down from America for the closing of the deal. Lethabo and his own team were also in attendance. Later in the evening, he and Imani were hosting a dinner party for some acquaintances and business associates.

He interlocked their fingers and she also raised her glass. He looked down at the woman next to him. None of this would've been possible without her. She'd been his rock through everything. He had thought he would come into town with her, and everything would be straightforward. Wrong.

There was one new demand after the other. So many times, he wanted to give up the whole idea and head back to New

York. He could buy any winery or vineyard he wanted in the States. Imani reminded him that he could, but there was a reason he chose and wanted this one.

Some days, he came home from negotiations and needed to vent. She let him and listened. She also shut it down when she thought he had gone on long enough. She kept him focused on the big picture, explaining the cultural differences between the way he and the sellers viewed things. Neither one of them were wrong, but they were shaped by their culture. Imani kept him focused on the fact that business is business, but culture plays a huge part.

"I want to thank each one of you for the hard work you put in." He nodded to each one of them. "I want to especially thank this woman here. It's cliché, but I'm being as real as I can get. Without her, there'd be no me. Love you, Manny."

She winked at him and smiled. That small gesture sent Brice over the edge. He pulled her to him and unleashed all the pent-up frustration from the past several weeks on her lips. He thought she would push him away as she always did when he got carried away in front of company. But she didn't. She kissed him back.

He explored her mouth and ravished her lips like a man without manners. He didn't come up for air until he heard someone clear their throat. He looked into her eyes. There, deep within her orbs were desire and confusion, the latter of which he was eager to clear up. He kissed the back of her hand and whispered in her ear.

"We need to talk."

Imani nodded and he faced their guests. "Here's to a job well done!"

Everyone echoed their cheers and lifted their glasses to clink with their neighbor. The group resumed eating, drinking, and discussing plans for the next phase.

After visiting the vineyard a couple of times, Imani got to work on her vision. Brice hired her just like they'd agreed and put her in contact with his team. The money he transferred to her was more than her asking price, causing her to be mad and sulk for several of hours. He let her do that, as long as she didn't talk about refunding him a portion. They hadn't talked about her current job and how she would balance both. But he wasn't worried because by the time they had their talk, he was sure she'd quit her job. She didn't have to start on the vineyard for two months, so there wasn't any rush. That would give his marketing executive enough time to get situated and settled in Stellenbosch before she joined them.

Brice looked over at her and admired how easily she commandeered the room. Over the last several weeks, they'd worked hard and played harder. Most days started the same; with their normal morning routine completed, they'd get dressed for meetings with the sellers, different vendors he wanted to hire and anyone else Lethabo thought he should be in contact with. Other days were spent sightseeing. In the evenings, they either cooked together, or allowed Chef Luan to spoil them before they retired or watched something on TV or a movie.

He couldn't imagine his life without her, or her belonging to someone else. The mere thought of it put him in a bad head-space. The last couple of weeks cemented that fact for him. It was now time to get her on the same page. The one thought that tightened his heart was what if he was too late? She made it a point to always remind him that this was only pretend. He hadn't corrected her because he didn't want to mess anything up. The deal was now done, so it was time to set the record straight.

BRICE LOOKED DOWN at his watch and lifted his eyes again to the driveway. He should've known that life always had a way of putting a monkey wrench in well laid out plans. His original plan was to ride with Imani out to Birkenhead House where the party was being held. Now he was waiting outside the canopied entrance for the limo carrying her to arrive.

He had been called away on an emergency at the winery, so he had to leave the villa a couple of hours earlier. Just as she had predicted, he didn't have time to go back to the villa, so he was glad he listened to her and carried his tuxedo with him. Bringing on a business manager who would hire and train was of the utmost importance. Although this was his passion project, he didn't want to be this involved in the day-to-day.

His phone buzzed in his breast pocket.

Breathe

It was the third text Imani had sent in the last couple of hours. Right after the lunch they had earlier, every time he tried to get a chance to talk to her, someone or something came up. The event coordinator for the night's festivities pulled her in for clarification of some last-minute details. He was pulled in another direction with Lethabo and some other business decisions for his other ventures in the States. In just under two months, his staff had gotten used to her running things, so they always went to her first instead of him. He wasn't complaining, but he desperately needed some time alone with Imani.

He lifted his eyes again and smiled when the limo carrying Imani came to a halt in front of him. He reached for the handle and opened the door. Offering a hand to help her out, he gasped when she stood in front of him. When she showed him this dress on the rack, it was gorgeous, but seeing it now on her body was something he wasn't prepared for. As his eyes roamed her frame, he thought of ways to get the fabric off her. That had to wait until they had their talk later tonight. Now they had to put on their last public, pretend performance.

"You look beautiful," he whispered in her ear as he ushered her into the hotel.

She glanced over at him. "Thanks, you always clean up nice." She ran her palm down her dress. "You're sure it isn't too much?"

She had on a black dress that clung to her curves and stopped right below her knee. His favorite part of the dress was the fact that it was backless.

"No. You look stunning. Let's get this over with. I have plans for us tonight."

When Imani told him what she had in store for the night, his imagination was nothing compared to what she'd actually put together with the event coordinator. There was a live band that played a variety of Western and African music all night long. There was a small table with a miniature mockup of the future Richardson vineyard and winery. The banners and balloons were mixed in with projections of the Richardson logo. Making the décor simple and elegant. The master of ceremony had the perfect mix of comedy and facts about the new venture to keep the crowd engaged. The meal itself was served with army like precision.

The night was winding down and Brice was chatting with a few businessmen that Lethabo insisted he'd want to get acquainted with. He lifted his eyes and they met Imani's from across the room. He excused himself and walked over to her. Without much thought, he grabbed her hand and led her out of the ballroom.

"Brice, have you forgotten we are the hosts?"

"No. But they can wait a few minutes."

"What's going on?"

Brice remained silent and moved them through the back

entrance of the building. He led her down the narrow path until they got to the beach. He bent down and took off her shoes. Dangling them on his fingers, he continued to lead her in silence, trying to form the words he wanted to say. He feared her rejection, but he would burst a vessel if he had to spend any more time containing what he felt for her.

"B, what's going on?"

He stopped and pulled her closer to him. "Manny, I've been looking for how to tell you this, but I can't seem to find the words."

"Since when can't you talk to me?"

"Since I watched your heartbreak from my recklessness."

He felt her stiffen in his embrace, so he rubbed her back to relax her. "For years we've texted, talked, had sleep overs, argued, fought, laughed, and cried. I even took your virginity when we both knew the time wasn't right. Our bond has survived things that others don't. However, what I won't survive is you belonging to someone else. For years, I've settled for what you were willing to give me because I messed up. I was okay with having some of you and keeping you happy. In the last several weeks, I've come to realize that I'm no longer okay with that. Especially if it means some dude comes in and—"

The ringtone assigned to Hakeem interrupted their concentration. Imani looked at his phone which was in her hand.

"Y...yo...you should answer him."

"Nah, don't worry about it. I'll call him later." He brushed his lips against hers. "Breathe baby."

Imani blinked and opened her mouth to speak when the phone rang again. "B, you should really answer. It's not usual for him to call at this time. It must be important."

Brice sighed and took the phone from her. "Bro, this

better... When? The plane is at the house now? Okay. I'm on my way. Stay with Mari."

"Is everything okay?"

"Sir Wilcox suffered a stroke and asked to see one of us, but Mari's in the hospital so Hakeem can't travel. I gotta go to London tonight."

"Yeah, yeah, go." She started to turn back toward the direction they came.

Brice grabbed her arm. "Aye, we haven't finished talking. You wanna come with me?"

"Brice, you have things to tie up here. I'll stay, you go, but hurry back. I have two more weeks before I have to go back to work."

Brice stared for a few seconds, then cupped her face and drew her in for a kiss. "I'll be back before you know it."

THIRTY-EIGHT

Imani caught herself nearly skipping down the hall as she left her bedroom. She was sure she heard Brice arrive in the early hours of the morning. What they thought would be a three-day trip to London ended up being a seven-day trip. She'd filled her days with daydreams of their future, sightseeing and working on the branding strategy for the winery. To her surprise, Brice's team had scheduled her for a couple of meetings while he was gone.

She and Brice connected via Facetime, texts, or calls at least once a day. They weren't long conversations due to their schedules, but they always made sure to say good night to each other. Mari was out of the hospital and the client, who was in critical condition, was now stable. Apparently, he thought he was dying and asked for Brice or Hakeem to work with his financial managers to change his portfolio. Imani wondered why they needed to be there for that. But for rich people, whatever they wanted, they got.

The only thing that had the permanent smile on her face fade a little was Daphne Wilcox. Imani thought nothing of her, except when she began having Brice on her Instagram page again. In some shots, her hand was on his, or she was so close to him that she was almost in his lap. Other shots were of them in the hospital. She wanted to bring it up but didn't want to sound insecure.

Truth was, she did feel that way sometimes. They hadn't talked about them since he'd left. It was her idea to wait until he got back. At times, when their history took her down the scenarios of what ifs, she wished they had hashed things out. Her self-preservation mode was kicking in again. It was also what had her doubting the reality of her and Brice's unfinished business.

Imani's stomach growled and she decided to head to the kitchen instead of Brice's bedroom, which was her initial destination. Chef Luan should be preparing breakfast by now, but she wanted to eat with Brice, so she'd settle for some fruit for now. Rounding the bend, she heard Brice's voice. She hurried her steps to enter the kitchen, but she was met with his back to her and him on the phone.

"No, it's just Manny. It's nothing serious."

Imani's heart fell to her stomach when she heard Brice utter those words. He hadn't seen her, so who was he telling it was "just her and nothing serious?" Was he downplaying what they had? Bile rose to her throat as she backed away. Did she once again read meaning into what they shared? His possessiveness, his kisses, light touches, whispers in her ear, forehead kisses. As she hurried back to her bedroom, her mind replayed the things he did manage to say before he was called to London.

"especially if it means some dude comes in and…"

She chided herself because, despite all of that, he never actually said he was in love with her. Did he want to just have her by his side so nobody else did? When she mulled over the events of the last several weeks in her head, all his actions pointed to some sincerity. But then again, she thought the same thing when they made love years ago and he told her that he loved her but didn't. She couldn't lay the blame totally on him because she was a willing participant.

She entered the room and lifted her hand to her forehead. She was no longer a child or a college freshman. She was a grown woman making the same stupid mistakes. There was no way she'd make herself look like a fool for Brice again. She had made a promise to herself; if it didn't work out, she would put some space between them. She looked at the ring on her finger, and with tears rolling down her face, she slid it off. First thing in the morning, she was getting out of here with her head held high. Before then, she had to survive the day.

The following morning, Imani woke up to the text she had been waiting on.

I'm here.

When Brice knocked on her door the previous morning, she knew that surviving the day wasn't going to work out. She quickly moved to the next option.

Avoidance.

She wasn't in a good mood and all that thinking gave her a headache, so she stayed in her room. Brice was worried and came in many times to check on her, even threatening to get a doctor to the house if she didn't feel better by morning. Another thing that worked in her favor was he had to go out for a little while. The saying was right – more money, more problems.

I'll be ready when you get here.

That was Dineo. She had been talking to him sparingly since she was in South Africa. The man hadn't done anything to her, so she didn't see the need to ghost him or be rude and totally ignore him. Brice didn't like it, but she was never on the phone in his presence, so he didn't complain a lot. That was what was going to make the hour more painful for her.

She knew Dineo was in Durban, another part of South Africa, on business. When she thought of her exit strategy, she knew Brice wouldn't let her leave alone. On a whim, she told him to come and get her. If she stayed in Brice's presence any longer, she would break down. She didn't want him feeling sorry for "poor emotional Imani." With Dineo, he'd be so angry that he would let her go. At least she was hoping he would.

Showered, dressed, and packed, Imani left the room luggage in tow. Her steps quickened when she recognized the raised voices coming from the great room. *When he said he was here, I didn't think he meant on the grounds. And who let him through the gate. Brice is going to go crazy.*

Imani left her luggage at the entrance to the room, walking in on a furious Brice and Dineo, who had a smirk on his face she wanted to slap off.

"Dineo, what are you doing here?" she asked.

"I—"

Brice turned to her, his eyes blazing with anger. His eyes traveled to her luggage and his jaws clenched.

"That's what I'd like to know, and where do you think you're going?" He rubbed his hand over his head and cocked his head at her. "Did you invite this joker to my house?"

Imani narrowed her eyes at his tone. *Yeah, he must be very angry or out of his mind to be talking to her like that.*

"Brice," she warned.

"Answer me," he roared.

Both of them glared at the other, completely ignoring they were in the presence of a third party. Dineo cleared his throat and their gazes dropped. Imani turned to look at him, a weary smile plastered across her face. The satisfaction she thought she would get from texting him to come get her the previous evening had waned tremendously.

"Imani, you look well. I'm glad you called me," he said.

"You called this dude? Why?"

"I wanted—"

"I need to talk to you in private. Now!" he thundered. Not giving her a chance to respond, he walked up to her, took her hand, and dragged her to his office.

"Would you slow down."

"Why? You in that much of a hurry to leave?"

"No, so you don't remove my arm from its socket."

Brice ignored her but slowed down. When they entered the office, he slammed the door behind them. Imani knew she couldn't be in this office long. Brice could talk her into anything for him. She was weak for this man. She loved and hated it at the same time. He'd had her mind, body, and soul since she was fifteen, and she didn't know how to break free. Now she needed to for her own sanity. She had put her heart out there, and once again he hadn't taken care of it.

"Do you mind telling me what's going on?"

Imani moved away from him and folded her arms across her chest. "I don't know what you're talking about. You asked me to help you with this deal. It's over and it's time for me to go."

"Just like that? What about everything we shared?"

"It was a good performance, but it's time we get on with our real lives."

"Real lives? Are you kidding me?" He blew out a breath in frustration.

"Brice, I return to work next week. I'm sure you haven't forgotten. I need to get back home and get settled."

"What happened between the day before I left for London and yesterday? I thought we were getting somewhere."

"And where is that?"

Imani watched as he rubbed his hands over his head and let out another harsh breath. He couldn't even get himself to say the words she so desperately needed to hear. She needed to get out of here before she broke down.

"Imani, I can't lose you. I've shown you in every way I know how that I want you to be with me."

Imani's lips quivered as she held back her tears. Why was it so difficult for him to express his undying love for her? If he felt it, it wouldn't be so hard to say.

"Brice, you'll never lose me. I'm your best friend after all, but I gotta go." She turned to leave but stopped when he called out her name. She held on to the doorknob without turning around. Her heart thudded against her rib cage waiting for the words she hoped he was going to say.

"Don't get too comfortable," he said.

Imani sighed and removed the ring from her pocket, placed it on the bookcase and walked out. A tear rolled down her cheek. She couldn't get too comfortable because she had to be back here soon to start on the rebrand project. In the meantime, however, she was going to try like crazy to get over him.

"WAIT, tell me the story again. Because this makes no sense. I talked to you almost every day while you were out there—"

"Nic, you forget that Brice and I are best friends. We're always going to have a good time." Imani picked out a dress from her closet and walked back toward the bed.

"No, this was different. The things you were telling me weren't best friend stuff. I've been around both of you for years. It was a man expressing his love stuff."

"Remember this has happened before. I misread his intentions and ended up with a bruised ego and a broken heart."

"This is different," Nicole insisted.

Imani turned her face toward her phone that was on speaker. "Look at you. Married and suddenly, you're team Brice."

"I'm team common sense and your happiness."

It had been three weeks since she had been back in Harare. Her mother was shocked when she walked in the door with Dineo and not Brice. Thankfully, she hadn't questioned her. All Imani told her was it didn't work out with Brice, and she accepted it. Or rather pretended to accept it. Because suddenly, she was a social media addict, dropping hints of him being with someone at one event or the other. Imani thanked her lucky stars that she had removed herself from that situation. She and Dineo had been getting to know each other better and later, he was taking her on their first official date.

"Manny?"

"What, Nic? I'm on the side of mending my heart. Please let it go. You see he has gone back to his harem."

"Girl, you of all people should be able to tell how miserable he looks in those pictures."

"I can't go there again. I thought we were going somewhere, but I told you—"

"Yes, I heard you the first million times you said it. And I'm going to tell you again that you were wrong. You should've asked him who he was talking to and what that was about," Nicole said.

Imani thought about it but decided what was done was done. She had known Brice for years. If he really wanted something, he would fight for it. If he really wanted her, no matter what she said, he wouldn't have let her walk out of his house with Dineo.

"Can you just drop it, please?" Imani had only stopped bursting into random tears a few days ago. She wanted to move on. No, she needed to move on.

"Okay, I'll say this, and I'm done. I never hated Brice; I hated what I thought was him taking you for granted. Now I see why two of you get along so well. You are both as stubborn as bulls. You love him, and from what you've told me, I can tell he loves you, but because of something that can be cleared up with a simple conversation, the two of you are opting to be miserable?"

Imani plopped down on the bed and decided against countering her friend's statement. It was pointless. She was the one wearing the shoe and knew exactly where it hurt. Instead of responding, she changed the topic. After a sigh, Nicole decided to move from the topic as well. They chatted a little more before they disconnected the call.

Several minutes later, Imani was admiring her reflection in the mirror when there was a knock at the door. She answered, tucking a loose tress behind her ear. She turned to meet her mother's intense stare. When she moved back home, she decided to move into her parents' house to keep her mother and little sister company, especially now that her dad was gone.

"Mama, why are you looking at me like that?"

"You look so beautiful, my daughter." She paused. "The young man you're going out with is here."

"Oh, thank you. I didn't hear the doorbell."

"That's because he arrived when I was on the veranda."

Imani stood and picked up her clutch. She felt her mother's gaze bore into her. She contemplated if she should keep ignoring her or give in. Knowing that either way her mother would still have her say, Imani asked.

"What is it mama?"

She was trying to move on, but everyone seemed bent on putting her and Brice together.

"I don't want you to make a mistake, my daughter. I have nothing against Dineo. I think he's a fine young man, but he doesn't put the spark in your eyes that Briceson does." She adjusted the wrapper on her waist. "My marriage was an arranged one and even though I loved and respected your father, it was a long process. I don't want the same for you. I want you to really love the one you end up with."

Imani walked over to her mother. The calmness of her tone stressed the sincerity of her point of view. Imani kissed her on her forehead.

"I hear you, mama. And I promise I know what I'm doing."

Imani walked out of her room and down the small hallway into the living room. When Dineo saw her, he stood and smiled. Imani returned the gesture. As much as she tried with him, there was no chemistry. The fire she felt even when she was feet away from Brice was absent with Dineo.

For the first time in weeks, she questioned if she really knew what she was doing.

"I thought I'd find you down here."

Brice glanced to the left at the sound of his sister-in law's voice. He gave the crew Captain final instructions and dismissed him. He walked over to Mariama and drew her in for a hug.

"What are you doing here?" He looked over her shoulder and frowned down at her. "Where's 'Keem? Aren't you supposed to be off your feet?"

"It was dehydration. You and your brother are working my nerves." She rolled her eyes at him.

"Shoot, you are working ours, not taking care of yourself."

Mariama swatted him with the paper in her hand. Brice chuckled and raised his hand in surrender. Out of habit, he raised his eyes to the entrance of the deck, still anticipating Hakeem walking in. A beat passed between them and there was no Hakeem, so Brice walked over to the bar area to fix them a drink.

While he was selecting the wine, he got caught up on the latest on his niece and nephew. Since getting back from South

Africa, he had drowned himself in work. He hadn't attended family dinners in three weeks and that was probably what brought about the unexpected visit. He walked over to her and handed her the glass of wine he poured.

"Is this from the new winery?"

Brice smiled and nodded. Apart from Imani, she was the only woman who was genuinely concerned about what he had going on. Before she disappeared on his brother, she was like his big sister. When she got back, she picked up right where she'd left off.

"Yeah. I got the sample yesterday. How do you like it?"

She smacked her lips together for a bit, then nodded with a smile spreading across her face. "I like it. How did you get it so fast? I thought it was a long process."

"Yeah, but this is not in production yet. It's just something that the vinter had couriered over to me."

"The lifestyles of the rich and famous."

"Considering how we grew up I make no apologies."

"And you shouldn't."

Brice's eyes darted to the clock on the wall. He had a few more things to get done before his yearly charity event set to take place in less than a week. The event for displaced children took place aboard his yacht every year. He was better off getting this conversation over with so he could concentrate on the matter at hand. The show had to go on despite his broken heart. Besides, from the look of his Instagram feed, it was going on fine with Imani. He hated it, but he loved her enough to take his loss and let her be happy.

"Are you listening to me?"

"Erm...yea."

"No, you're not." Mariama let out an exaggerated sigh and narrowed her eyes at him.

His eyebrows came together. "What? What did I do?"

"You are really going ahead with this event without Imani at your side? In the five years since you started it, she's been there every year."

"Imani and I agreed to give each other space. She's still the homie, but I gotta do something without her."

"And you're still a terrible liar and miserable at that."

He frowned at her. "Wow, what's with all the insults, sis?"

"I'll do more than that if you don't go and get your girl." She had her hands on her hips like she was ready for battle.

Brice chuckled. "You are my family. You're supposed to be on my side. Chill with the hostility."

Mariama shook her head at him. He knew it was all love and she wanted him to have what she and his brother had. He wanted that too, but he couldn't be in a relationship by himself. He wasn't like Hakeem; going caveman wasn't his style. He could be assertive when he wanted to, but he and Imani weren't like that.

"I'm on your side, but I don't get it." Her tone was softer.

"What's not to get? She helped me with a deal, but at the end of it, she called her boyfriend over to get her." Brice's body still got heated any time he remembered the dude with the smirk on his face standing in his house. The security team that manned his gate that day got fired. The excuse that he was here to see "*your wife*" didn't cut it. It was all the more reason Dineo shouldn't have been let in without proper clearance.

"And you just let her go? I know she's in love with—"

Brice's eyes bugged. "Whoa...that's going a little far. She has love for me, but she isn't in love with me."

"Are you serious right now? How can everyone see it except both of you?" Mariama massaged her temples.

Brice snickered at her. She was the one that came on his yacht, interrupting his day, but she was acting like he was the one giving her a headache. This was the exact reason he stayed away. He wasn't ready to talk about Imani. At least not until after this event. If he allowed himself to stop and think about her, he would act totally out of character. Like go and drag her back to the US, something he promised her he wouldn't do.

"Look Mari, I know you want me to be happy. I ain't gonna lie and say I am, but I'll get there. Don't worry about me. Imani and I will be fine. She knows I love her. We just need space right now."

Brice watched Mariama as the fight in her disappeared. He gave her a faint smile and after she made him promise to come by the house for Sunday dinner, she stood to leave. She walked toward him and placed her hand on his shoulder.

"If you told her you love her and she still walked away, then it's her loss."

"She knows..."

Mariama raised a brow. "You keep saying she knows...did you tell her?"

He furrowed his brows, curious at her insistence. "Errm, not exactly, but she knows."

Mariama punched his shoulder.

"Ouch sis, that hurts. I'm about to call 'Keem to come get you."

"Brice, listen to me carefully. Did you *tell* Imani that you are in love with her? The words... did you say the words?" She stretched out the last part of her statement like he was slow.

"No, I didn't say the words. My actions should have shown her that." He stood and strolled over to the bar and set his glass down. "What's the big deal?"

"To refrain from hitting you again, I'm going to stay over here." She let out an exaggerated breath. "The big deal is you have to establish where friendship ends and you wanting her to be your woman begins. You've always straddled that fine line, overprotective, buying her gifts, taking vacations together, fighting, and makeups. You even say love you. Then you ask her to be your pretend bae for some deal; how is she supposed to know you want the real thing if you don't say the words?"

Brice stood up straight. "What do you mean, how is she supposed to know? I kissed her deeply, told her I wanted us to be forever. I...." His thoughts trailed as the reality hit him that he didn't say anything he hadn't said to her in their decade-long friendship. But he was more intimate. Shouldn't she have known? His eyes met Mariama's.

"Yeah, there you go." She secured her bag across her shoulder and turned to leave. "And you're welcome."

As the click of her heels faded, Brice picked up his phone to make three calls. To his assistant, crew captain and lastly, his pilot. If what Mariama said was correct, he was really about to act out of character.

THIRTY-SIX HOURS LATER, Brice got out of his car and looked at the Sharif home in Harare. He had been here several times, so the gateman let him in without having to alert the family. He rubbed his tired eyes that were desperately in need of rest. He hoped to get it after he got his answers. This wasn't a conversation he wanted to have over the phone. He wanted Imani to look him in his eyes when she answered him. He walked up the three stairs that led to the front door and rang the bell.

A few minutes later, Mrs. Sharif unlocked the door. Her surprise was evident but was quickly replaced by her signature smile.

"Ah, Brice, my son. What are you doing here? Welcome. Come in, come in." She opened the door wider and moved to the side to let him in.

Brice walked into the house and her embrace. She had been calling him her son ever since he could remember. At first, he was confused by the term of endearment, but then Imani explained to him it was an African thing. To be called a son or a daughter didn't really have anything to do with blood. Neither was being called an aunt or uncle.

"*Mhoroi*," Brice greeted in her native tongue. It was something he had done since he heard Imani say it. "How are you doing? Looking as beautiful as ever."

She giggled. "I'm fine, thank you. You always flatter me. Come, you must be tired." She walked toward the living room.

Brice locked the door and followed her. "Where's everyone?"

"They're in the dining room. I was coming from my room when I heard the doorbell. I hope you brought your appetite; we were about to start lunch."

Brice's mouth watered. His appetite was another thing that hadn't been in sync lately. He wanted to address the matter for which he came but knew it would be offensive to refuse a meal. As they approached, he heard Imani laughing. The sound swelled his heart and set his body on fire at the same time.

Especially when he heard the other voice that laughed along. This was no time to lose his head. He was determined not to give her any reason to be upset with him. He only hoped he could control himself long enough to get through lunch.

He entered behind Mrs. Sharif, and the silence that enveloped the room was almost comical. Imani's little sister was out of her seat in a flash and in his arms. He hugged her and inquired about school. She dragged him over to sit next to her, which he did. It gave him the perfect view of Imani's face. She still hadn't said anything, although her eyes told him she was stunned and curious. Dineo looked as though he was about to blow a gasket. Brice decided he'd allow them both to stew. He had waited three weeks. What was a couple more hours?

"What's up, Manny? We're not speaking today?" He raised his brow.

She cleared her throat. "Hey, Brice. Wh…what are you doing here?"

"Came to clear some things up, but I'm starving, so I'm about to eat first." Out of his peripheral, Brice saw one of the maids walk up and set an empty plate and cutlery in front of him. "'Preciate it."

"Oh, okay. Well, you know everybody here." She glanced over at Dineo.

Imani knew better than to introduce him to dude sitting next to her. For the sake of her mom, and not wanting to be rude, Brice gave him a head nod. He had nothing else for the guy who thought he was about to take Imani from him. Unlike the last time, the smirk on his face was gone, replaced with uncertainty.

An hour later, lunch over, Brice walked into the living room. He'd stayed back in the dining room after lunch to talk to Imani's sister about school. She knew she could always call him if she needed anything. But it was a message he had to keep reiterating, even to Imani sometimes. All money did was change his tax bracket and give him the flexibility and lifestyle he wanted. It didn't change him from the Brice that walked home with Imani in high school.

He saw Imani sitting on the sofa with her ex. Whatever he was now, Brice wasn't sure, but he knew for certain he was about to be her ex in a few minutes. Time was up.

"Aye Manny, let me holla at you for a few minutes."

Dineo and Imani turned their heads toward him. Brice inclined his head to the front door. If dude moved funny, there was no telling what Brice would do, and since he didn't want to disrespect her parents' house, they needed to take it outside. Imani stood and so did Dineo.

"I wasn't talking to you, bruh." Brice clenched his teeth. He had tolerated enough.

"Imani is my intended. Where she goes, I'll go," he said.

Brice laughed and turned his head to Imani. "Yo, did he just say intended?"

Imani pinned him with a warning look, but that ship had sailed. No more Mr. Nice Guy. Brice continued to chuckle, shook his head, and opened the door. "Come on, intended, I need to holla at you."

"Brice, stop it."

"What? You ain't say nothing when he said it."

Brice moved to the side to let her out, before walking out himself. If dude wanted to come, he was welcome to, but he had to open the door himself. The screen door slammed behind them and Imani looked at him and rolled her eyes.

"Just petty for no reason," she murmured.

Brice ignored her and took her hand. The sun was beginning to set, and the evening breeze was cool enough for them to hang outside.

"Okay, what's going on? What's the real reason you're here? Is everyone okay? 'Keem? Mari? The kids. On second thought, they should be if you had a whole meal before—"

"Breathe, woman. You right, everyone's cool, but I gotta ask you something. And don't even think about lying to me."

"You flew all the way down here for a question?"

"Yep. I need to see your eyes and your body language when you answer."

She folded her arms across her chest. Brice unfolded them. "Nah, I need to see all of you."

"Brice, we agreed to space. You could've asked your question over the phone."

He was about to respond when Dineo walked out of the house toward them.

"Imani, you can't be seen outside alone with—"

Brice cut him off. "What century is this dude from? Man, I've—"

Imani placed her hand on his chest to calm him down. She knew he was getting agitated. It did the trick. Brice took in a breath and faced her.

"Look, I don't know who this dude is. Or what you have promised him, but I need to know something because that will determine my next move." He was two seconds from throwing him over the fence.

"What?"

"Do you know I love you?"

Imani stared at him for a few seconds. As he waited for her response, he could hear his own heart beating, so he knew she could hear it too.

"Yes, Brice. I know you love me."

Brice raised himself from the car he was leaned on and adjusted his stance. "Do you know that I'm in love with you?"

Imani took a step back. Mariama's words came back to him and so did his annoyance. Anger that he had been in misery for three weeks because he wasn't in tune with the woman that he intended to spend the rest of his life with.

"Imani, please tell me that you know I'm in love with you."

She shook her head. "I can't because I don't."

"What do you mean you don't?" Brice's eyes caught Dineo's approach. "You might wanna back up. Now is not the time." He returned his eyes to Imani. "How can't you know, Manny?"

"How am I supposed to know? You never told me. The one time I told you that I was in love with you, it backfired remember?"

"I remember and for the millionth time I'm sorry. But baby, all the nights we spent in Stellenbosch, didn't it feel different?"

"It did. But..."

"But what Imani, because you're about to make me lose my mind." He rubbed the back of his neck.

"The day you got back from London, I was on my way to the kitchen and overheard you on the phone with someone," she explained.

He lifted his shoulders. "And?"

"I'm not sure what the person said, but you said, 'No it's just Imani, nothing serious'."

Brice put his hands in his pockets. "Baby, please make it make sense."

"I love you so much, but you dismissed me to whoever you were talking to. I got scared and panicked. I had flashbacks to college and felt the weeks we spent together really weren't anything serious to you. After all, we were supposed to be pretending."

Brice raised his hand and ran it down his face. He grabbed her shoulders. "Listen to me because after today, I don't want any more excuses. I was young and quite frankly, we weren't ready. If we had entered a relationship, I would've cheated and that would've ruined everything. Worse than the damage I ended up doing. I've been in love with you since we graduated, but I was scared to hurt you again, so I settled for what you gave me, just so you could be happy. But I draw the line when you start thinking about marrying someone else.

"Imani Sharif, for the last few weeks I've driven myself into the ground with regret that I had lost you. Make this the last time you jump to conclusions where you and I are concerned. Do you understand me? I don't even remember that conversation and it's what ruined us? I'm in love with you and I want to spend the rest of my life with you."

Imani smiled. "Is that a proposal?"

"I've already given you your dream proposal. Do you want another?" He removed the ring from his pocket and slid it on her finger. He cupped her face and drew her to him. "Don't ever take that off again."

"Okay. And no, my proposal was perfect," she whispered.

Brice captured her lips and launched a smoldering tongue battle. In the background, he heard tires screeching. Brice was glad dude knew how to exit the stage. He really didn't want to have to show him.

THE END

EPILOGUE

"Helloooo, world. I love my wife *and* I'm in love with my wife. These are my confessions."

Imani turned her tired body under the covers to face her husband who she was two seconds from throwing overboard. With his stupid blowhorn. She rubbed her eyes and sat up against the headboard. Her eyes darted toward her phone. It was only a little past seven in the morning. As much as Brice had worked her body last night, she was surprised that even he was up early. She admired him through the glass sliding doors that led to their balcony. He had the door slightly open, allowing the clean ocean breeze to waft up her nostrils.

They'd gotten married four months ago at their villa in Stellenbosch. Neither of them wanted to have a long, drawn-out engagement or have anything elaborate. Imani smiled as she remembered the most intimate ceremony that she had ever been a part of. At a point during the reception, Brice had them bring some water, then he kneeled and washed her feet. At first, she was confused, before he had her sit and told their family and friends that this was a demonstration of his commitment to honor, love and serve his wife and their future children. It was a symbol of humility that brought her to tears.

She rubbed her stomach. She wasn't showing yet, but in about seven months, he'd have another person to cater to.

Currently, they were on his yacht on the second week of their two-month cruise through the Caribbean loop. She had been on his yacht a couple of times, so its elegance was no longer surprising.

The sliding door opened, and she turned to lock eyes with her husband. He was shirtless with his pajama bottoms hanging low on his waist. He set the blowhorn to the side and sauntered over to her.

"Like what you see?"

"I love what I see, but I might have to hurt him if he keeps waking me up this early with his confessions."

Brice placed his hand on her neck, kissed her and sat on the side of the bed. "Ever since I found out you need clarification, it's my duty to ensure that happens."

"Every morning, Brice? Really?"

"Heck yeah. How many weeks did you allow me wallow in misery?"

"That wasn't my fau—"

"Aht. Aht, Aht. How many weeks, woman?"

"Three." She pouted and folded her hands across her chest.

"Okay then. You got one more week to wake up to my confessions." He kissed her lips, and made his way down to her neck, chest and finally her stomach. His hand lingered on her stomach, caressing it. "A'ight get up so you can feed my son. We're about to dock in the Cayman Islands."

"Move, meanie." She tried to untangle her legs from the sheets.

Brice cased her in with his arms. "Why I gotta be all that? Because I love my wife?"

"No, because you insist on disturbing my sleep."

His hooded eyes spelled mischief. "You need me to put you back to sleep? Just say the word. You know that's my favorite past time."

Brice slid her down onto the bed and leaned on top of her and proceeded to give her what she craved.

"I love you, Brice."

"I love you too, Manny Richardson."

FINAL NOTE

I hope you enjoyed Darius, Hakeem & Brice's journey to love. Please don't forget to leave a review.

Also, you can keep up with me and be in the know by signing up for my newsletter and subscribing to my website at www.UnomaNwankwor.com

Before you go, check out some of my other titles.

The Ultimatum Series (Complete Series)

The Christmas Ultimatum

The Final Ultimatum

Sons of Ishmael Series (Complete Series)

A Scoop of Love

Anchored by Love

Mended with Love

Redeemed Through Love

Stand Alone Books

An Unexpected Blessing

He Changed My Name

When You Let Go

The Invisible Shackles Books (Complete Series)

To Live Again

To Breathe Again

The DuBois-Arazi Family Novels (Uncompleted Series)

A Promise Fulfilled